APHRODITE'S ISLAND

A captivating and emotional historical fiction novel

HILARY GREEN

Revised edition 2022
Joffe Books, London
www.joffebooks.com

First published by Robert Hale in Great Britain in 2014

This paperback edition was first published
in Great Britain in 2022

Cover art by Jarmila Takač

ISBN: 978-1-80405-121-4

PART ONE

THE BRITISH COLONY OF CYPRUS, 1955

CHAPTER 1

The soldiers came to our village just as we were finishing the midday meal. They told all the men and boys over twelve to go to the village square. Then they started searching the houses. They were all large men, clumsy in their heavy boots, but very young. The one who came to search our house, who seemed a little older than the others, was blond, his skin reddened by the sun. He seemed embarrassed by what he had to do. To our great surprise he spoke to my mother in Greek.

'Forgive me, *kiria*. I have to carry out my orders. It will not take long.'

I said, 'Who do you think you are, bursting in here, turning everything upside-down? You are supposed to be here to protect us, to keep the peace, not to terrorize innocent women and children.'

He looked at me and smiled and said, 'I think it would take more than the British army to terrorize you, *despoina*! I promise I will not turn anything upside-down, or if I do I will put it back again.'

'But what are you doing with my husband, and my sons?' my mother cried out, with tears in her eyes.

He said gently, 'Do not worry, *kiria*. They are quite safe. We just need them out of the way for a few minutes. When the search is over they can come home again.'

'What are you looking for, anyway?' I demanded.

He said, 'I think you know the answer to that. Two days ago someone threw a bomb at a British army lorry. Someone is hiding bomb-making equipment somewhere, and we have to find it.'

'Do you really think,' I exclaimed, 'that you are going to find bomb-making equipment in my mother's oven?'

He smiled at me again. 'No, *despoina*. I'm sure no terrorist would dare to take such a liberty, with you to reckon with.'

But he searched the kitchen just the same, and the rest of the house, though I have to admit he didn't make a mess.

Later, when the soldiers had gone, my brothers pulled the oilskin bag with the rifles in it up out of the well and returned them to their hiding place under the floorboards.

The soldiers are everywhere in the city, driving around in their armoured cars, manning checkpoints. When they are off duty they stand on the street corners or sit in the bars, watching the girls go by. Sometimes they call out to us. We do not answer, of course. We have our reputations to consider, and the anger of our fathers and brothers. Then, a few days ago . . .

'*Despoina* Ariadne!'

I did not recognize the voice. I looked around. To me, at that time, all British soldiers looked the same.

'*Despoina* Ariadne!' He was running across the road towards me. It would have been rude to turn away, having once stopped and looked round. 'You remember me?'

'Of course. It was you who searched our house.' I spoke coldly, with dignity.

'Yes.' His eyes were very blue and he looked at me appealingly, like a small boy who knows he has done wrong. 'Don't be angry with me, *despoina*. You know I have to carry out my orders.'

'You are wasting your time,' I said. 'You found nothing.'

As I spoke there was a tremble of fear in my stomach, thinking what he might have found if he had come at another time.

He smiled. 'But it was not a waste of time. After all, I met you, *Despoina* Ariadne.'

'How do you know my name?'

'It was easy. I asked someone, "Who is the beautiful girl with the black hair and the proud walk who lives in the house near the church?" And they said, "Ah, that is the *Despoina* Ariadne, the schoolmaster's daughter."'

His eyes were teasing me. I saw that the skin of his face was no longer red and sore-looking but tanned a light gold, and without his army cap his hair was almost silver in the sunlight. I knew I should not be standing here, talking to a British officer in the public street, but I did not know how to get away.

He went on, 'I did not expect to see you here in Nicosia. Are you shopping?'

'No,' I said. 'You can see from my uniform why I am here. I am on my way home from school.'

He looked at my clothes as if he had not noticed them before. 'I thought you were too old for school. I'm sorry. I mean, you seemed so grown up . . .' I was pleased to see that he looked confused.

'I am seventeen,' I said. 'I am in the Girls' Sixth Form at the Gymnasium. My father believes in the value of education, even for girls. Now I must go. I cannot stand here talking to you.'

'How are you going to get back to your village?' he asked.

'On the bus, of course.'

'Let me give you a lift. I have the jeep just here.'

I confess I hesitated, just for a second. His eyes were so blue, so sparkling with life. Then another soldier came out of a shop across the road and shouted, 'Hey, you coming?'

He said quickly, 'Let me introduce you to my friend. He's a nice chap, really.'

But the interruption had given me time to collect myself. I lifted my chin and spoke very coolly.

'No, thank you. I have to go now. My father would not like me to be seen riding around with two British tommies.'

On the bus all my friends were asking me about the handsome Englishman, but I made them promise not to say anything to anyone in the village.

Next day, when I came out of school, he was sitting in his jeep outside the school gates. He waved to me but I pretended not to see him. I knew it was impossible for us to meet, but I couldn't stop myself from imagining what we might have said to each other if things had been different.

Next Sunday afternoon I was sitting with my family in the shade of the grapevine behind our house. My father was reading the paper and my mother was sewing and my two brothers, Iannis and Demetrios, were playing backgammon and arguing, as usual. When the knock came at the door they all stopped what they were doing and looked up. Any neighbour would have walked straight in. Who could this visitor be? Then they all looked at me, so I left my homework and went to open the door.

He was outside — my English soldier. Before I could speak, he took off his cap and said, 'Forgive me for disturbing your Sunday afternoon, *despoina*. I am not here on official business. I wish to speak with your father. Is he at home?'

The expressions on my brothers' faces when I led him out into the courtyard would have been enough to intimidate most men, but he appeared not to notice. Instead he said, politely, 'Good afternoon, *kirios, kiria*. Please excuse this intrusion. My name is Stephen Allenby. Before I joined the army I was a student of Greek language and literature and now that I am here on Cyprus I am anxious to learn as much as I can of your history and culture. I know that you, *kirios*, are a schoolmaster and I have been told that you are also an expert in the history of this island. I have come to ask if you would do me the honour of allowing me to study with you, if we can arrange a time that is mutually convenient. Perhaps an hour a week? I should, of course, pay for my lessons.'

There was a silence. We all looked at my father and I knew none of us believed what the Englishman had said. I knew, too, that my brothers saw a very different explanation for the subterfuge than the one that was making my heart race.

After a moment, my father rose to his feet. 'Let us go into my study, Lieutenant. We can discuss this matter there in private.'

As soon as they had gone indoors, Iannis let out a growl of fury. 'What is he doing here? Studying our history? What sort of fools does he think we are? He is here to spy on us.'

'Calm yourself,' my mother ordered. 'He may be telling the truth. In any case, you will do us no good by making your hostility so obvious. He has behaved with perfect courtesy and you will do the same while he is under our roof.'

'I will not stay in the same house with that man!' Iannis declared. 'He is the enemy, however good his manners! If he is going to be received here, then I am leaving.'

And he slammed out of the house. I sat very still, pretending to get on with my work, but all I could think was 'His name is Stephen and he has come here to find me'.

It was some time before my father came out again, with Stephen beside him. I was sent to fetch wine and honey cakes and for half an hour we sat and made conversation. In all that time he only looked at me twice but when he did my heart jumped in my chest and my pulse beat even faster.

After Stephen had gone, Iannis came back. He was furious to learn that my father had agreed that Stephen should call on us every Sunday afternoon for his lesson.

'What are you thinking of?' he demanded. 'He is a spy! It's obvious. Why are you inviting him into our house?'

'Think a moment,' my father said quietly. 'Who will suspect a humble schoolmaster who entertains an English officer in his own home every week? What better camouflage could we have? And if you keep your temper under control, what reason could he have for suspicion? There is nothing here to incriminate us. And if he is a spy, is it not better for us to make a friend of him? He could be very useful one day.'

Three days after Stephen's visit, during our English lesson, we became aware of noise from the street outside. To begin with it was some way off, a low roar like a distant stormy sea. Then it came closer and we realized it was men shouting. Our teacher told us to remain in our seats and concentrate on our work, but the noise grew louder still and we knew something important must be happening. Someone near the window called out that the street was full of people and we all jumped up and went to look. There was a great crowd, waving Greek flags and banners proclaiming our desire to be united with the Motherland. Everyone was chanting in rhythm and it sounded even more like waves crashing against a cliff.

'Enosis! Enosis! Enosis!'

One of the girls shouted, 'Let's join them!', and everyone crowded towards the door. The teacher called to us to sit down and get on with our work but no one paid any attention. We flew down the stairs and out into the street. The crowd pushed and jostled us but we stuck together and forced our way with the rest along the narrow streets. The heat was stifling and the smell of sweat made me gag but it was exhilarating to be part of such a mass of people and we all joined in the chant.

'Enosis! Enosis! Enosis!'

Eventually we found ourselves opposite the building that houses the British Institute. The police were lined up outside to prevent us reaching it. The crowd milled around, jeering at them and calling them traitors, and boys began pushing their way through the throng, selling bottles of Coca-Cola. We were all parched by that time and the bottles were sold as fast as the boys could bring them from the cafés and bars round the square. I remember that they were warm by the time they reached us and I can still recall the violently fizzy, sickly-sweet taste. Then someone threw the first bottle at the line of policemen. The girl who had led us out of the classroom yelled, 'Let's get them! Let the traitors have it!', and we all surged forward, hurling our bottles at the men's heads. I have a good aim and I saw my bottle knock off a man's helmet.

Suddenly I remembered Stephen and wondered what he would think if he could see me. The line of police broke under the rain of bottles and some of the crowd surged forward into the building but I held back. The other girls had all rushed on ahead. I waited until the crowd had thinned out and then I began to walk back towards the Gymnasium.

I thought of Stephen and wondered how it was possible for us to be enemies. I realized, of course, that he was not acting of his own free will. His government had ordered him to do National Service and he had to obey orders.

Later that afternoon I heard that the British Institute had been burned to the ground.

The following Sunday, when Stephen had finished his session with my father, he came and sat with us in the courtyard, as before. I suppose it was only natural that he should ask my father's opinion about the riot. My father replied that it was regrettable but as long as the British government refused to allow us to determine our own fate, the situation could only get worse.

'But, *kirios*, as I understand it,' Stephen said, 'my government has offered you a large degree of self-determination, provided only that we retain control over defence and external affairs.'

'That is not true independence.'

'Perhaps not, but it's a start, surely. You have to see the British point of view. Cyprus is a vital strategic base in the Cold War. We have to protect our oil supplies through the Suez Canal.'

As the discussion went on, the feeling of confusion that had been growing in me since the riot deepened. Until now I had accepted what my father and my brothers had told me — that the British were the enemy and the soldiers an occupying force determined to crush our people. I could no longer reconcile that image with the handsome man who sat in our garden, discussing the situation so earnestly and reasonably. When he said, 'It breaks my heart that we cannot find some way of existing side by side as friends,' I believed him. I could only hope that my father did, too.

The discussion was interrupted by Demetrios. He had been up on the hills, watching the wild creatures. Demetrios loved animals and birds and everything wild and natural and his ambition was to study zoology, but a village schoolmaster cannot afford to send his sons to university. Instead, Demetrios was apprenticed to a local tailor and had to confine his studies to his evenings and days off. That day he was distressed and furious because he had discovered that one of the shepherds up in the hills had shot an eagle. Stephen immediately expressed an interest. It seemed he too liked to study birds and he asked Demetrios if he could show him where to see the eagles. In a moment, all talk of politics was forgotten and Demetrios was arranging to take Stephen up into the hills with him the next weekend. I was delighted! I knew Iannis would be furious, but Demetrios was a kind soul, willing to make friends with anyone. I thought that if he and Stephen started spending time together it would be much easier for me to see him.

Just before Stephen was about to leave, I suddenly 'remembered' that I had to talk to Ferhan. I told my parents that I had lent her a book that I needed for school next day, so I would have to walk over to her house to collect it. Ferhan is Turkish so she doesn't go to the Gymnasium with me but when we were small we both went to my father's school in the village. She would like to have studied further but her parents did not see the point of higher education for women, so I often lent her some of my books. She lived on the other side of the village, about a mile away. As I hoped, Stephen offered to give me a lift and, of course, my mother said I couldn't go in his jeep on my own. But then Demetrios, bless him, said he would come with us. He wanted a lift into Kyrenia anyway!

So, off we went. I sat beside Stephen. We couldn't say much, with Demetrios in the back seat, but once, when he was changing gear, he reached his hand across and touched mine. It was only for a moment but he looked at me and I could see that he felt the same way I did. The combination of happiness and fear made my chest so tight I could hardly breathe.

When he dropped me off at Ferhan's house he said, 'Goodbye, *Despoina* Ariadne. We'll meet again soon.' He winked at me and at that moment I knew that in some way my life had changed forever.

Ferhan was very surprised to see me. Of course, I hadn't lent her a book, but I was dying to talk to someone about Stephen and I knew I could trust Ferhan. She was shocked, of course. She would never dream of meeting a man without her parents' consent. I told her we don't live in the middle ages anymore and a girl should be able to make up her own mind about the men she goes out with. At least, being Turkish, Ferhan does not regard the British as being our enemies. How I wished my father and brothers would give up all this nonsense about *enosis*! Then we could all get on with our lives without being afraid that someone might find out what they were doing. And perhaps they wouldn't mind me seeing Stephen. Perhaps.

CHAPTER 2

On the Monday after Stephen's visit, I couldn't stop thinking about him and wondering if he might be waiting outside the school gates again. The last lesson was English and I could see into the street from the classroom window. Mr Durrell reprimanded me twice for inattention because I kept gazing outside. Then, suddenly, he was there, just like before! I knew I couldn't talk to him in front of all the others when we came out of school, so I told Mr Durrell that I was feeling unwell and asked to be excused. Of course, he thought that was why I hadn't been paying attention earlier and he was quite concerned. I felt bad about lying to him but he let me go and a few minutes later I was outside. I jumped into the jeep beside Stephen and told him to drive away quickly so that we couldn't be seen from the school. He drove round the corner and stopped in a quiet side street.

He said, 'I'm so glad to see you. How did you manage to get away before all the others?'

I told him how I had lied to my teacher and he looked at me with those wonderful blue eyes and smiled that smile that makes me feel as though I have just stepped off a cliff into thin air.

'Thank you,' he said. 'Thank you for doing that, so we can have a chance to talk.' Then he put his hand on mine and I thought I was going to faint with pleasure.

He went on, 'I think you must guess how I feel about you. I can't get you out of my mind. But I know it is not possible for me to ask you to come out with me, as I would an English girl. I understand that things are done differently here. I wanted to ask you, would it be acceptable for me to speak to your father? If I asked him, would he let me take you to the cinema one evening?'

I felt panic gripping my throat. 'No! No, you mustn't do that! I couldn't . . . he wouldn't allow it. No girl can go out alone with a man unless they are engaged to be married.'

'Then can I come and ask him for your hand in marriage?'

I could hardly breathe. 'But we hardly know each other.'

'No, not yet. So what happens in your society? If I'm not allowed to be with you until we are engaged, how can we get to know each other? What do other couples do?'

'If . . . if the parents on both sides approve, then the boy comes to call on the girl and in the evening they go walking together — but with the girl's parents as well. Then, later, sometimes they might be allowed to sit together for a while alone.'

'Then can I come calling?'

'You come already, every Sunday.'

'But I never have a chance to talk to you alone — or to walk out with you. If I explain to your father that my intentions are honourable . . .'

'No! If you tell him that you are interested in me he will forbid you to come to the house anymore.'

'But why?'

'Because . . . because you are English. Don't you understand? The people here resent the British occupiers. If anyone saw us together my whole family would be dishonoured.'

'Then what can we do?'

'Nothing. There is nothing we can do.'

'Do you mean that?'

Our eyes met and I knew that I had to find some way to be with him.

'When are you off duty next?'

'On Thursday, from midday onwards.'

'I will meet you then. But don't come to the school. Wait for me in the square by the Selimiye Mosque.'

'What will you tell the school?'

'I shall tell them I am ill.' I was surprised how easily the lie came to me. I opened the door of the jeep. 'I must go now. Wait for me on Thursday.'

'I'll be there. Don't worry. Nothing on earth will stop me from being there.'

That evening Iannis came home from work with a look on his face that made me afraid. He was excited, but it was a harsh, cruel excitement that turned him from my brother into a dangerous stranger.

'Have you heard the news?' he demanded of my father.

'What news?'

'There has been a running battle in the streets of Famagusta — our people against the British troops. At last the Brits are going to see that we mean business. This is just the beginning!'

'Careful, my son,' father warned. 'We have a long way to go yet before we can take on the British with any chance of winning. It is a mistake to show our hand too soon. We must be patient and circumspect. Remember, there are still those who would be happy to betray us.'

I crept up to my bedroom and sat gazing out of the window. I knew Stephen could not have been involved with the fighting in Famagusta because he had been with me but if the fighting spread, as Iannis obviously hoped it would, how long would it be before he and Iannis came face to face on opposite sides of the battle?

That night at supper we listened to the report of the fighting on the radio. When it finished I said, 'I don't see why we have to fight the British. The soldiers are only here because their government forces them to come. They don't mean us any harm, I'm sure.'

My father and brothers stared at me as if I had said something obscene and my mother said quickly, 'Help me clear the table, Ariadne. You don't understand these things.'

'I do!' I said passionately. 'I've heard you all talking about it for long enough. *Enosis, enosis!* What does it matter? Why can't we just live at peace, the way we always have?'

Iannis began to speak but my father silenced him with a gesture. He reached across the table and took hold of my hand.

'Ariadne, I am disappointed to hear you speak like this. You have been brought up to have pride in your Greek heritage and to believe in the importance of liberty. We Greeks have the right to choose who should govern us. We are not slaves, to be ruled by foreigners.' Then he smiled and patted my hand. 'You are young and, after all, you are a girl. Leave these matters to those who understand them. Archbishop Makarios has given his blessing to our cause. That should be enough for you.'

On Thursday I took the school bus as usual, but on the way I kept clutching my stomach and groaning and telling everyone nearby that I felt sick. In school I kept up the pretence and at morning break I told my friend Penelope that I felt too ill to be in school and I was going home. She wanted to come with me but I persuaded her that I could manage on my own and asked her to make my excuses to the teachers. I walked out, heading in the direction of the bus stop and, as soon as I knew I was out of sight, I slipped away down a side street.

I pulled off my school blazer and stuffed it into my bag and covered my head with a dark scarf so that I looked like any other girl out shopping. When I reached the square I was shaking. I was terrified that Stephen would have changed his mind or been prevented from keeping our appointment. There was no sign of him outside the mosque. I looked at my watch. It was still ten minutes before midday. I waited for a while, but I felt foolish and conspicuous standing around and I was afraid that someone who knew me would come by

14

and recognize me, so I slipped into the mosque. Inside it was cool and the vast, white-painted space was calming but I still felt out of place. What was I, a Greek, doing here in what had once been a Roman Catholic cathedral and was now a Muslim mosque? After a few minutes I went outside again. Stephen's jeep was not there, but then I saw him, hurrying through the crowds towards me. I forced myself to stand still and behave with dignity.

He stopped a few feet away from me and we both said 'Good morning' in an unnatural, formal way. Then he said, 'Thank you for coming. I was afraid you might have changed your mind. I hardly slept a wink last night for worrying about it.'

I lifted my chin. 'Do you mean that you thought I wouldn't keep my word?'

He looked so confused that I wanted to laugh. 'No, no! I didn't mean it like that. I was just afraid that you might have decided it was—well, a mistake.'

I said, 'It probably is a mistake — but I'm here anyway.'

He smiled then, and I smiled back and after that things felt easier.

He said, 'I left the jeep round the corner. I thought it would be less conspicuous.'

As we walked I asked him how it was that he always managed to have a jeep to drive around in and he grinned.

'I'm supposed to be in Military Intelligence. It means I'm allowed to go wandering round the island poking my nose in wherever I find something interesting. My superiors haven't twigged yet that what interests me isn't necessarily anything that might be useful to them.' Then his grin faded. 'Mind you, if we have any more incidents like what happened yesterday in Famagusta I may find it harder to get away. You heard about that?'

'Yes,' I said. 'I heard.'

When we got to the jeep he said, 'Where shall we go?'

The question took me by surprise. I had expected him to decide. He saw that I was lost for an answer and went on, 'I

15

don't know the island well enough yet. I thought you might be able to suggest somewhere quiet — somewhere we're not likely to run across anyone you know. That would be best, wouldn't it?'

I was thinking hard. 'Have you ever been to the little church of St Antiphonitis?'

'I don't think so.'

'You would remember if you had. I'll take you there.'

We drove back towards Kyrenia and I kept my scarf pulled round my face. It was difficult to talk because of the noise of the engine and the wind whipping past our ears but I was glad of that. All I could think of was that I, a Greek girl, was riding alone with an English officer. Once we were stopped at a road-block but when the soldiers manning it saw Stephen's uniform they saluted and waved us through. I looked back as we drove away and saw them grinning and pointing and realized how easy it is for a girl to lose her reputation.

I told him not to take the main road, but the one which crosses the mountains to the east of Kyrenia. When we got to the top of the pass, I directed Stephen off onto the narrow mountain road that winds along the top of the ridge. Soon we were deep among the trees, where only the occasional forester goes, or a villager searching for firewood or a lost sheep. We were truly alone now but I was not afraid anymore. I knew that Stephen would never harm me.

After we had bumped along the track for some time, he looked at me and said with a laugh, 'Where is this place? I don't believe it exists.'

'It does,' I said. 'Truly! Be patient, it's only a little bit further.'

He took his hand off the wheel and touched mine. 'It's all right, I trust you. I know you wouldn't lead me into an ambush.'

The words were spoken lightly but then he looked away and said nothing for a while and I knew he was thinking similar thoughts to my own. He was thinking how very foolish we were both being, in the eyes of the rest of the world.

We came to a point where the track widened enough to turn a car.

'Stop here,' I said. 'We have to walk the last bit.'

I led him down the steep, rocky path into the clearing where the tiny church stood, completely hidden among the trees.

'This is incredible!' he exclaimed. 'I should never have found this on my own.'

I pushed open the heavy wooden door and he followed me inside. For a moment or two we were both blinded by the sudden transition from sunlight to the dim interior. Then I heard him draw in his breath in amazement.

'It's so beautiful! All these frescoes. They must be hundreds of years old.'

'Many hundreds,' I agreed.

We walked together round the walls and stood staring up at the face of Christ above us in the dome. I discovered that he knew more than I did about Byzantine art and about the stories of the saints pictured in the frescoes. After a while I asked, 'Do you have churches like this in England?'

'Not like this. Some of them are very grand and very beautiful but not . . . not so colourful. I have seen churches like this in Greece, though.'

'Do you go to church often?'

'Not any more. When I was younger I believed fervently in—' He hesitated and gestured at the pictures '—in all this. Sadly, not any longer.'

'Sadly?'

'Yes. I have lost my faith, but I respect and admire those who believe, like the people who made these beautiful pictures.'

We went outside and sat down on a grassy bank in the shade of the building.

He said, 'Thank you so much for bringing me here. And thank you for being here yourself. I think you know I haven't been able to get you out of my thoughts since the first day I saw you.'

'And I have thought of you, too, all the time.'

He kissed me then. It was the first time I had ever been kissed by a man and my first instinct was to struggle free but his arms round me were so gentle and I felt so safe in his embrace that my alarm lasted only a second. His lips were warm and slightly roughened by the sun and when they parted and I felt his tongue flicker across mine, something happened inside me that I had never experienced before. Of course I had fantasized about this moment for years, like any young girl, but I had never imagined that my body could come so vibrantly alive, obliterating all self-consciousness in the torrent of physical sensation.

I do not know how long we lay in each other's arms, just kissing, but eventually he drew away and looked down into my face.

'My darling girl, we must stop this. I want you so badly, but I know we mustn't let it go any further. It wouldn't be fair to you.'

I longed to reach out and pull him back to me, to tell him I wanted him, too. But some remnant of honour — or was it fear? — prevented me. He sat up and ran his hand through his hair and I straightened my clothes and tied the scarf back over my hair. He got up and held out his hand to me.

'Come on, I'll drive you back to Nicosia.'

When we got back to the jeep I said, 'When shall I see you again?'

He took hold of my hands. 'Do you want to?'

'Of course. You know I do.'

'If we go on seeing each other, something will happen, you know that. If I can't ask you to marry me . . .'

He left the sentence unfinished but I understood his meaning.

'We can't stop. Not now!'

'Then we need somewhere to meet — somewhere safe and private.'

'I know. I'll think of somewhere. When shall I see you again?'

'On Sunday, when I come for my lesson with your father.'

'I'll find some way to give you a note. When can you be free again?'

He shook his head, frowning. 'I don't know. Things are getting difficult. You know there is going to be a General Strike tomorrow? That means trouble. I'll get a message to you somehow.'

We looked at each other and suddenly I felt empty and hopeless. He put his arms round me and kissed me on the forehead.

'We'll find a way. Don't look so sad. Things will work out, somehow.'

I nestled against him. 'Yes, of course they will.'

CHAPTER 3

The Girls' and Boys' Sixth Forms at the Gymnasium have formed a joint committee to organize protests against the British occupation and when the General Strike was announced they made it clear that we were all expected to join the demonstrations. On the day after my date with Stephen we all walked out of our normal lessons to attend a meeting to discuss tactics. The teachers are too intimidated to protest. There is a feeling that anyone who is not whole-heartedly in favour of action is a traitor.

I realized this at the meeting, when I tried to find an excuse not to join in. I said I didn't think my parents would allow it but all the others immediately turned on me.

'Of course you must be there!'

'You're not chicken, are you?'

One of the boys said, 'I know your brother Iannis. He's with us all the way. I'll talk to him, if you like. He'll persuade your parents.'

I saw that I had fallen into a trap. My father and brothers were already suspicious because of my outburst the other evening. I couldn't afford to make things worse. Also, I was not sure if the boy who had spoken was a sworn member of EOKA or not. Either way, Iannis would not be happy about him poking his nose into our affairs. I muttered something about talking my parents round myself and promised that I would be at the demo.

When the day came, we gathered outside the school and marched towards the government offices. Penelope and I had made a banner demanding 'ENOSIS OR DEATH' and we each carried one of the poles that supported it. Although it was the end of October, the Mesaoria was still parched and Nicosia was like an oven. By the time we reached the street leading to the square where the offices were situated, we had joined up with several other processions and with so many people packed into the narrow confines between the buildings I began to feel I was suffocating. When we got near the square, the whole procession came to a halt and word was passed back to us that soldiers were blocking the end of the street. The crowd began to get angry. Craning on tiptoe, I could just make out the ranks of British soldiers in battledress and behind them two or three armoured cars. For the first time I felt angry too. What right had these people to treat us like enemies in our own country, to prevent us from walking the streets of our own capital city? Boys at the front of the demonstration began yelling insults at the troops and the chant of *'Enosis!'* filled the street and echoed off the walls. Soon the first missiles were thrown and small groups of soldiers charged into the crowd and dragged the throwers back behind their lines. That made the mood of the crowd even uglier.

I was chanting and shouting with the rest, carried away by the heat and frustration at not being able to move. Then a girl on my left grabbed my arm.

'Look up there! On the rooftop!'

I looked up. Three soldiers stood on the flat roof just parallel to where we were. One carried a rifle, one a camera and the third, an officer, was scanning the crowd through a pair of field glasses.

'They're spying on us! Taking pictures!' my companion shouted in my ear.

I dropped my head and tried to duck behind her shoulder. My stomach was tying itself in knots. The officer with the field glasses was Stephen. Had he recognized me? What would he think? Would he see me now as an enemy, as I had begun to see the other British soldiers? I tried to edge away towards the side of the street, where I would be out of his line of vision, but Penelope held fast to her end of the banner and would not move. More demonstrators were pressing in at the far end of the street and the crowd was becoming so dense that any movement was almost impossible anyway. I could only keep my head down and hope that he would not spot me among the crowd.

Something was happening at the front of the demonstration. The soldiers had started to move forward, pushing our front ranks back. The people behind me were still trying to force their way forward and suddenly I was very much afraid. I could not move in either direction and the crush was so great that I could hardly breathe. A surge of bodies ripped the banner out of my hands and it went down, to be trampled under a dozen feet. I was terrified that I might lose my balance and suffer the same fate. In my panic I looked up at the rooftop where Stephen stood. He was not looking in my direction but talking into a walkie-talkie radio.

A moment later a voice came over a loudhailer.

'Do not try to move forward. The road ahead of you is blocked. If you do not give way some of your people may get hurt. I repeat, move back! Disperse quietly and go to your homes. There is nothing you can do here.'

The appeal was met with a new bout of chanting and insults but the pressure eased a little. Looking around me, I saw a narrow alleyway just behind and to my left. A few people were already slipping quietly away down it. I squirmed and shoved my way through the crowd until I reached it. The relief of being out of the crush of bodies and into the comparative coolness of the alley made me feel light-headed. I followed the others towards the road at the far end, with very little idea of where I intended to go next, and just as I reached the junction a jeep pulled up across the end of the alley. Two soldiers jumped out and came towards me.

One of them took me by the arm and when I struggled he said cheerfully, 'No need to panic, miss. Our officer wants a word, that's all. We're not going to harm you.'

They marched me to the jeep and pushed me up into the passenger seat. Stephen sat behind the wheel.

He said, 'OK, lads. Get back up on the roof and keep an eye on what's going on. I'll join you in a minute.'

The two men turned and ran back down the road, their boots clattering on the paving stones. I gazed straight ahead of me and tried not to let him see that I was shaking.

He said, 'Are you all right?'

'Yes.'

'Thank God! I was terrified you were going to get hurt. It's lucky I was able to see what was going on and warn the officer in charge. The last thing we need is a death or a serious injury.'

I glanced sideways at him. 'It was you who made them stop shoving us?'

'I radioed the CO and told him what was happening.'

'Thank you.' My voice was tight and my throat ached.

He put his hand over mine. 'Ariadne, darling, why couldn't you stay away? Did you have to get involved?'

I pulled my hand away. 'Why can't you people stay out of the way? We only want to make our feelings known. It's our city, after all.'

'You know why. Remember what happened to the British Institute? We couldn't let the government offices be burned to the ground, could we?'

'Why not? It's not our government. Why should we be governed by some British aristocrat who doesn't know anything about our country?'

'Darling, Sir John Harding is not a British aristocrat. He's a career soldier and he knows this island and loves it. I'm sure he only wants what is best for all of you.'

'Don't call me darling! Your soldiers have just nearly crushed me to death.'

'I'm sorry. You know I would never have wanted this to happen.' His voice was anguished. 'Ariadne, please! Don't let this come between us. I have to carry out my orders. You know that.'

People were still coming down the alley and they gazed at us curiously as they passed. I moved to get out.

'I can't be seen sitting here with you.'

He restrained me with a hand on my wrist. 'It's all right. Tell anyone who asks that I had you brought in for questioning because I thought you were one of the ringleaders. That's what I told my men.'

I looked at him properly for the first time and felt the usual quiver in my stomach, as if I had just stepped into thin air.

He said, 'I love you! We mustn't let this make any difference. Please!'

I knew he was right. Whatever happened between our people, nothing could alter the way we felt about each other.

I said, 'Shall I see you on Sunday?'

'Yes, of course. But I want to see you alone. When?'

'When can you get away?'

'Any day. I'll find an excuse, somehow.'

'Tuesday, then. About four o'clock.' A plan was beginning to shape itself in my mind.

'Where?'

'I'll give you a map on Sunday. Bring some papers with you and put them where I can knock them off.'

'I understand.' His smile wiped away the last traces of my anger. 'Thank you, my darling girl.'

I started to get out of the jeep. He said, 'Won't you let me drive you out of the city? I could drop you somewhere you could get a bus back to Ayios Epiktetos.'

I shook my head. 'I've got to find the others. If this is going to work, they have to think I'm committed to the cause. Don't worry. I'll be careful. I'll see you on Sunday.'

I crouched on the sandy floor of the cave and peered out between the branches of the fallen pine tree that almost hid the entrance. My brothers and I had found the place years ago, when I was still young enough to be allowed to roam the hills with the boys. It had been our secret hiding place for a long time — a pirates' cave, a spaceship, an outlaws' hideout — until Iannis and Demetrios grew out of make-believe and exchanged their toy pistols for real guns and I was told it was time I began to behave like a young lady. I had almost forgotten it existed until the day of the demonstration.

The pine tree had blown down in some long-ago storm but had clung to the rocky slope with enough roots to keep it alive, so that the sunlight filtered in through green branches and scented the air with resin. Where I sat the cave mouth was fairly wide and we had thought at first that it was no more than a sheltered overhang in the side of the rock face. When we looked closer we discovered that further back there was a narrow passage leading into the hillside. Iannis and Demetrios had wanted to explore it but the sunlight did not penetrate beyond the opening and within a few yards they found themselves in total darkness. We often talked about making torches out of the pine branches and going deeper but we never had — at least not to my knowledge. Iannis tried to tell us that he had gone in once alone and that after a short distance the passage opened out into a huge cave, but he spoiled the story by adding that the cave was full of gold bars and jewels left by pirates long ago and now guarded by a fire-breathing dragon. Even then, young as I was, I knew there were no such creatures. Just the same, when I arrived that afternoon I had taken the precaution of throwing a few small rocks into the dark opening, just in case some less than mythological serpent had taken up residence there.

I had given my parents the impression that the events at the demonstration had fired me with patriotic resolve. As far as they knew, I was even now attending a meeting to plan further action. I craned forward, watching the narrow path that slanted up the steep slope through the trees. It was just after four. Surely, I told myself, Stephen could not have misunderstood my directions. My plan had worked perfectly.

He had left his books and papers on the arm of his chair and when I passed to collect his coffee cup it had been easy to knock them to the floor, and easy as I knelt to collect them to slip the map I had drawn in among them. He must know his way around well enough to recognize the landmarks. I had even marked the tree at the beginning of the narrow path, as I had promised in my note, by hanging an old Coca-Cola can from one of the branches.

A rock clattered down the slope, dislodged by somebody's foot. A moment later I saw him, moving cautiously, one hand on the revolver at his hip. For an instant I felt afraid. Could he really think I was luring him into an ambush? Then he stooped on the far side of the screen of branches, trying to peer into the darker space beyond.

'Ariadne?'

I caught my breath. 'I'm here!'

He pushed the branches apart and scrambled through. There was no need for words. We went straight into each other's arms. His kisses burned my mouth. I could feel the sun-heat of his body and smell his sweat. The rest of the universe vanished.

At length he lifted his head and looked down into my face. 'Ariadne, what do you want — from me?' I frowned, unsure what he was asking. Did he think I was spying for the terrorists — or looking for money? He went on, 'You know, if things were different I would be coming to speak to your father, to ask for your hand in marriage. But you tell me that is impossible as things stand. I would take you away from here and marry you anyway, if I could. But neither of us is a free agent. I have to serve out my two years' National Service and you will not come of age for longer than that. If I thought that at the end of that time we could marry, I would wait — if that is what you want. I know long engagements are normal here. But I can't do it like this. Not if we are going to meet secretly, alone. It's more than flesh and blood can stand. Do you know what I am saying?'

I knew. I had little experience of men except for dark hints from my mother but I was not completely naive. I had thought of little else since I slipped the map into his papers and I had come to my decision. My heart was thumping so hard that it seemed to shake my whole body.

'I understand. I can't help what my father thinks — and three years is too long to wait.'

'You're sure? You've thought about this?'

I reached my arms round his neck. 'I'm sure.'

I had heard fearsome stories of the pain and embarrassment of a bride's first night, whispered in the twilight by friends who had heard it from older sisters and cousins. It was nothing like that. Already every nerve in my body was pricking with desire, so that when his hand slipped inside my blouse and found my breast the nipple was already as hard as an almond and when he eased the blouse off and unfastened my bra I was proud that my breasts were full and firm enough to please him. He undid my skirt and I lifted myself so that he could pull it down and my knickers came with it. I kept my eyes closed but the knowledge that he was looking at my naked body sent a thrill of ecstasy through me. There was a moment of awkwardness when he drew back and I was aware of him fumbling with something but I understood what he was doing. Then he slipped his hand between my legs and my body took control so that all conscious thought ceased. When the pain came it was sharp but brief and I felt it as a kind of triumph. Sensing the urgency of his desire and hearing him pant and groan with pleasure as he came, I was suddenly flooded with a sense of power, of what it meant to be a woman.

CHAPTER 4

Karaolis will hang! He was condemned to death for the murder of a policeman the day after I let Stephen make love to me. Iannis says he will be our first martyr. Since then, five British soldiers have been killed. I am terrified for Stephen. I know he goes wandering about the island alone and everyone thinks he is a spy. Perhaps he is. How do I know what he does when he is not with me? Am I a traitor to my own people?

Two nights ago I was woken by the sound of footsteps and low voices outside my window. Looking out, I saw five mules standing in the street below. Men were coming and going from the house, carrying packages wrapped in oilskin, Iannis and Demetrios among them. I recognized the packages. They were the rifles that had been hidden under the floorboards for months. Some of the mules were already loaded with unfamiliar crates and boxes. I wondered whether they were arms that had just been acquired somehow or whether they had been hidden all along in other houses in the village. Whichever it was, I could understand why the decision had been taken to move them. Every day we heard tales of other villages that had been surrounded at night by troops who travelled in convoys without lights through the mountains. At dawn the search would commence and there was no time to move the arms to safer hiding places.

The night air was cool and I wrapped myself in my shawl, but it was not the cold that made me tremble. I had no idea what EOKA's plans were, except for the hints Iannis gave when he talked of 'giving the Brits a taste of their own medicine', but there had already been deaths on both sides and the situation was getting more tense every day. It occurred to me that perhaps these guns and whatever else was in the crates were not being moved to a safer place but were being prepared for an attack or an ambush. In that case, should I warn Stephen? How could I, when my own brothers might be the ones caught or killed in the confrontation?

I knew most of the men down in the street but there was one I had never seen before, a short, powerfully built man who seemed to be in charge of the operation. When the mules were all loaded he beckoned the others to him and they gathered by the wall of the house, just below my bedroom window. Voices were lowered but in the still night air I could hear every word.

'Which of you knows the way to this cave?'

'I do.' It was Iannis's voice. 'We played there as kids. I'm the one who suggested it.'

'Right. You lead the way. Let's get going.'

I sat rigid by the window until the clacking of the mules' hooves had faded into the distance. My brain felt as paralyzed as my body. Eventually, I dragged myself back to the bed and lay down, pulling the blankets close around me to try to still the trembling that gripped me like a fever. Later that same day I was due to meet Stephen at the cave. How could I stop him from going there? He had warned me never to try to contact him at his base in Famagusta and I had no idea where he would be during the earlier part of the day. And even if I could contact him, what excuse could I make for changing our meeting place? I could stay away; tell him later that I had been taken ill. Then, if he found the cache of arms, at least I could not be accused of betraying their hiding place. But

I had told him that Iannis knew about the cave — that we three were the only ones who did. He would immediately connect the arms with my family. How could I inflict that dilemma on him? Another thought struck me. Suppose they had left someone to guard the cache. Stephen would walk in on them, all unsuspecting, and would probably be shot. At all costs I must prevent him from doing that. I would have to wait for him on the track below the cave and find some excuse not to go there. But what? The sky was light before I managed to sleep again.

Next day I cut my last lesson in order to be sure of getting to the cave before him. I took the bus, as I always did, to the next village to Ayios Epiktetos and walked from there. There had been rain during the morning and the air was clear and cool, making the climb into the hills much less arduous, but I suddenly noticed that I was leaving footprints in the softened ground. It didn't matter here, the track was often used by people moving between the two villages, but if I took the path up to the cave they would give me away. My stomach clenched with alarm as a new thought came to me. Had Stephen and I left telltale prints and other traces in the cave? Would Iannis have seen them, in the dark? Could he possibly guess that I had been there? And what of last night's mule train? They must have left tracks. Would Stephen notice them?

When I reached the place where the path to the cave branched off, I was relieved to see that the rain had turned it temporarily into a watercourse. All traces of any passing had been washed away, leaving the rocks swept clean and gleaming dully in the sunshine. I stood quite still, listening for any movement above me. It had occurred to me with the daylight that it was unlikely that anyone would have been left to guard the cave. All the men I had seen last night had jobs and families. They could not disappear into the hills for hours on end without raising suspicion. And the cave had been chosen specifically because no one was likely to stumble across it. Still, I had to be sure that I was not allowing Stephen to walk into an ambush.

After a few moments I began to creep cautiously up the path, pausing every few steps to listen. There was no sound except for the rustle of the wind through the branches. I reached the final bend in the zig-zag track and flattened myself behind a large rock. Beyond the cave mouth the path ended in a tumble of loose earth from an old landslide. There was no sign of movement and the branches of the fallen pine appeared to be undisturbed. I began to wonder if I had mis-heard the conversation below my window, or even dreamed it. Silently, I moved out of the shadow of the rock and crept up to the fallen tree. Beyond the branches I could see nothing but darkness. For a while longer I crouched there, nerving myself to enter. Then I pushed aside a branch and scrambled through.

Once my eyes grew accustomed to the dimness I saw that the front of the cave was empty and, moreover, someone had swept the sandy floor with a pine branch so that it was smooth and trackless. To anyone else it would have seemed that the cave had not been entered for years but I knew that Stephen and I must have left our footprints in the dust and we had never bothered to wipe them out. Had anyone else seen them? Or perhaps with so many men coming and going they had been obscured by others before they were noticed.

For the first time I had brought a torch with me. I made my way to the back of the cave and found the narrow slit in the rocks that led back into the interior. There was still no sound. If anyone was in there, they were sitting in silence and complete darkness. I switched on the torch and edged into the cleft. It was so narrow that my shoulders touched the rock on either side and a man would have had to turn sideways to pass through. A few yards in there was a turn to the right and once I had passed it the last trace of sunlight was obscured. My heart was pounding and I had to force myself to go on. I had never believed Iannis's stories, but they had left their mark none the less.

The passage was shorter than I expected and quite sud-denly I found myself at the entrance to the inner chamber.

It was smaller than I had imagined from Iannis's description but with a high-vaulted ceiling where the beam of my torch failed to penetrate the darkness. There was no treasure, and no fire-breathing dragon, but on the far side, stacked in a pile, were the crates and bundles I had seen loaded onto the mules.

As soon as I was sure of what I was seeing I was seized by a new wave of panic. I was convinced that someone would come into the cave behind me and to prevent me from revealing the secret would somehow block the narrow passageway leading to the open air. A terror of being closed up in the dark gripped me and I blundered back towards the mouth of the cave, choking and almost sobbing with fear. Once I was in the light again, I sat down on the floor and tried to regain control of myself. The arms were here, but well hidden. Stephen had never shown any inclination to explore the back of the cave and I had never mentioned the existence of the passage. Rather than arouse his suspicions by making some excuse to change our meeting place, would it not be better to try to behave as if nothing had happened?

I scrambled to my feet and seized the dead pine branch that had clearly been used as a broom to wipe out tracks last night. In a frenzy of haste, I began to brush away my own footprints. It was only when I reached the passageway in the rock that I realized I must obliterate them all the way through to the far chamber, so that when the others returned to collect their cache they would not know someone else had been there. I swallowed and tasted bile. It was harder this time to force myself into that dark hole than it had been before but somehow I half stumbled, half crawled to the entrance of the second chamber. Then, working backwards, I wiped out all traces of my presence until I was once more crouching by the cave mouth with the dappled sunlight on my back.

I had only just finished when I heard a step on the path outside. I scrambled to the edge of the cave, pressing my back against the wall. A man's shadow fell across the sandy floor. Then the branches were pushed aside and Stephen stepped through. Without thinking, I cried out in relief and he stopped short, his hand going to his revolver. Then he recognized me and held out his arms.

'It's all right, silly! It's only me. Who did you think it was?'

I clung to him, trying to hide my shaking voice in laughter. 'I don't know. I wasn't expecting you so soon. You took me by surprise.'

'I'm early, I know. I didn't think you'd be here. Were you as impatient as I was?'

'Yes. Yes, I suppose I am. I couldn't wait to see you.'

'Me, too. Oh, darling, I hate every moment I'm not with you! I think of you all day and dream of you all night.'

He kissed me and drew me down onto the ground. He had brought drinks, beer for himself, Coke for me, and I drank greedily. My throat was parched from nerves as much as from my exertions. Afterwards he began to make love to me but this time I was unable to give myself up to him as unreservedly as before.

He felt my tension and said softly, 'What is it, my love? You're all wound up. Is it the usual monthly thing?'

I blushed at the mention of such a thing but nodded and muttered, 'Probably.'

He stroked my hair. 'We don't have to do anything, if you'd rather not. I can be patient. We can just cuddle and chat, if you'd rather.'

I felt on the edge of tears. 'Yes, please. I'd like that.'

So for the first time we talked in the intimate way of lovers. He told me about his unhappy boyhood, sent away to boarding school by his adoptive parents who, he said, must have decided after a year or two that the adoption had been a mistake and wanted him out of the way. He told me how he had been bullied, until he had learned to fight back, and how later he had discovered that he was cleverer than most of the other boys and had achieved some self-respect. He spoke of the relief and delight of his time at Cambridge University and the misery of being cast back into the brutal atmosphere of army life.

'Thank God I got a deferment until I had my degree! At least that meant I could apply for a commission. I don't think I'd have survived two years as a squaddie!'

I asked him what he would do when he left the army.

'I thought of becoming a teacher but I realize now it was for all the wrong reasons. I've always loved to travel and to write, and I thought the long holidays would give me a chance to do both.'

'So have you changed your mind?'

'I think so. While I've been here I've seen so many things that — well, things that ought to be brought to people's attention, so they can understand what's really going on. And I've seen the correspondents from the various national papers hanging round the bars and hotels, trying to make sense of the situation. I can't write about how things are here, of course, not while I'm in the army, but once I get out . . . How do you fancy being the wife of a journalist — a foreign correspondent?'

My breath caught in my throat. 'Here? You know my father would never permit it.'

'How could he stop us, once you're over twenty-one?'

'You don't understand. Age makes no difference here. We could never live here as husband and wife.'

'Then would you come away with me? To England or wherever else in the world I happened to be sent? I know it's asking a lot, for you to leave your family and the place where you grew up. But it seems as though it's the only chance for us. Would you do that, Ariadne?'

I should have hesitated. I should have been afraid but I only felt complete certainty. 'Yes. If you will come back for me, when you leave the army, I will come with you to the end of the earth.'

He kissed me then, and very soon I forgot my fear, forgot even the guns hidden at the back of the cave, and we made love.

There has been a battle at Soli, the first real face-to-face engagement between our people and the British. How can I still think of them as 'our people'? I have cut myself off from

34

my father and my brothers as surely as if I was already married to Stephen. Iannis and Demetrios disappeared for three days and returned filthy and exhausted. Demetrios looked sick and distressed but Iannis was wild-eyed with excitement and fury. Two of our men have been killed, Zakos and Michael, and Iannis can talk of nothing but revenge. I dare not point out to him that the British have good reason to feel the same. Only a week ago there was a shocking incident at the Ledra Hotel in Nicosia. Two of the regiments serving here are from Scotland and there was a Caledonian Ball at the Ledra. In the middle of the dancing, when everyone, I suppose, was enjoying themselves and trying to forget all the trouble, a grenade went off. Four people were injured and later, after the place was evacuated, an unexploded grenade was found under the table reserved for the governor, Sir John Harding. When we heard the news Iannis banged his fist on the table and called the men who had planted the grenade incompetent fools. I asked him what good it would have done if it had gone off, because Sir John was not even there at the time. He just glared at me and called me a stupid girl. All I could think of was thank God Stephen was not invited to the ball.

Things are getting worse. First the attack at the Ledra, then the battle at Soli. Now the latest news is that two British soldiers have been gunned down in broad daylight while out window-shopping. Is it possible that Christmas might bring a time of peace? No, that is a foolish hope.

Yesterday I met Stephen at the cave as usual. We have been meeting three or four times a week, although we know we are both taking a terrible risk. So that we can have more time together, I have been slipping away from school during the lunch hour. I tell them various stories: that I am unwell, that I have to visit a sick relative, that I am going to the library to do some research. The times are so disturbed, with the whole school in upheaval with meetings and demonstrations, that no one has paid much attention to my absences — yet, but I don't know how much longer it can go on.

After we had made love, Stephen said, 'My darling, it is going to be difficult for me to meet you so often from now on. There's going to be a crackdown on security. It's not just the shootings the other day. Bombs have been thrown into three bars in the city. We've been instructed that from now on we have to go around in pairs for protection. I've managed to convince my superiors that I am following up some useful Intelligence contacts, who would be frightened off if I showed up with another soldier, but it's getting harder.' He sighed and sat up, running his hand over his hair. 'The problem is, I don't actually have any information to give them. I'm going to have to justify all the time I've been spending away from base somehow.'

I thought of the weapons hidden in the back of the cave. He had never shown any sign of wanting to explore and I had begun to forget my anxiety. Now it struck me that I had the means at hand to provide him with exactly the kind of information that his superiors wanted. After all, I hate what the men of EOKA are doing. The loss of the rifles and grenades in the inner chamber might mean that lives would be saved on both sides. A word from me and Stephen would regain the confidence of his superiors and his freedom of movement. The temptation was so strong that it made me tremble, but in the same instant I knew I had to resist it. It would be an act of betrayal that might lead the authorities straight to my own brothers.

CHAPTER 5

Demetrios is dead! No one will tell me exactly how it happened. Father will only say that he and Iannis were 'on active service'. Iannis has disappeared, gone into hiding somewhere. Demetrios, my gentle brother who never wished harm to any living creature, is dead. Is this part of my punishment? I have betrayed my people and disgraced my family. I always knew that I should have to suffer for my wickedness — but why should my brother suffer too?

Today I went to the cave, hoping that Stephen would come to find me. I have to speak to him! As soon as I left the main path I knew what had happened. There were footprints, broken branches, spent ammunition littering the ground. I understood then how Demetrios died. But I had said nothing! I never breathed the faintest hint to Stephen, and he cannot have suspected what was hidden in the darkness at the back of the place where we made love. So it must have been pure chance that someone else discovered the hiding place. Unless he was followed — or I was. Did I, after all, betray my brother?

There was a sentry posted at the mouth of the cave and other men sitting inside. I suppose they were waiting to see if anyone else comes to look for the weapons. Fools! Every member of EOKA will have heard about their loss by now.

But it means I can never meet Stephen there again and I do not know where else to find him. He no longer comes to have his lesson with my father on Sundays. That finished months ago, when the security situation got so bad. The troops no longer stroll around the streets of Nicosia as they used to. They drive round in their jeeps, rifles at the ready. It is impossible to arrange what might look like a casual encounter. Yet I must contrive some way of speaking to him — and soon!

As if this isn't enough, the school has finally become suspicious. The headmaster has written to my father, asking why I have missed so many lessons. I told my parents that I had lost patience with my teachers, who seem not to care about the struggle for independence, and was spending my time helping to write leaflets and organize demonstrations with other activists among my classmates. My father pretended to reprimand me but I could see that he was not really angry. I have been careful in the last few months not to speak against *enosis* and he is glad to think that I have accepted the error of my previous opinions. So, I have deceived him in yet another way and if he ever asks any of the real activists from the Gymnasium what I have been doing he will learn that. But what is that compared with the greater sin I have committed and for which my punishment is only just beginning?

Demetrios is dead and I am pregnant!

The guard at the gate of the British army camp did not want to let me in. I told him that I was a friend of Lieutenant Allenby, but he said it was against his orders to let anyone pass. I begged and pleaded. It went against my pride, but I was desperate. Then I had an idea. I told him that I had been acting as an informant for the lieutenant and that I had something vital to tell him. He made a phone call then, and I thought he was speaking to Stephen. When he told me to follow another soldier into the camp, I thought my problems were over. I would see Stephen and explain to him and he would look after me. I wasn't sure how, but I knew he would take care of me.

Instead of taking me to Stephen, the man led me to an office and I found myself facing a man in a colonel's uniform. He had grey hair and a grey face with not a trace of kindness in it.

'You have information? Well?'

I drew myself up and tried to speak with dignity, although my legs were trembling.

'I need to speak to Lieutenant Allenby. My information is for him.'

'If you have information which may be of use in the current emergency, then you must give it to me. If not, you had better be on your way.'

It was no good! His coldness and his overbearing manner were too much for me. I began to cry. I told him that Stephen and I were lovers and that now I was expecting his child. I said that Stephen did not know this and that I must tell him.

That man! He was a monster, not a human being. He sat behind his desk and looked at me as if I was a slut from the slums of Famagusta.

'My dear girl, if you have been foolish enough to get yourself into this predicament that is something for you to sort out with your family. The British army cannot take responsibility for your bastard. Lieutenant Allenby has behaved very stupidly, and he will be dealt with accordingly. But there is no question of your being allowed to see him. I suggest you go home and make a clean breast of things to your parents. Good day.'

A moment later I found myself being led back along the corridor. I was shaking all over and I could not control my tears, although I was ashamed for the soldiers to see me like that. At the gate the sentry jerked his head towards the road and told me curtly to 'push off'. I understood that he had reason to hate my people, but still I wondered how he could be so callous when he must have seen my distress.

Once out of the camp I walked for a long time without thinking where I was going, until I found myself on the beach. The sea was angry and the waves thundered against the shore. A fine rain was falling and I realized for the first time that I was wet through and shivering with cold. I looked at the sea and contemplated walking straight into the waves. How could I go home and tell my mother and father what had happened to me? It was bad enough that I had allowed myself to become pregnant out of wedlock but that the father was a British soldier, a representative of the hated enemy who were occupying our island, was unforgivable. Moreover, he was a man who had represented himself as a friend of the whole family. He and Demetrios had gone bird watching together. The thought of my brother dragged me deeper into my misery. Demetrios had been killed in an ambush outside the very cave that Stephen and I had used as our meeting place. When that came out, as I knew it must eventually, Iannis would immediately conclude that it was I who had betrayed them. I would be branded a traitor as well as a whore. I would be lucky to escape with my life. I looked again at the sea. I believe if it had been a calm day I should have walked into the water and let it take me but the fury of the waves terrified me. I remembered that my father was a good man and that he had always loved me. I knew that I had forfeited that love forever but I had to trust that his goodness would not allow him to have me killed, along with the child I carried. I turned away and began to trudge back towards the city.

PART TWO

LONDON, 1973

CHAPTER 6

'Stephen Allenby?'

Stephen stopped short, feeling the familiar tingle down his spine that spelt 'trouble'. His first thought was that this was the parent of one of his pupils, lying in wait for him to complain about the fact that his boy had been disciplined. He had heard plenty of stories from colleagues of being shouted at and even threatened by irate fathers. But a second glance dispelled that idea. Stephen had not lost his journalist's eye for detail and ability to sum up and categorize people at first sight. The man standing by his car had close-cropped grey hair. His clothes were clearly intended to look casual — blazer and cavalry twill trousers — but only succeeded in giving the impression that he would have been happier in a suit, or in uniform, perhaps. There was something about the set of his shoulders that said ex-military.

'Yes?' he agreed cautiously.

The man reached into an inner pocket and produced a card. 'My name's Warrender. I wonder if we could have a word in private.'

Stephen looked at the card. It said, 'Matthew Warrender, Personnel Solutions,' and gave an address in the City. 'What about?'

'It's not something I want to discuss standing in the car park. Suffice it to say that I have a proposal to make that I think will interest you. Is there somewhere we could go? It's too early for the pub, unfortunately. Somewhere we could get a cup of tea, perhaps?'

Stephen scrutinized his face. His expression was bland and friendly. 'Look, if you're trying to sell me a time-share or something, I'm afraid you are wasting your time.'

The stranger laughed briefly. 'It's nothing like that, I assure you.'

Caution suggested that it would be wise to refuse the invitation but Stephen's curiosity was piqued. Once upon a time, sensing a story, he would not have hesitated.

'All right. There's a café across the road. It's a bit of a greasy spoon but I'm afraid that's the best we can do round here.'

Neither of them spoke as Stephen led the way through the early rush-hour traffic. In the café they found a corner table well away from the half-dozen or so elderly women and overalled workmen who made up the rest of the clientele. Warrender went to the counter and came back with two mugs of tea and a couple of bath buns.

As he sat down Stephen said, 'How did you know my name? And where to find me?'

'We've had our eyes on you for some time. You see, we think you have the expertise and the background that we're looking for.'

'What sort of expertise?'

'You used to be a journalist, didn't you?'

'So?'

'And you have spent time in Cyprus.'

The tingle was back down Stephen's spine. 'Many years ago, yes.'

'I imagine that you still take an interest in what is going on out there. In which case, it will not have escaped your attention that trouble is brewing again. You were there during the EOKA rising. Did you know that EOKA has been re-formed? They are calling themselves EOKA B and the old agitation for *enosis* is back on the agenda.'

'I had read something in the papers about that, yes.'

'Right. Well, my clients are looking for someone who would be prepared to go out there, on a long-term basis, and send back in-depth reports.'

'Your clients?'

'I'm not at liberty to divulge who it is at the moment. I seem to remember that you reported for several of the quality broadsheets, back in the day. All I am asking at the moment is whether you are sufficiently interested to come to a formal interview. At that point I should be able to be much more explicit.'

Once again, Stephen studied the other man's face. He knew that if any of the papers he had once worked for wanted him back on the staff the invitation would have come in an informal telephone call. There was something else going on here — but what?

'What did you mean by long term?' he asked.

'That's hard to define. A year? Maybe longer. You can be assured of one thing. My clients are prepared to pay quite well — better than the average teacher's salary, anyway. And, of course, your family could accompany you. You have a small daughter, I believe.'

Stephen knew he should end the conversation there. These people, whoever they were, knew too much about him. But he was being offered the chance to get away from London, from a job he had never liked and now hated more with every passing day. Above all, he was being offered the chance to go back to Cyprus. The temptation was too much.

'When would this interview take place? And where?'

'You have the address there.' Warrender indicated the card which Stephen had laid beside his saucer. 'As for when . . . I presume you can't get away during school hours. How would 5 p.m. the day after tomorrow suit you?'

Stephen hesitated, drew a breath, and said, 'OK. Five o'clock it is.' He put the card in his pocket and rose. 'Thanks for the tea.'

Warrender smiled. 'My pleasure.'

Driving home, Stephen told himself he was being a fool, but he could not dismiss the throb of excitement in the pit of his stomach — an excitement he had not experienced for years. It would be good for all of them, he told himself. God knew, they needed a change!

As he stepped through the front door, his small daughter threw herself at him and clung to his legs. Her face was red and streaked with tears. He bent down and lifted her into his arms.

'What's the matter, Cressy? Don't cry, darling. Tell Daddy what's wrong.'

'Mummy cross. Mummy shout at Cressy! Horrid Mummy!'

'No, you mustn't say that. If Mummy's cross with you I expect it's for a good reason. You must have done something wrong.'

'Didn't! Didn't!' The small face creased up and the tears began to flow again.

Stephen felt an all-too-familiar sinking at his heart. 'Come on. Let's go and see what Mummy has to say.'

Laura was in the kitchen. Stephen took in the half-smoked cigarette on the ashtray and the opened bottle of wine on the kitchen table. Almost half of it was gone and the kitchen was in a fog of tobacco and the smoke from pork chops being fried in too hot a pan. The radio was playing 'Tie a Yellow Ribbon Round the Ole Oak Tree'.

She said, 'Oh, you're back then.'

'Yes. Sorry I'm a bit late. I got held up.'

'Oh yes? Little Miss Blue-eyes needed a shoulder to cry on, did she?'

'Miss Blue-eyes' was Laura's name for a young teacher who had recently joined the staff in Stephen's department. She was having a difficult first year and he had gone out of his way to help her, but Laura insisted on construing his kindness as the beginning of an affair. Stephen controlled his temper and said evenly, 'No. It was nothing to do with school, actually. I'll tell you about it later. Why are you angry with Cressida?'

Laura looked round. 'Oh, Daddy's girl's been telling tales again, has she? You ought to know better. She turns it on like a tap, as soon as she sees you. You spoil her, that's the trouble.'

'No, I think she's genuinely upset. What happened?'

'Nothing! It's all very well for you, swanning in expecting your meal to be on the table. I've had a hard day at school, too, you know. And then I have to pick Madam up from the child-minder, and she's done nothing but whine and grizzle ever since we got home. *'Play with me! Play with me!'* As if I had time!'

'That's not fair, Laura!' he protested. 'I don't swan in expecting my meal to be on the table. Very often I do the cooking. And Cressida only wants a bit of your time and attention. After all, she doesn't see you all day.'

Laura slammed plates into the oven. 'That's right! It's all my fault. I knew it would be. It was your idea that I should go back to work.'

'I only suggested it because you seemed miserable stuck at home all day.'

'Anyone with half a mind would be miserable stuck here with no one to talk to except a toddler. You should try it one day!'

'So that's why I thought you might be happier if you went back to work. Come on, Laura! You can't have it both ways.'

She put down the pan of potatoes she was draining and sat at the table. 'I can't have it any way! I'm wrong whatever I do.'

He set Cressida down on her feet and went to put his arm round his wife. 'No, you're not. You're just tired. We both are. Come on. Let's get the dinner on the table and then I've got something to tell you.'

He reached across and re-tuned the radio. The chimes of Big Ben vibrated around the kitchen.

'Oh, why can't you leave it alone?' Laura exclaimed.

'I want to listen to the news.'

'I can't think why. It's the same every evening. I'm sick to death of hearing about Nixon and Watergate, strikes, prices going up, Edward Heath moaning on—'

'Hush!' Stephen said sharply. 'Just listen a minute.'

The announcer was saying, 'In Athens today it was announced that the Greek junta which has been in control of the country since the revolution has abolished the monarchy and declared Greece a republic.'

'Well, hurrah for them!' Laura said, with a hint of sarcasm.

'You don't mean that! The colonels' regime is one of the most repressive in Europe. It depends on the secret police and the use of torture to maintain itself.'

She looked at him with an expression of affectionate mockery that reminded him of the old Laura. 'OK, calm down. I know the Greeks are your special pets.'

'I love Greece. I love the country and I love its history. And it sickens me to think of what is going on there now. But there's something else . . .' He fell silent as he took in the possible implications. If EOKA was rearing its ugly head again, this news could only encourage it. He took the plate that Laura held out to him. 'Come on. We need to talk. There's something I want to tell you.'

Two days later Stephen presented himself at the address on Warrender's card, which turned out to be an anonymous office block just off the Strand. A board in the foyer directed him to the fourth floor and a secretary in an outer office ushered him through to the inner room. Inside the door, Stephen came to an abrupt halt. Suddenly everything was becoming clearer. Warrender was standing by the window but it was the man who rose from behind the desk who jolted Stephen back twenty years.

'Major Henshaw!' It was all he could do not to come to attention.

Henshaw came round the desk smiling, his hand extended. 'Not major any more. I left the service years ago. Good to see you, Stephen.'

'How are you, sir?' Stephen asked as they shook hands, struggling for the right social tone.

'Pretty well, all things considered. And you?'

'Not bad — all things considered.'

'Have a seat.' Henshaw waved him to an easy chair near the window and took one opposite him. 'You've met Matthew, of course. Have a drink. Scotch?'

'No, thank you.'

'Ah, no, of course not. Something else? Tea? Coffee?'

'Coffee would be good.'

Henshaw signed to Warrender, who busied himself at a side table where a coffee machine stood beside a collection of bottles. Henshaw leaned back in his chair, a glass of whisky in his hand.

'Well, you'll be wondering what all this is about. The fact is, we think you may be able to help us.'

'Why me?' Stephen asked. 'How did you know where I was?'

'You won't realize it, of course, but we've been keeping a fatherly eye on you ever since you left the army.'

'Why? What on earth for?'

'Your activities in Cyprus gave us cause for concern, for a start. You allowed yourself to become involved with a family that was in the forefront of the EOKA terrorist organization, while ostensibly working for British Military Intelligence.'

'I had no idea they were terrorists! My only interest was in—'

'In the young lady concerned. Yes, we came to that conclusion in the end. Your efforts to track her down when you were finally demobbed convinced us.'

'You knew about that?'

'We knew that you went straight back to Cyprus and then to Athens. We even knew that you paid a private detective to track her down — but to no avail.'

'Her father had married her off to some family friend. I didn't even know her married name.'

'Probably the best outcome, under the circumstances. Anyway, we lost sight of you for a while after that, until we started to read articles by you in some of the quality papers. It was obvious that you had a knack of turning up wherever there was trouble brewing and worming your way into the confidence of the people involved. We were particularly impressed by your despatches from Vietnam, for example. You have a way of getting to the heart of matters. It's a great pity that you finally succumbed to the trap that ensnares so many foreign correspondents, stuck in hotel rooms far from home.' Henshaw held up his glass so that the evening sunlight coming through the window turned its contents to liquid gold.

'That's all in the past,' Stephen said sharply. 'I've been clean for five years now.'

'We know that, and I applaud you for your strength of mind. And for finding a new career. But,' Henshaw leaned forward, holding the glass between his knees, 'I must admit that I find it hard to believe that the humdrum routine of a schoolteacher's life really suits you.'

Stephen hesitated. This was too close to the truth for comfort. He said, 'I'm not ideally suited to it. Perhaps I'm not very good at it.'

'But you were a very good foreign correspondent. Wouldn't you like to go back to that life?'

'I have a wife and child to support.'

'Ah yes. Laura, isn't it? I seem to remember that she was involved in the anti-Vietnam war protests.'

'Do you keep tabs on everyone?'

'Only those who bring themselves to our attention. A war reporter and an anti-war protester. Isn't that a rather unusual alliance?

'Not at all. I've seen enough of war to hate everything about it.'

'I take your point. So you will be all the more anxious to help us avoid future conflicts. To get back to my previous point. Wouldn't you like to get back to what you do best, as a journalist?'

'Ideally, yes. But no one would employ me now.'

'Oh, I think that could be arranged. Let me put my cards on the table. We are concerned about developments in

Cyprus. We want someone out there who knows the people and speaks the language, someone who was familiar with the old EOKA, who can report back on what these new chaps are intending. How do you fancy being based out there?'

'We're not talking about being a foreign correspondent, are we? That's just a cover.'

'Yes, but I can promise you that, provided your articles are up to your old standard, they would appear in some prestigious newspapers. Of course, you would not be telling the general public quite what you would be telling us, but there would still be plenty of scope for in-depth reporting.'

'So who would I be working for, really? Military Intelligence again?'

Henshaw shrugged slightly. 'A rose by any other name . . . You would be serving your country, and I can promise you that when the assignment was over you would find that there was a generous — what shall I call it — severance settlement. Plus the fact that you would have had the opportunity to re-establish your career.'

'You are asking me to relocate my family, on a long-term basis. Suppose my wife doesn't want to go?'

Henshaw sat back with a smile. 'Here's a suggestion. Why don't you take her there for a holiday? Easter is in a few weeks' time. If she likes the place you would be able to work out your notice for the summer term and move permanently in July.'

'There's a snag to that. I can't afford foreign holidays on my pay.'

'Oh, that won't be a problem. I'm sure *The Telegraph* would be happy to commission you to produce a report for their Travel section. I believe Cyprus is becoming a popular tourist destination. All expenses paid, naturally.'

Stephen gazed at him. He felt breathless. The chance to get his career back on track; to go back to Cyprus; perhaps to see Ariadne again — He stopped himself sharply. There was no chance of that. She was in Athens, a married woman with children. But all the same, just the chance to be back on that magical island . . .

He said, 'And if I did decide to relocate, in the long term, how am I supposed to be supporting myself? The occasional article in the British papers won't be enough to convince people.'

'I suggest you might look for a small business — a shop, a B&B, something that wouldn't take up too much of your time. There are plenty of ex-pats out there, eking out a living that way.' Henshaw rose. 'So, what about it? Do we have a deal?'

Stephen got up too. 'I'll have to discuss it with my wife. Not the real motive behind the move, of course, but the general idea.'

'Offer her the holiday,' Henshaw said. 'That should be enough for now.'

Laura was slumped in an armchair in front of the TV when he got home. A pile of exercise books was on the table beside her, together with a half-empty bottle of wine. Cressida, content for once, was playing on the floor with her doll's tea set.

Laura looked up. 'Well, how did it go — this mysterious interview?'

He knew from her expression that she thought the story of the interview was an excuse; that she still believed he was seeing another woman. He forced a smile.

'It went pretty well. I'll tell you all about it over dinner.'

She hauled herself to her feet. 'I'd better start cooking then.'

'No need. I picked up a Chinese on the way home. Come on, let's eat.'

Three weeks later they were sitting on the balcony of their hotel room watching the last light fade from the waves lapping the long sandy beaches of the east coast of Cyprus. Or Laura was watching, while Stephen tapped away on his ancient typewriter. In the room behind them, Cressida was sound asleep. He pulled a sheet of paper out of the machine, added it to a small pile beside him on the table, and stretched his arms.

'That's enough for tonight.'

'How's it going?'

'Nearly finished.'

He looked at her. Her face had softened and filled out, los-
ing the pinched, exhausted expression he had seen too often
over the last months. They had spent all day on the beach,
watching Cressida building sandcastles and playing with her
in the edge of the water, and they were both bathed in the
afterglow of sunshine and fresh air. In the gentle evening light,
she looked again like the young woman he had fallen in love
with five years earlier. He mentally corrected himself. Not
'fallen in love'. He had fallen in love once in his life, and it had
not been with Laura. But he had been attracted to her — to
her vitality and self-confidence — and it had seemed to him
then that she offered all he could hope for in a relationship.
That was before Cressida's birth had transformed her, knotted
her into an apparently endless cycle of alternate lethargy and
frantic activity. Now, he thought, perhaps at last they might
be able to break free. He stretched again and yawned.

Laura said, 'What shall we do tomorrow?'

'I'd like to go over to the north coast again. It's the area
I got to know best when I was here before.'

'Kyrenia? Yes, that sounds good. I think I liked that best
of all the places we've visited.'

'We can stop off in Kyrenia. But I want to go further
west, along the coast. It's pretty rugged but quite beautiful
and almost unspoiled. That OK with you?'

'Sure, fine. We've had a good day on the beach. It'll be
better for Cressy to keep out of the sun tomorrow.'

Around lunchtime next day they found themselves in the
village of Lapithos. Cressida was becoming fretful and Laura
said, 'Let's see if we can find a bar or a restaurant where we
can get something to eat and drink. I'm parched!'

At first it seemed there was nowhere, then as they drove
out of the village Laura exclaimed, 'There, look!'

Three whitewashed Moorish arches shaded a terrace set
with tables, at which half a dozen men and women were

drinking. Stephen parked the car and left Laura and Cressida at a table while he went inside. As his eyes adjusted to the dim light of the bar, he saw a tubby grey-haired man polishing the counter. When he asked, in Greek, for two Cokes and a lemonade, the response took him by surprise.

'Sorry, chum. You'll have to slow down. My Greek's a bit dodgy, even after all this time.'

'You're English? So am I.'

As he poured the drinks, the man explained that he and his wife had bought the bar on an impulse, after discovery it on holiday.

'We fancied retiring to somewhere warm and this was a way of funding it — and I must say we've never regretted it. But now it looks as though we're going to have to put it on the market and go home.'

Stephen felt the same tingle down his spine that he had experienced when meeting Warrender. Could this be a set-up? Or was it just a genuine coincidence?

'Business not good, then?' he hazarded.

'Oh, business is fine. No, it's not that. Our daughter's expecting her first kid and she's on her own. Her fella went off and left her as soon as he knew she was pregnant, the bastard! So she needs some help with the baby so she can go back to work. We don't want to leave here but it looks as if we shall have to.'

Outside, while they sipped their drinks and waited for the Greek salads he had ordered, Stephen said, 'This is good, isn't it?'

'Mm!' Laura agreed. 'Bliss!'

'How would you fancy living here permanently?'

She laughed. 'Join the lotus eaters? Chance'd be a fine thing.'

'We could do it.'

'Oh yes? And live on thin air, I suppose.'

'No, I'm serious. The people who recruited me, they're a sort of agency for several papers and they want someone out here on a semi-permanent basis. The job's mine if I want it.'

She frowned at him. 'Is that what all this has been about? Bring me here, get me hooked on the place, before you come out with the full story?'

'Not exactly,' he mumbled. 'I told them I couldn't take the job unless you agreed, so they suggested we came on holiday to see how you like it.'

'And they are offering you the job on the strength of work you did six, seven or more years ago?'

'Partly. But mainly because I know the place and speak the language. Anyway, what do you think?'

'Well, I can see the attraction for you, but what am I supposed to do all day?'

'Ah, well, I was coming to that. The writing job probably won't pay enough to keep us on its own, so I was thinking we might buy a small business of some kind. We could run it together.' He leaned forward. 'Think about it, Laura. You know things weren't going well for us back in England. You hated being at home with no one but Cressida but you find it too much of a strain working and looking after her. This way, we'd both be around, and she wouldn't have to go to a childminder. It's worth a try, isn't it?' He knew he was being duplicitous but he told himself that, whatever his motives, there was truth in what he was saying.

Laura gazed out at the Mediterranean glittering in the distance. Then she turned back to him. 'And what sort of business did you have in mind?'

He could not suppress a grin. 'Ah, well, that's the point. The couple who own this place are English. I got chatting while I was ordering the lunch. They want to go home to be with their daughter, who is expecting a baby, so they want to sell up.'

She stared at him. 'You're not serious, are you? My God! You are serious! Stephen, you are a recovering alcoholic — and you are thinking of *buying a pub*!'

He was momentarily taken aback. The contradiction had not even occurred to him. 'But I'm past all that. You know I haven't touched a drop for five years. Look, if I can watch you working your way through a bottle of wine without feeling the slightest temptation, doesn't that prove it? If anyone has a problem with the amount of alcohol they consume, it isn't me!'

Their eyes met and he realized he had shocked them both. He was suddenly aware that Laura's drinking had been worrying him at a subconscious level but he had refused to acknowledge it.

After a pause Laura said briskly, 'Don't be silly! That was just a way of relaxing after a hard day. I haven't had more than the odd glass with my dinner since we've been out here.'

'Exactly!' he said. 'That's just the point I'm trying to make.'

'And if we were to buy this place, how are we supposed to pay for it?'

'That wouldn't be a problem. Our house in Croydon would fetch more than enough to cover it. Think what we would be going back to. Strikes, rampant inflation — and winter's on its way.' He waved a hand in the direction of the view. 'Just imagine waking up to this every morning, picking your own oranges and lemons and figs, no more rush-hour traffic, no more struggling to keep order with 4C. And Cressida's happier here, too. Now you are so much more relaxed, so is she. Look at her now.'

Cressida was sitting on the steps leading down from the terrace, absorbed in the activities of a small colony of ants.

'But that's another thing,' Laura said. 'What about her education?'

'She's not due to start school for a year yet. And she'll soon pick up Greek. It's supposed to be good for children's general intelligence to learn to speak another language.' He reached across and took Laura's hand. 'I'm only suggesting we try it. Why don't we give it a year, and see how it goes.'

He was not sure, even as he spoke, why it was so important to him that she should agree. It had to do with saving their marriage, certainly, and with re-starting his own career. But there was something else; a visceral urgency that he felt but could not fully explain. The island had him in its thrall and he knew he must stay.

A plump, grey-haired woman, who looked like the feminine equivalent of the man behind the bar, came out of the house with the salads.

Laura said, 'My husband tells me you want to sell up.'

The woman sighed. 'Yes, sadly. It'll break our hearts to leave. We've really loved it here. But we're needed at home, so that's that.'

They chatted for a while about life on the island, and the business of running the bar. When the woman had left them to eat their lunch, Laura looked up at the name on the board above the central arch.

'What's this place called? You know I can't read Greek.'

He looked at the sign for the first time and laughed. 'It's called the Café Anonymou — the nameless café.'

Laura wrinkled her nose. 'That's rather sad. It sounds as though someone ought to adopt it and give it a name.' She smiled suddenly. 'OK, I agree. Provided the business checks out and is as good as they say, and they don't want a silly price for it. I'm probably mad but let's give it a go.'

PART THREE

THE TURKISH REPUBLIC OF NORTHERN

CYPRUS, 1998

CHAPTER 7

'Miss Allenby?'

I look up from my guidebook and my breakfast coffee, prepared to be irritated by the interruption. As I focus on the speaker, annoyance is replaced by a visceral twinge of appreciation. He is young — well, youngish — a few years older than me. Mid-thirties perhaps. He is taller than most of the local men, but dark haired and olive skinned like them, with a lean, athletic figure. It is the eyes that hold my attention: heavy lidded, with a direct, brooding gaze, under arched brows.

He smiles. 'Forgive me for interrupting your breakfast. My name is Karim Mezeli. The hotel employs me to take parties to visit some of the ancient sites on the island. We're about to leave for the temple of Aphrodite. Would you care to join us?'

My initial irritation returns. So that's it. Just another local touting for business. I shake my head. 'Thank you, no. I have other plans for today.'

He bends his head in a gesture that is almost courtly. 'A pity. Another time, perhaps? The island has a fascinating history.'

'Yes, I know.' For a moment I am tempted to pursue the conversation, but I restrain the impulse. 'Yes, another time, perhaps.' It was not what I intended to say.

He nods again. 'I shall look forward to it.'

I watch him move away towards the foyer, where he is immediately surrounded by a gaggle of enthusiastic tourists. I have a general impression of men with beards and baggy shorts and women in floral dresses that expose too much sagging flesh. With his dark eyes and strong, aquiline nose, he looks like a bird of prey among pigeons.

I feel a chill of dismay. Perhaps this whole holiday is going to turn out to be a mistake. *'It was your choice,'* I remind myself. *'You could have gone to Corfu with the rest of the girls.'*

It is true. I remember Sue insisting, in her usual bossy I-know-what's-best-for-you voice, 'You've had a rough time lately, what with your mother's illness and the funeral and everything. What you need is a break, a chance to get away from it all and have fun.'

The trouble was, Sue's idea of fun was the last thing I felt I needed at that moment. Baking on the beach all day and plunging into the stifling cacophony of a nightclub each evening has lost its appeal. I've had enough of the effort to repel the attentions of sweaty-handed men looking for a one-night stand and of waking in the morning to the bitter flavour of solitude and too much alcohol. Perhaps I've grown out of it. Perhaps I'm growing up. Perhaps I'm getting old!

But the doctor who had looked after Mother told me I ought to take a holiday. 'You look worn out,' he said. 'You need a rest.' Yes, that's it. Above all else I wanted a rest. I can't remember ever before feeling so completely exhausted. And when I found the photographs, hidden at the bottom of a drawer when I was going through Mother's things, that decided me.

Mezeli shepherds the group out towards a waiting bus and as the last of them pass him he looks across the room and for a moment his eyes meet mine and I feel an electric tingle at the pit of my stomach. He turns away and goes out, the doors closing behind him.

I finish my coffee and go up to my room. The envelope containing the photographs is in the drawer of the dressing table. I take it out and the feel of it, the smell of old, slightly mouldy paper, transports me back through the days to another place altogether. Sunlight slanted through gaps in the curtains that covered the grimy windows, illuminating firefly hordes of dust motes. The bedstead stood naked, its stained mattress consigned to the dump. The empty wardrobe gaped like a hungry mouth. There was a lingering, musty odour, a mixture of stale alcohol and *Je Reviens*, my mother's favourite perfume. I took the photographs from their hiding place and went downstairs. Then I closed the front door for the last time and walked to the garden gate. The house watched me expressionlessly from its blank windows. Along the path Grandmother's once-prized roses had grown leggy for want of pruning, but still flaunted their blooms above the encroaching dandelions and buttercups. Close by, on the verge, the dustbin awaited collection, its lid bulging open to reveal its cargo of empty sherry bottles.

I twitch my shoulders, physically shaking off the memory, telling myself it's too late now to have regrets, too late to feel guilty. I did my best, after all. All those interminable weekends, trying to persuade my mother to go for a walk, visit friends, take an interest in current affairs — anything to distract her from the lure of the bottle. It was useless but I did try. And it cost me more than my time. In the end it cost me Paul. What more could have been expected of me? But there is a further memory that I cannot suppress. 'Sorry, Mum, not this weekend . . . No, it's work — well sort of . . . Paul's got to entertain some important clients. He wants me to be with him . . . I'll be down next weekend, without fail . . .' The hospital telephoned on the Monday morning. 'I'm sorry, your mother passed away during the night . . .'

I open the envelope and slide the contents onto the polished surface of the table, spreading them out, my eyes flicking from one image to the next, until I find the one I am looking for — a couple with a small child. The man is tall and very fair, his face and arms deeply tanned; the woman is less striking, her hair in the picture neither dark nor blonde, her face rounded and without make-up. He wears flared jeans, she a loose caftan of some light material. Between them a child of three or four with a mop of silver-blonde hair screws up her face at the photographer. I pick up the picture and study it more closely. In the background there is a house; white walls supporting a riot of purple bougainvillaea, a terrace with tables and umbrellas, beyond that three pointed Moorish arches leading into the dark interior; above the door a painted sign. *Café Anonymou*. On the back Mother has written: *Stephen, me and Cressida outside the bar — Lapithos, 1974*. Was that child really me? Why is it that I have no recollection of that time or that place? *Café Anonymou* — the nameless café! Why did they call it that? Looking back, it almost seems a sign of impermanence, as if they had felt it was not worthwhile giving the place a name; like a child not expected to live. And why did Mother keep these pictures hidden away? Why have I never seen them before?

I put the photograph down and pick up another. The same fair-haired man, much younger, in army uniform, with two others. They are laughing, leaning on each other's shoulders, their eyes screwed up against the light. On the back, in a handwriting I do not recognize, are the words: *Self, Jonno and Dempsey — Famagusta, 1955*. So, my father served here as a young man, doing his National Service, presumably. Was that why he came back, with his wife and child? What was it that drew him back? And why did he wait nineteen years?

I half close my eyes, struggling to fix a distant memory. Surely I must have a mental picture of some sort! But all I can recall is a tall presence and a hand holding mine as we walk along a leafy English lane. I shuffle the photographs back into the envelope, except for the one showing the three of us in front of the café. That I put into my handbag. Then I pick up my hat and head for the lift.

Coming out of the hotel I draw a deep breath and my mood lightens. Later it will be very hot but at this hour the air is pleasantly fresh. A breeze sets the fringes of the sun umbrellas on the terrace fluttering and whips the waters of the harbour into a thousand small waves that reflect the sunshine in brilliant shards of light. A few dozen brightly painted fishing boats dance on the water and beyond them the honey-coloured bulk of Kyrenia Castle glows in the sunshine. I stroll along the harbour front until I come to the office of a car-hire firm. I arrange a car for the day and when the formalities have been completed I say, 'Do you have a map of the island? I want to find a place called Lapithos.'

The man behind the desk frowns. 'You mean Lapta. All the places are called by their Turkish names now.'

'Oh, I'm sorry. I didn't realize. Can you show me where it is?'

He produces a map and prods a finger on a spot about fifteen kilometres to the west. 'Here. You take the coast road. You will see the signs.'

I collect the car keys and drive out of the town, relieved that in this erstwhile British colony traffic still drives on the left. Soon I am heading west on the coast road. To my right the land drops away to a sea patterned in sapphire and turquoise. To my left the narrow coastal plain is bounded by a range of mountains that rise almost sheer to a rampart of jagged peaks, like the broken teeth of a saw. In between the landscape is patched with the silver of olive groves and the umber of dry pastures and punctuated with the dark exclamation marks of cypresses.

As I drive, I feel myself relax. The tension goes out of my shoulders and my hands cease to grip the steering wheel as if the car were some unruly animal. I have thought a lot about Cyprus recently but I never imagined this beauty. Was this what drew my father back, this brilliant light, this glowing landscape? Since finding the photograph of him in his army uniform I have tried to imagine why the island had such a lasting hold on him. Once, before she died, my grandmother let slip the fact that I had lived there as a small child but when I tried to get Mother to talk about it she always put the questions aside with a brusque 'I really don't remember' and then changed the subject. Eventually I learned not to bring it up.

Now, looking around as I drive, I begin for the first time to sense the magic that might draw a man back after twenty years. I find myself recalling the story of Odysseus and the land of the lotus eaters, the island where the lotus grew and any man who tasted it immediately forgot home and family and wanted only to lie and rest and listen to the music of the place. Isn't there a poem by Tennyson? *'There is sweet music here that softer falls, Than petals from blown roses on the grass . . .'* Or was that Shakespeare in *The Tempest*? *'The isle is full of music, sounds and sweet airs that give delight and hurt not . . .'* Oh, to be able to write like that! It has been my dream since childhood but so far my only successes have been a short story published in *Writers' News* and a couple of poems in obscure magazines.

The blare of a horn brings me back to reality and I realize that I have allowed the car to drift perilously close to the centre of the narrow road. *'Watch out,'* I tell myself, *'Looks like the lotus has got you in its grip already!'*

I pass through a village or two of dusty-fronted shops, their wares crowding the pavements, and houses where small children study my passing with vast dark eyes. There are some hotels, closer to the sea, but not the solid wall of concrete that ruins so many other Mediterranean resorts, and in the spaces between them the waves break in creamy foam on a rocky shore. I pass an army barracks where a sentry sits drowsily behind a table, then more hotels, and finally come to the turning signposted Lapta.

The road climbs and twists past white villas enclosed behind high walls. The village is spread out along several narrow lanes and for a while I drive around without any clear sense of direction. Eventually, at the highest point, where the escarpment of the mountains rises so steeply that any further building is impossible, I come to a place where a spring spouts from the rock face below a building which proclaims itself a bar and restaurant. A glance at the photograph is enough to be sure that this is not the Café Anonymou, even by another name, but I am thirsty by now, so I park the car and find a table on a terrace overlooking the village and the steep drop to the sea.

I order a Coca-Cola from the owner, a dark, wiry man with a drooping moustache, and when he brings it I ask, 'Is there another bar in the village, called the Café Anonymou?'

He frowns and answers in heavily accented English, 'No places with Greek names here.'

'No, of course not,' I correct myself hastily. 'It used to be called that, a long time ago. Perhaps the name has been changed.'

'I come here twelve years ago, from Turkey,' he says. 'No place like that here then. No Greeks here — not no more.'

'It wasn't Greeks who owned it,' I tell him. 'The owners were English — my father and mother.'

'You live here then?'

'Yes, but I can't remember where it was.'

'Your mother and father not remember?'

'They're both dead.'

'Dead?' His face softens a little. 'That is sorry.' He begins to wipe the table and it looks as if I have drawn a blank. Then he looks up, his eyes brightening. 'English man and lady living here, in village. Old people. Maybe they remember?'

'Oh, yes. Perhaps they might. Can you tell me where they live?'

The route takes me back over a road I have already traversed but, as I draw up outside the house, I experience a shock of recognition. There are the three Moorish arches and the terrace, now empty of its tables and bright sun umbrellas. The sign above the door has gone, but I am in no doubt that this is the house in the photograph. As I walk up the path from the road, I have an uncanny sense of familiarity, almost as if I have become a small child again, wandering home after playing with friends in the village.

My knock at the door is answered by a small, grey-haired man with a face like an elderly gnome and thin legs protruding from oversized khaki shorts.

He greets me with a cheerful smile. 'Good morning. Can I help you?'

Suddenly I don't know what to say. I have not given any thought as to how to introduce myself.

'I'm sorry to disturb you. My name's Cressida Allenby and I think I used to live here once. I wondered if — if . . .' I dry up. What do I want from these people? What did I expect to find?

Surprisingly, his face lights up. 'Allenby? Allenby? Come in, please, come in.' He stands aside and beckons me in. 'Come through to the back, where it's shady. Can I offer you a drink? Beer? Lemonade?' He leads me out onto a patio shaded by a large fig tree, and shouts down the garden, 'Meg? Meg! Come up here. There's a young lady called Allenby come to see us.' Then, turning to me. 'Do sit down. I'm sorry, what did you say your first name was?'

'Cressida,' I reply automatically. My brain seems to have gone into freefall. I have sat here, on that step, squeezing open the ripe figs, digging out the pulpy flesh with its crunchy seeds with my fingers. The green, earthy smell of the fruit comes back to me so strongly that I feel a sudden wave of nausea. I ate so many figs that my stomach was upset for days! Mother said . . . Mother was sitting at the table, shelling peas into a green plastic colander. Her hair was not mousy. In this light it was a complex, interwoven mass of amber and gold, hanging in a loose braid over one shoulder. I said . . .

My host's voice jerks me back to the present. 'I'm sorry. What did you say? I was just . . . This place brings back so many memories.'

'Not to worry!' He smiles at me cheerfully. 'I can quite understand that. I said, you must have been very small when you lived here.'

I stare at him. 'You know when we left? I mean, otherwise . . .'

''74, wasn't it? Must have been.'

A tall woman with a rope of grey hair wound precariously on top of her head comes up from a lower terrace, carrying a trug full of cucumbers and tomatoes. The little man jumps up.

'Meg, this is Cressida Allenby. Cressida, this is my wife, Meg. Oh, just a minute! I'm being stupid. I haven't even introduced myself. My name's Oswald Wentworth. Please call me Os, everyone does.'

'How do you do?' I say automatically. The sight of this tiny man beside his tall, large-boned wife makes me think of a Jack Russell terrier beside an Old English Sheepdog.

Mrs Wentworth is saying, 'Allenby? Did your people own this place when it was a pub?'

'Yes, yes, we've already established that,' her husband breaks in. 'Where's that box? Do you remember where we put it?'

'Yes, I remember quite well.' His wife has a grave serenity that contrasts with his excitability and reinforces the doggy image. 'I'll go and find it.' She smiles at me. 'Would you like a drink? I'm going to bring some lemonade for us, anyway. But perhaps you would rather have a beer?'

'Lemonade would be lovely, thank you.'

'Good. Do sit down and make yourself at home. I shall be back in a minute.'

As we seat ourselves again, Os Wentworth says, 'It's such a pleasure to hear an English voice! We don't get many visitors these days.'

'Did you know my parents?'

'No, sorry. Never met them. Heard them spoken of, but never actually ran across them. We were living in Nicosia then. We bought this place when I retired six years ago — bought it from the Johnsons, who bought it from your parents when everything calmed down after the invasion — sorry, "peace operation". We wanted to be sure that it had always been in English hands, pre '74, you see. Dodgy business buying anything expropriated from the Greeks. If we ever get a settlement they might come and demand it back — with some justification, I suppose. And recently the chances of a settlement seem to be rather better.'

I feel lost and stupid. 'I'm sorry. I'm afraid I really don't understand what you're talking about.'

'You don't?' He looks surprised. Then, 'No, of course, why should you? It's all ancient history to you. Very much part of everyday life to us here, I'm afraid.'

His wife calls from the house, 'Os, can you come and carry this, please? I can't manage the tray and the box.'

He jumps up with a murmured 'Excuse me a minute' and scampers into the house, to return a moment later carrying a tray with a jug and glasses. Meg follows him bearing a rather battered and discoloured cardboard box, which she places on the table in front of me.

'We found this when we moved in, in the little box room that Os now uses as a study. I suppose the Johnsons put it in there out of the way, in case anyone came for it. We didn't know how to contact you — or your parents, rather — so we just tucked it in the bottom of a cupboard.'

I look inside the box. There is an A4-size notebook with faded maroon board covers and a sheaf of papers that appear to have been torn from a loose-leaf pad. I open the book and glance at the first page.

'It's my mother's writing!' I scan the opening lines. 'It seems to be some kind of journal. I had no idea she ever kept one.'

'Well, they were exciting times, in a way. Perhaps she felt she wanted to keep a record of what was going on,' Meg Wentworth replies, in her calm, easy voice. 'Then, I suppose, in all the panic of getting out, these got left behind.'

'Panic?' I query. 'I'm sorry, I feel I should know, but I don't. What happened?'

'That was when the Turks invaded. This strip along the north coast was a war zone for several days and all the ex-pats were evacuated. It was chaotic at the time. I'm not surprised things got left behind. You don't remember anything about it?'

'No, I don't think so. At least . . . vaguely. But I've always thought it was just a bad dream.'

Meg leans over and pats my hand. 'I'm not surprised. It was a nightmare for all of us.'

'Were you evacuated too?'

Os chuckles. 'No, not us! We stuck it out. We've been here right through the whole lot, haven't we, Meg? Right from '55.'

"'55?' The date sparks a recollection. 'That was when my father was stationed here, in the army.'

'Ah well, then you'll know all about it,' Os says.

'No, he never spoke of his time here — as far as I can recall. What happened?'

'The Greek-speaking population wanted independence from Britain and to be governed from Athens. What they called *enosis* — union with the motherland. There was a very active terrorist organization that went by the name of EOKA — *Ethniki Organosis Kyprion Agoniston*. Your father was probably sent out here to fight them.'

'So was it still going on in 1974, when we came back here?'

'We had a quieter spell after independence but then it all started up again, with EOKA B, as they called themselves. Of course, the Turkish minority didn't want to be ruled by Athens. It was when the Greeks looked like going ahead with *enosis* despite them that the mainland Turks invaded.'

'And the island has been divided ever since?'

'Sadly, yes.'

'Why did you stay, if there was so much trouble?'

'It was my job. I worked in the Governor's Office until independence. When that came we didn't fancy going home. We'd made a life here, and come to love the place in spite of everything. I got a job with the British Consulate and we stayed on. Then, when retirement came, we bought this place. We've always wanted to be here on the north coast, even though it did mean crossing the border.'

'Anyway,' Meg says, 'your parents decided to go home. Where are they now?'

'I'm afraid they're both dead.'

'Oh no! Oh, I am sorry!'

'But your father got out all right, didn't he?' Os says. 'I mean, I remember there was a problem of some sort. That's why the name was familiar. We had some dealings with your mother at the Consulate. He was missing, wasn't he — just before the invasion?'

'Was he?' I stare at him. 'I didn't know.'

'Well, of course, you wouldn't remember anything about it. But I'm sure there was something . . . We even had troops out looking for him. But anyway, he did get out, when the evacuation came?'

'Well, yes, he must have done. I remember him coming back to England with us. At least, I remember him *in* England, when I started school.'

'How did he die?' Meg asks gently.

'I don't know. I was only six years old. I just remember my mother telling me that he was never coming back. He travelled a lot, you know, as a foreign correspondent. Journalism was his proper job, not running a pub.' I don't want to talk about this so I turn to the box in front of me. 'Thank you so much for keeping this all these years. I shall really enjoy reading my mother's journal.' I pick up the sheaf of loose papers again. 'I don't know what these are. They seem to be written in Greek.'

'May I see?' Os reaches out a hand and I pass him the yellowing pages. 'Yes, it's Greek script all right.'

'It's odd. I'm pretty sure my mother couldn't even speak Greek. Let alone write it.'

Os hands back the papers. 'Look, I don't think I should pry into these. I've just glanced at the first one and it's pretty obviously a love letter.'

'A love letter? Who to — and who from?'

'I couldn't say. The first one just begins "my only beloved". There isn't a name.'

'You understand Greek?'

'Yes. It was part of my job to translate documents.'

I free the first few sheets from the sheaf and turn them over. Were they letters addressed to my mother? If so, who from? Then I look at the bottom of the page.

'There's a signature here. *Stephen!* They're from my father. But why would he write in Greek?'

I look from Os to his wife. Both return my gaze with widened eyes and lifted eyebrows. Their expressions say as clearly as words, *it's none of our business*. I finish my drink and shuffle the papers together.

'Look, I really must be going. Thank you so much for the drink, and for these.'

'Won't you stay for some lunch?' Meg asks. 'It's only a salad, but you're most welcome.'

Suddenly I want very much to be alone, to think. 'It's very kind of you but I can't stay. I promised to meet someone.' The lie comes easily.

'Well, come and see us again while you're on the island. How long are you staying?' Os gets to his feet and begins to shepherd me back towards the front door.

'Just ten days. Thank you. I'd like that.'

'Perhaps you'd like to look round the house, see if it brings back memories,' Meg suggests.

'Yes, I would, another time. Thanks again.'

They escort me to the car and wave me off, calling, 'Don't forget. You're welcome any time.'

I head downhill towards the sea, but I have only gone a few hundred yards when I become aware of a sudden trickle of fluid from my nose. I put the backs of my fingers to my nostrils and they come away with a bright smear of blood. Hastily, I pull the car in to the side of the road and scrabble in my bag for a tissue. There is only one, and that so worn and crumpled as to be almost useless. Clasping it to my nose, I scramble out of the car. After the air-conditioned interior, the heat almost takes my breath away. A few yards further along an ancient fig tree leans over the wall of an abandoned garden. I stumble into the shade and bend over, supporting myself with one hand on the wall. Heavy drops of blood splash onto the ground and are swallowed up almost immediately by the parched soil. I feel dizzy. I pinch my nostrils to staunch the flow and sink to the ground. At that moment I feel the tremor of a distant explosion.

I am a child again, screaming as the noise rips the air just above my head. There is a crash like thunder, very close by, and huddled against the protective wall I feel the earth shudder, while the tree above my head is shaken by a great wind which sends leaves and unripe figs showering down upon me. Sobbing, I cry out 'Mummy! Daddy!' but the sound is lost as the sky splits open with another roar. There is a blinding flash and another crash which sends me cowering against the earth, my hands over my ears. Then my arm is seized and I am lifted to my feet. A voice shouts something incomprehensible but I recognize the face. It's the angel boy who comes to visit my mother sometimes. His face is streaked with dirt and his golden hair is matted with sweat, but he smiles reassuringly and I cling to him as tightly as I can as he picks me up. He begins to run with me up the lane towards my home. The terrifying roar comes again, this time accompanied by a sharp rattling noise. The boy gasps and checks his stride for an instant, and I see that the sleeve of his shirt is suddenly red with blood, but he keeps his hold on me and runs on. Watching the blood run down his arm, I notice that he is carrying something — some rolled-up bits of paper. I wonder why he doesn't drop them. Then we are at the gate, running up to the terrace and in, under the archway, to the cool darkness of the house.

I open my eyes. The air is still and the only sound is the rasping of cicadas in the long grass. I am soaked with sweat and there are bloodstains down the front of my shirt. I struggle unsteadily to my feet and get into the car. All I can think of is an urgent desire to get back to the cool security of the hotel.

CHAPTER 8

Back in my room I shower and change my clothes. Then I sit down in front of the dressing table and study my reflection in the mirror. What happened back there under the fig tree? Did I doze off and dream the explosion and the boy with the angel face? Did I pass out — faint at the sight of my own blood? Surely not. I, Cressida Allenby, who can party all weekend and still arrive for work bright eyed and bushy tailed on Monday, ready to inspire even 4WZ with an interest in *Macbeth* or the poetry of Wilfred Owen. Behaving like a Victorian lady with an attack of the vapours? What was that all about?

I examine my face. My mother's doctor said I looked washed out. It's true. I am pale. Pasty, Mother would have called it. There are blue shadows under my eyes. I run my fingers along my jawline, aware for the first time of a softening and loosening of the flesh — the first faint signs of inevitable deliquescence and decay. Twenty-eight. In just over a year I shall be thirty. Already there is a faint tracery of lines at the corners of my eyes. At my age my mother was married, with a child. Well, so what? That was expected for her generation. But being unmarried is one thing. It is altogether different being single, unattached, unspoken for. For a moment Paul's face floats into my memory, but I close my mind to it. It is over; finished.

I open the box the Wentworths gave me and take out my mother's journal. As I open it the same faint odour of damp and decay that the photographs have comes to my nostrils, and with it the ghost of *Je Reviens*. Or is that my imagination? I turn a page or two, then close the book and put it back in the box. I can't face it now. What I need is some lunch and perhaps a swim.

It seems the tour party has not returned, so I eat lunch on the terrace in solitary splendour. Afterwards, I change into my swimming costume, lather my limbs with sun cream and stretch out on a lounger by the pool. Sometime later I come to with a headache and an uncomfortable feeling that my legs have been too long in the sun. There is movement and voices nearby and I see that the other guests have returned and are settling themselves around the pool. A couple nearby smile and nod in a friendly manner but I don't feel inclined to chat, so I smile back and get up and dive into the pool.

I have always thought of myself as a strong swimmer and I have made a habit of going to the local baths at least once a week. I set out to swim twenty lengths, an easy target, but by the time I have accomplished five my legs feel heavy and my heart is thumping. Is it really possible to lose condition to such an extent in a few short weeks? I press on grimly for another three but finally have to give in. Even the effort of hauling myself out of the water makes my head swim and for a moment I have to double over at the side of the pool.

'Miss Allenby? Are you all right?'

I straighten up as quickly as I can. Karim Mezeli is standing beside me. His hand is outstretched as if to take me by the arm, but as I look at him he apparently thinks better of it. Instead he says, 'Can I get you anything? A glass of water?'

I force a smile. 'No, really, I'm fine. Thank you. Just a bit too much sun, I expect.'

He nods gravely. He is casually dressed in a polo shirt and jeans but there is something formal and restrained in his manner. 'You must be careful. English people so often fail to understand how powerful the sun is here. It can be dangerous, especially for someone as fair as you.'

'Yes, I'll be more sensible from now on. I think I must have fallen asleep.'

There is a pause, and I sense that we are both trying to find a way of prolonging the conversation. Embarrassed, I turn away and sit down on the sun-lounger. He says, 'Well, I'll leave you to . . .'

'I hope your visit this morning was a success.' The words come out before I have time to analyse my reasons.

He turns to look at me again. 'Yes, it was, thank you.'

'Where did you go?'

'To the temple of Aphrodite at Vounos. What is left is mainly Roman in origin, but it is built on the site of a much older temple.' He pauses. 'You're not interested in history?'

'Well, I've never been very keen on ruins and, well, you know, trenches with bits of pottery in them.'

He laughs, his teeth very white against his tan. 'Perhaps that's because you don't know what they stand for — the stories they could tell us.'

'Ah, stories!' I find myself smiling back at him. 'Now there you have caught my interest. I love stories.' I realize that he is still standing, looking down at me, and add, on an impulse, 'Won't you sit down? That is, if you have time.'

He seems to hesitate for a moment, then he draws a chair closer and seats himself. 'As it happens, I have the afternoons off. Perhaps I could order some tea for both of us?'

What am I doing? I ask myself. Aloud I say 'Why not? Tea sounds great.'

Mezeli beckons to a waiter and orders tea, then turns back to me. 'You're here alone?'

A warning bell goes off at the back of my mind. 'Yes. Why do you ask?'

'Only that it's unusual. People usually come either as couples or in a party.'

'Yes, well — I just felt like having some time to myself. I've been — rather busy lately.' *Why am I telling him all this?*

'Work?'

'Partly.'

'What do you do?'

'I'm a teacher.'

'Oh, what do you teach?'

I can't resist this. 'The classical answer to that is "children".'

He acknowledges the barb with a smile. 'I'll rephrase the question. What is your subject?'

'English.'

'That explains the interest in stories. Where do you work?

'London.'

'Ah! The hectic metropolitan life.'

The waiter returns with a tray. 'Your tea, Dr Mezeli.'

I look up, startled. '*Doctor?* I'm sorry, I didn't realize . . .'

He grins. 'Oh, not a real doctor. Just a Ph.D.'

I am embarrassed. I had assumed that he was just a local tour guide. To hide my confusion I turn my attention to the tea. As I pour, something occurs to me. 'You know my name. How?'

He lifts his dark brows. 'It's not difficult. I looked in the hotel register. All the other guests belong to the tour group.'

I keep my eyes on my cup. So, he was sufficiently interested to look me up. I feel a stir of gratification and take myself instantly to task. *This is exactly the sort of thing you came here to avoid!*

'What made you choose to come here, particularly?' he asks.

I am not sure where to begin — or if I want to begin at all. 'It's a long story.'

He looks away. 'Then I mustn't pry.'

'No!' Suddenly I feel I am being ungracious. 'I didn't mean it like that. It's just — well, I don't want to bore you.' He does not respond and to break the silence I say, 'You speak very good English.'

'I should. I studied for six years in Newcastle.'

'Newcastle! That must have been a bit of a shock after Cyprus.'

'I loved every minute of it. They were the happiest years of my life.'

'But you came back to live here.'

His face grows serious again. 'I was born here. It is my home. There was work to be done here.'

'Well, I'm sure if I had to choose between all this,' indicating the view across the harbour, 'and the River Tyne I'd choose to live here.'

'Would you?' He looks at me quizzically. 'I wonder. So, what did make you decide to come here?'

'An old photograph I came across. You see, we used to live here once, when I was very small. I'd almost forgotten until I saw the photo. My mother and father ran a small bar in a village called Lapithos. Do you know it?'

'Lapta,' he says.

'Oh, yes, sorry. I forgot we have to use the Turkish name now.'

'Yes, I know the place. What made your parents come here to run a bar?'

I laugh. 'God knows! I think it was some mad idea of my father's. My mother never talked about it, but I think he was rather inclined to crazy impulses like that.'

He looks at me. His gaze is sharp, attentive, slightly disconcerting. 'Was?'

'I never knew him very well. He left us when I was six and died soon afterwards.'

'And your mother? You speak of them both in the past tense.'

'She died six weeks ago.'

'I'm so sorry. So you came here out of — what? Nostalgia? Curiosity?'

'A bit of both, I suppose. It was just an impulse, really. My doctor said I ought to take a holiday and then I happened to come across the photograph so I thought, Why not? I had no idea it would turn out to be so complicated.' I hesitate, not wanting to appear ignorant. 'I'm afraid I don't really understand what happened here. I don't have much time for politics and that sort of thing.'

He smiles wryly. 'You're fortunate. Here, everything is political. Anyway, I hope you will enjoy yourself, now you are here. It's a very beautiful place. It's just a pity you can only see half of it.'

'Is it quite impossible to cross the border?'

'Completely. Unless you are a diplomat or a member of the UN peace-keeping force.'

'Well,' I finish my tea, 'it doesn't really matter. The part I'm interested in is round here — where my parents lived, well, where I lived briefly.'

'Why don't you join some of our excursions? It would give you a different perspective on the history of the island.'

My first instinct is to refuse. 'Oh, I couldn't do that. After all, these other people have paid for the privilege.'

His nostrils flare and his eyes narrow and I think that he is not a man to be thwarted by convention or red tape. 'I don't see that it makes any difference to them. There is room in the coach and one more in the group will make no difference. Come as my guest.'

The idea appeals, but I suspect for the wrong reason. But I give in. 'Well, if you're sure it's OK . . .'

He smiles. 'I'll make it OK.'

I look at him. I have always gone for fair, very English-looking men before but there is no denying the quiver of excitement at the pit of my stomach. He glances at his watch. 'Forgive me. I must leave you. I have to prepare a talk for this evening. I hope you'll come and listen?'

I promise that I will and watch him walk away. He moves lithely, like a dancer or someone more used to walking bare-foot than in shoes.

After dinner I feel more like turning in for an early night than going to a lecture, but I made a promise and I find I do not want to disappoint Karim Mezeli. So I treat myself to a brandy from the bar and make my way to the room set aside for the talk. Most of the rest of the group are there and a couple near the back make room for me with friendly smiles. They introduce themselves as Alan and Mary and I learn that he is a lecturer in maths at an FE college in Guildford and she teaches history at a local comprehensive. 'Bit of a busman's holiday,' she says with a laugh. I am relieved of the need to admit that I am a teacher too, with the inevitable comparing of notes and sharing of grievances that would follow, by Mezeli's arrival. A projector and a screen have been set up in readiness and one of the hotel staff stands by the machine.

'I hope you enjoyed our excursion this morning,' he begins. His manner is pleasant; unassuming but at the same time authoritative. 'Now I want to give you some background to that and to other temples we shall visit. As I told you, the worship of Aphrodite goes back many centuries before Roman times, or even the classical Greek period. Now, I know we are all familiar with the conventional image of Aphrodite, or Venus as the Romans would have called her. To us she is the goddess of love. Usually she is presented in a rather romantic, even sentimental style. We have all seen the Botticelli painting of a buxom, rather coy lady standing in a seashell. But the Aphrodite who was worshipped in Cyprus from prehistoric times would have been a much more powerful figure; an incarnation of the Great Mother Goddess who was worshipped all around the Mediterranean. She was primarily the goddess of fertility, as this ancient statuette makes clear.' He taps the lectern and a photograph appears on the screen. It shows a terracotta figurine of a squat female shape, huge breasted and obviously pregnant. He smiles at the murmur of surprise from his audience. 'Not quite what we think of as a love-goddess. Aphrodite symbolized the natural process of birth, maturity, death and regeneration. She had a triple nature, represented by the phases of the moon. At the new moon she was the virgin goddess, whom later Greeks called Artemis. At full moon she was the mother goddess and as the moon waned she became the goddess of death. One of her Greek names was Aphrodite Epitymbria — Aphrodite of the tombs. Of course, we don't know precisely how her rites were celebrated but it seems that at some temples young girls were required to offer up their virginity to the first man who asked them, before they could marry. Then, there is this Bronze Age model that was found near Bellapais.' He taps again and a new image appears on the screen. 'This suggests that a bull was sacrificed to the goddess, or perhaps a man wearing a bull mask. He was probably the sacred king, chosen by the High Priestess to be her consort at the spring equinox and then sacrificed the following spring, when his blood would be sprinkled on the ground to fertilise it . . .'

I only half listen to the rest of the lecture. Perhaps it's the brandy, or the heat of the room. I find myself drifting into a drowsy state where the images he has conjured up seem to take concrete form. I see a girl, sitting in a temple courtyard. Other girls sit all around her but she does not speak to them. Her head is bowed and her hair falls forward to cover her face. Men stroll between the rows, examining, choosing. Some of the girls weep and tremble, others stare back brazenly. Some are obviously waiting for one particular man. When a man sees a face that appeals to him he throws a piece of silver into her lap, takes her by the wrist and leads her out of the temple. As a man pauses beside her, the girl I saw first raises her head and I see why she keeps it lowered. Her face is disfigured by an ugly red scar — a burn perhaps. The man draws back, shakes his head and passes on. She droops forward again, letting her hair cover the scar. Poor girl! How long will she have to wait?

I wake with a jerk as people around me start to chatter and get up from their seats. Mezeli has stopped talking but the pictures that have formed in my mind are still as vivid as a sequence from a film. I want to use them somehow. I'm not sure how. A short story, perhaps? A poem? What matters is to get something down while the ideas are fresh in my mind. I go to my room, pull my laptop out of the wardrobe and boot it up.

CHAPTER 9

I wake suddenly with a confused impression that the window of the room is in the wrong place and the morning traffic heavier than usual. Then I remember the geography of my hotel room and recognize the steady hum of the air conditioning. I have been dreaming, a dream that haunted my childhood but which has not troubled me for a long time, until tonight. I am a small child again, running beside my mother, dragged along by the fierce grip on my hand, tripping and stumbling on uneven ground. Around me is a forest of legs, blocking the light, kicking up dust that chokes my nostrils and my mouth. Then the hand that holds mine vanishes and I am alone in that huge, moving forest. I fall, but the feet keep trampling over me. I try to scream but my mouth is full of sand. At that point, as usual, I wake up, my body drenched in sweat. I force myself to get up and pour a glass of chilled mineral water from the fridge. The sweat dries on my body in the cool air of the room and after a little while I get back into bed and sleep fitfully until woken by the noise of the chambermaids busy in the next room.

I shower and dress and take the box containing the journal down to breakfast with me, determined to make a start on reading it out in the fresh air by the pool. However, as soon as I sit down Mezeli appears at my side.

'Good morning, Miss Allenby. I wondered if you would care to come with us today. We are going to Salamis. I think you would find it interesting.'

I hesitate. The idea is appealing, but on the other hand I want to make a start on reading my mother's journal. 'It's nice of you to ask, but I'm afraid I have some research of my own to do. Thank you, Dr Mezeli.'

He smiles. 'Karim, please. My name is Karim.'

I smile back. 'And you must call me Cressida.'

'Cressida. It's very appropriate!' He looks at me for a moment. 'You know what it means? It is from the Greek *chryseis*, meaning golden. I imagine your parents must have known that and given you the name because of your colouring. Did they understand Greek?'

'My father would have done,' I say. 'He had a degree in Classics.' A thought strikes me. 'I'm rather surprised that you speak it, though.'

He arches an eyebrow ironically. 'You mean because I am Turkish Cypriot? But of course I speak Greek. Until the partition in 1974 I grew up with Greek friends. We were all bilingual.'

The waiter approaches to refill my coffee cup and Mezeli nods towards the box. 'Is this connected with your research?'

'Yes, it is. I managed to find the house where we used to live. It belongs to some people called Wentworth now. They gave me this. It's some papers my parents apparently left behind when they moved out. Isn't it amazing that they've been kept all these years?'

'Are they important papers?'

'Oh, nothing vital. Just a diary and some . . . some letters. But it will be interesting to find out a bit more about the time they spent here.'

'Extremely interesting! For a historian like myself the discovery of original documents is always exciting.'

I can see from his face that he is genuinely fascinated and I laugh. 'It's a bit out of your period, isn't it?'

'You think so? To me, this is part of my own history. May I ask you, when did you leave Cyprus?'

'In 1974, I think. At least, that's what Mr Wentworth thought. During the — what did he call it? The peace operation.'

His lip curls ironically. 'Ah yes. The peace operation.'

'What was it all about, Karim?' I ask. 'Why did you invade?'

His face changes and the heavy eyelids come down like shutters. 'I didn't invade anyone. I am Turkish Cypriot. I was born here. My family has lived here for generations.'

'I'm sorry,' I murmur, disconcerted by his change of mood. 'I wasn't intending to imply any sort of criticism.'

'Please, there's no need to apologize. I don't expect you to understand the situation here.' He looks at his watch and rises to his feet. 'Now, if you will excuse me, I must collect the rest of my party.' He inclines his head with his curious, old-fashioned formality and walks away.

I am tempted to call after him, but I cannot think of anything to say. I feel I have been tactless and am annoyed with myself, but at the same time I can't help thinking that he is being unreasonably sensitive.

Later, by the pool, I set the box on a table and spread out its contents. I pick up the letters, the paper stained and ragged at the edges and so yellow that in places it is hard to make out the writing. The back of the bottom sheet is marked with several large, rust-coloured blotches, as if something has been spilled on it. I study the unintelligible Greek characters and then turn the page over and look again at the signature, quite clear in ordinary script — *Stephen*. '*My only beloved*' he had begun. But if these were addressed to my mother, why had he written in Greek? And if they were not — and the implications of that give me pause — then how did they come to be in the same box as my mother's journal?

I put the letters aside and open the notebook. My mother's handwriting, instantly recognizable, sends a pang of anguish through me. I picture her as I saw her in the last days, skeletal, tremulous but still defiantly reaching for the sherry bottle. How different from the round-faced, smiling woman in the photograph outside the *Café Anonymou*. Was there some clue here, in the journal or in these letters, as to what had brought about the change?

LAURA ALLENBY — JOURNAL, 1974

5 April

So, here we are, installed in what I suppose I must start to think of as our new home. I have to admit I find it hard to believe that we now live here permanently. It's very different from when we were here last Easter on holiday. Then everything was new and exciting. Even going to buy a loaf of bread was an adventure. But today I went to get some groceries at the little shop in the village and I was suddenly almost overcome by a great feeling of homesickness. No more popping into the local Spar store on the way home from work. No more Sainsbury's or Waitrose! I'm going to have to learn a whole new way of cooking, with different ingredients. And I suppose I must keep struggling with my Greek. Stephen is in his element, of course, nattering away with the locals. At least most of the customers at the bar are English ex-pats, so I can chat to them.

Not that they offer much in the way of intellectual stimulus! I'm just beginning to realize how much I've given up to come here. Not just familiar shops. That's not really important. I mean friends, good conversation — my job. That's why I have decided to keep this journal. At least it will force me to put my ideas into some sort of coherent order and stop me from becoming completely brain-dead.

I just hope this move will make Steve happy, at last. He hated England, and he hated teaching — and I'm afraid he would have begun to hate me if we had stayed. So, as long as he is happy here, I can stick it out. At least Cressida seems to have settled down all right. Stephen says she will soon pick up the language and make friends. I suppose he's right, but God knows what we'll do about school when the time comes. Oh well, sufficient unto the day . . .

I skim over the next pages, which are mainly concerned with my mother's efforts to adapt to her new life and the struggle to establish a regular clientele for the bar. There are references to tentative contacts with neighbours and some deft character sketches of some regular patrons but nothing of any significance. Then an entry catches my attention.

25 April

I am really confused by the political situation here. The local Greeks seem quite friendly but everywhere you go there is graffiti in support of enosis *and EOKA. Even the church is involved. Now people are talking about an invasion from mainland Greece. Lalage, who comes in from the village to help in the bar, says the ordinary people just want to get on with their lives but they are afraid to speak out against the terrorists for fear of reprisals. Most of the houses fly the Greek flag but she says it's only because they are afraid of EOKA. I thought all the unrest here had settled down, or I wouldn't have agreed to move out here. Now it seems it is all starting up again.*

27 April

I'm worried about Stephen. He's taken to disappearing for hours at a time. He says it's research for the articles he's been commissioned to write, which involves interviewing people all over the island. That's all very well for him! Meanwhile I am stuck here with a small child and a bar to run. I know I have Lalage to help, and it's not as if we're exactly rushed off our feet with customers. And I've got quite friendly with some of the regulars so there's usually someone to chat to . . . But if I'd wanted a career as a barmaid I wouldn't have bothered going to university and then getting my teaching qualification. I loved my job! Stephen could never understand that. To him teaching was just something he'd been forced into to support a wife and child. Nothing would do but we must move out here and buy this bar. And now we're here he has no more interest in it than he had in his teaching job!

I must stop this. It isn't helping. It's the wine talking. That's the one comfort about this place. At least it's cheap and easy to drown your sorrows esp. since S. never seems to notice how many bottles of vino are unaccounted for! I shall have to watch it or I'll end up like some of the gin-sodden old ex-colonials propping up the bar night after night.

I put the journal down and gaze out across the harbour. So that was when it had all started. I imagine my mother sitting alone in the bar, waiting for a customer to turn up, with a bottle and a glass at her elbow. Why did my father leave her to cope alone like that? Didn't he care for her? For either of us? And where was I? I try to see myself as the small child in the photograph. What was I doing while my mother slowly sank into this slough of despond? I have fleeting memories of endless sunny days, of my mother cooking, picking strange, exotic flowers and fruit, but no recollection of her drinking. Somehow I was protected from that — during those early years, at least. I give up with a sigh and tuck the journal back into the box and lower myself into the pool.

After my swim I take a stroll round the town, buy some postcards and write them at a table outside a restaurant facing the harbour. A waiter brings me a 'village' salad — (it would be a Greek salad in England) — and a glass of lager and I eat slowly, watching the passing scene. It is Easter week in England, but thinking of the packed beaches of Spain or the Greek islands, Kyrenia seems pleasantly uncrowded and relaxed. Many of the visitors are families who appear Middle Eastern in origin, Turks from the mainland, I assume. Most of the women are in summer dresses but a few are shrouded in headscarves and long robes. One such group takes a table next to mine. The children have curly dark hair and expressive faces and the father is muscular and macho in shorts and a tight-fitting T-shirt, but of the mother I can see nothing but her eyes. It comes as a shock to hear that their accents are pure Birmingham.

When I get back to the hotel the tour group have returned and Mezeli is sitting at a table on the terrace with Alan and Mary. She sees me and waves me over but I hesitate, worried that after this morning Mezeli is still offended with me. But he rises with a smile and courteously offers me his chair. Mary leans forward. Her blue eyes are vivid with enthusiasm.

'It's such a pity you couldn't join us today. We've been to the chapel of St Barnabas and then on to Salamis and it was absolutely fascinating.'

'Salamis?' I say. 'Wasn't there a battle there?'

Mezeli shakes his head. 'That was a different Salamis, a naval battle off the coast of Greece. But don't worry, most people confuse the two until they've been there.'

Mary says, 'Dr Mezeli is *so* informative! I never realized that it was the place where St Paul first preached the gospel to the Jews of Cyprus.'

'Oh, really?' I try to sound impressed.

Mezeli's expression is sardonic. 'Not that it made much impression, to begin with, anyway. The idea of a god who died and rose again on the third day would not have seemed particularly revolutionary to the people there.'

'How do you mean?' Alan asks.

'They were already accustomed to the rites of Adonis, who was slain by Zeus in the shape of a boar and then restored to life after a season in Hades. People here still say that the anemones that flower every spring arise from his blood. It is another re-telling of the ritual by which the sacred king was sacrificed every spring to bring fertility to the fields.'

'Human sacrifice?' Mary shudders. 'How horrible! Thank goodness we've got beyond that!'

Mezeli lifts an eyebrow. 'Have we? It seems to me this island has been regularly fertilized with new outpourings of blood. It is an inextricable fact of our history.'

Alan says, 'I suppose you're referring to the EOKA business in the fifties. But surely it's only natural that the Greek Cypriots should want to be governed by their own people instead of by us — I mean, us Brits.'

'Why?' Mezeli turns his hawk-like gaze towards him. 'Cyprus was never part of Greece.'

'Never? I know it was a British colony until recently. Wasn't it Greek before that?'

'No. For several hundred years before that it was part of the Ottoman Empire. And before that it belonged to Venice and before that to the Norman French who took it in the First Crusade.'

'The Crusades?' Mary exclaims. 'Oh dear, Christianity against Islam — and now it all seems to be coming round again. Is the trouble here about religion?'

Mezeli shrugs. 'Religion and politics together. Cyprus has the misfortune to lie at the crossroads between east and west, between the Muslim world and the Christian. But that's nothing new. Before that it stood at the crossroad between Christianity and paganism.'

'Which brings us back to St Paul,' I say and he smiles and nods.

Next morning he stops by my table again. 'We are going to visit the castle of St Hilarion. It's not far. You must have seen it, up there above the city. Will you come with us?'

I have seen it, of course. Perched on a precipitous crag, its towers and turrets look like something out of a child's picture book. I am tempted, and besides, it would be rude to keep refusing.

'Well, if you're sure no one will object . . .'

'I'm sure.'

'Thank you. I'd like to come.'

As we climb out of the coach, one of the party, a large woman with dyed blonde hair and hands covered in enough rings to make effective knuckle dusters, exclaims, 'Ooh, isn't it romantic-looking! A fairy-tale castle!'

Mezeli, overhearing, smiles. 'Funny you should say that. It was actually used by Walt Disney as the model for Snow White's castle.'

I follow the others through the massive gateway and into a maze of steeply climbing, cobbled roadways.

'Of course,' Mezeli is saying, 'St Hilarion was not the original name of the castle. As you can see, it is built on two peaks and its original name was Didymos, meaning Twins. St Hilarion was a hermit who was reputed to have lived up here and later a monastery was built in his memory. It is from that that the castle gets its present name. However, when the

Franks under Guy de Lusignan took over they must have mis-heard, or misinterpreted, the original name. That was the era of the troubadours and the cult of courtly love, so perhaps it's not surprising that they opted for something more in keeping with their way of thinking. They called it not Didymos but Dieudamour — god of love.'

'There!' says the blonde. 'I said it was romantic.'

'There are romantic elements in its story,' Mezeli agrees, 'but I'm afraid they are outweighed by the more gruesome episodes. Siege warfare could be very cruel. Shall we move on up to the Royal Apartments?'

On the topmost summit we come to a large, airy chamber with a wide window embrasure looking out westwards along the coast. The sun is at its zenith and in the confined space of the narrow streets the heat was suffocating but here, thank God, there is a breeze. I sit down on the windowsill and gaze out. Below me the wooded slope drops precipitously down to the narrow strip of fertile land, where villages cluster among their olive groves and citrus orchards. Beyond that is a sea of such transparent turquoise that every reef and rock shows up as a cobalt stain and away in the west land and sea, silver and green and blue, melt into the amethyst haze of the horizon.

'You will be told by the local guides,' Mezeli is say-ing, 'that this is where Richard Coeur de Lion married the Princess Berengaria of Navarre. I'm sorry to disappoint you, but it's not true. They were married in Cyprus, certainly, but in the chapel of St George in Limassol. Richard was on his way to the Third Crusade and the ships carrying his bride-to-be and her entourage were driven onto the south coast by a storm. However, it is true that when Richard left for the Holy Land he left Berengaria behind with his sister, Joan. This castle became the favourite summer residence of the new Frankish rulers, so it is quite possible that Berengaria spent a lot of time sitting in this room, which has always been known as the Queen's Chamber.'

I lean my head back against the embrasure of the window and close my eyes. Mezeli's voice murmurs on, but I am no longer listening. I am imagining Berengaria, sitting here day after day, yearning for her father's palace in Navarre, wondering when, if ever, her husband would return. Not that it was a love match! I remember my history lessons. Richard needed a political alliance, and an heir, but no man was ever a more unwilling bridegroom. Poor Berengaria, languishing in the castle named after the god of love, must have thought that she had as much chance of being impregnated by Cupid as by her husband. A child born from the union of a god and a virgin. How such a blasphemous thought would have shocked her! There is the beginning of another story here. If I had pen and paper with me I would write it down, but as I do not I memorize it to be typed up later.

CHAPTER 10

I sleep badly and wake the next morning with an amorphous sense of anxiety. This island seems to have a strange effect on me. To dispel the feeling, I go down to the pool. No one else is about and I have it to myself, but once again after a few lengths I feel exhausted. This is more than normal tiredness, brought on by stress and too many late nights. I remember my mother's doctor looking at me and muttering something about anaemia. Perhaps I should have it checked out when I get home.

To distract myself I go back to my room and open my mother's journal. I don't know what I am looking for and flick through the pages aimlessly until an entry catches my eye.

3 May

I met an angel today! At least, that's what he says his name is and I must say he looks the part. Blond hair, like a helmet of silver feathers, but eyes the colour of amber and the sort of profile that wouldn't disgrace a Michelangelo statue. His name is Evangelos, but he says everyone calls him Angel! He must be about eighteen, I suppose, and he came into the bar and asked for a part-time job. He says he wants to learn English so that he can go and work as a waiter in England, to learn the restaurant business. We don't really need anyone else, but he is willing to work for nothing in return for English lessons, so I told him he could come and help out whenever he feels like it. Stephen wasn't around when he came — surprise, surprise — but I described the boy when he got back and mentioned how extraordinary I found it that a Greek Cypriot boy could be so fair. Stephen says he is probably a throwback to some Frankish soldier who came here with the Crusaders and got one of the local girls into trouble. I suspect it's more likely to be something much more recent — some Scandinavian tourist, or perhaps a soldier with the UN peace-keeping force. Anyway, he's a nice lad, extremely polite and helpful, and I'm going to enjoy having him around.

I lower the book. The angel boy! Angel . . . Do I really remember, or am I just imagining a tall, fair-haired boy who played hide and seek with me in the garden, among the lemon trees and the bushes of scarlet hibiscus?

4 May

More trouble! Old Jimmy Partridge, who is one of our regulars and has lived here for years, reckons the Turkish Cypriots will never stand for enosis *and if the EOKA fanatics push for it too hard the mainland Turks may come in to back them up. And that would mean war! Why can't the politicians leave people alone to get on with their lives in peace! With every day that passes I wish more profoundly that we had never come here.*

9 May

I don't know what's the matter with Stephen. He's becoming more and more morose and unpredictable. I thought perhaps it was the political situation and that maybe he was beginning to realize that dragging us all out here at this time was not a good idea. But when I mentioned it his response was that if I was that worried I'd better just pack up and go home. He's looking for something — or someone! I've always had the feeling that something happened when he was out here as a National Serviceman that he's never got over. I know, of course, that he was never really in love with me. I've never fooled myself about that. He was lonely and miserable and having a sort of mid-life crisis because he couldn't make a go of journalism. And I think he saw how desperately I wanted

him. He's a kind man, underneath the moody exterior, and I suppose
he thought at least one of us might as well be happy — and perhaps
he thought it would work out for him, too. And, of course, there was
Cressida on the way. We were happy, for the first year or so. At least, I
was. Oh, sod it! And sod him! Let's open another bottle.

I shut the book. 'Something happened . . . that he's never got over . . .' It must have been another woman, and those letters were written to her. 'My only beloved' . . . Who was she? What was there about her that had left such a vacuum at the centre of my father's life? What power had she wielded that, even after so many years, she could draw him back to this island? Did he find her? I feel a sudden spurt of anger. What right had this stranger to wreak such havoc on three lives?

Beneath these thoughts another phrase from the journal is struggling to the surface. 'Of course, there was Cressida on the way.' Had it been a mistake, or a deliberate trap to force Stephen into marriage? I try to push the thought down, but it demands my attention. My very existence is the result of a deception. I was used to entrap a man into a loveless marriage. No wonder he never cared for me!

I hire the car again and drive out to Lapta. The Wentworths are busy in their garden, as usual, but they both seem delighted to see me and before long we are all seated round the table under the fig tree with glasses of Meg's homemade lemonade.

'By the way,' Os says, 'did you find anything of interest in those papers we gave you?'

I have to clear my throat before I can answer. 'Yes, I did. As a matter of fact, that's what I wanted to talk to you about. I've been reading my mother's journal. It seems as though my father must have had some sort of affair with a local girl when he was here doing his National Service. Those letters must be addressed to her, not to my mother.'

'Then how could they have ended up in the same box with her journal?' Meg asks. 'Surely he wouldn't have left them where she was likely to come across them.'

'It's a puzzle,' I agree. 'Maybe he hid them and she found them. Or perhaps the people who bought the house found them, and put them in the box.'

'Ah, very likely,' Os says.

'Of course, even if my mother had come across them she probably wouldn't have realized what they were. Anyway, they obviously never reached the person they were intended for.' I hesitate. Should I be asking this? Curiosity gets the better of discretion. 'I was wondering . . . you said you could read Greek, Os. I would really like to know what is in those letters. Could you translate them for me? Or is that putting you to too much trouble?'

'My dear girl, it's no trouble! I quite enjoy little exercises like that.' Then he seems to have second thoughts. 'But are you sure you want me to? I shouldn't wish to pry into your private affairs.'

'Well, they're not really *my* affairs, are they? Since both my parents are dead now, I can't see that anyone can be hurt. Perhaps it sounds as if I'm being a bit voyeuristic, but you see I know so little about my father. I'm beginning to think that he never forgot this girl, whoever she was, and it ruined my mother's life. I should like to at least try to understand why it happened.'

'Oh dear!' Meg says, in shocked tones. Then again, more gently, 'Oh dear!'

'If that's what you want, of course I'll have a go at translating them for you,' Os agrees. 'It may take me a day or two, though. If I remember rightly the writing is pretty faded.'

I am beginning to regret my presumption. 'Look, I really don't want to be a nuisance. If it turns out to be too much of a pain, please don't bother with it.'

Meg smiles at me. 'Oh, you don't want to worry about that. He loves a puzzle, and it'll make a change from the *Telegraph* crossword.'

'Exactly!' her husband agrees. 'Have you got them with you?'

I produce the letters from my bag and hand them over. 'I'll pop in, in a few days' time, to see how you're getting on.'

'No, don't bother to come out here,' Os says. 'I've got to come into Kyrenia to do some shopping sometime soon. I'll drop them off at your hotel. Where are you staying? The Dome?'

'Yes, that's right.'

'That's no problem. As soon as I have something to show you I'll bring them in. If you're not there, I'll leave them at reception.'

'Well, if it's not too much trouble. Thank you very much.'

'Now,' Meg says. 'How would you like a look round the house?'

I follow her obediently through the various rooms. I have a disquieting sense of familiarity, as if some memory lurks just around every corner, but I cannot honestly say that I recognize anything.

'Well, why should you, after all?' Meg says consolingly. 'The place has had two different owners since you were here. All the furniture and decoration must be totally different. It's not surprising you don't remember it.'

I feel I have taken up enough of her time. 'I thought I might take a stroll round the village, see if that rings any bells. Do you think there is anybody living here who might remember my parents?'

Meg sighs and shakes her head. 'Not any more, my dear. This was a Greek village. All the inhabitants are Turkish now.'

'What happened to the Greeks?'

'All gone south in the exchange of populations.'

'You mean they were driven out when Turkey invaded?'

'Well, some of them fled to escape the fighting and some went voluntarily soon after, when it became clear that the Turks were in control of the north. The rest were told to go.'

'So they just had to leave everything, their houses, their land, just like that?'

94

'Yes. But they weren't the only ones. Thousands of Turkish Cypriots had to leave their villages in the south, to escape the National Guard and the EOKA terrorists. They were given the houses left empty by the Greeks. It's true they probably got the best of the bargain, but there must have been a lot of tragedy and heartache on both sides. Anyway, I'm afraid that the only people who might remember your parents would be a few old ex-pats like us. Most of them would have been retired even then, so it's unlikely that they're still alive, but I could ask around for you.'

'Would you? That's very kind of you. I'd really like to meet anyone who knew them.'

I say goodbye and thank them again and set off along the narrow lane into the village. I pass one or two shops where dark-scarved women chat over baskets of groceries, and wonder if it was shopping in one of them that caused my mother that pang of homesickness. Old men sip tiny cups of thick coffee outside the *cafénion* and click their worry beads. I feel their eyes following me as I pass and am suddenly aware of my shorts and bare legs, but whether the looks express disapproval or mere curiosity I cannot decide. I turn a corner alongside the wall of a house. From an open window above my head comes the sound of raised voices — a man and a woman shouting in Turkish. In the background a child is sobbing.

Suddenly I feel dizzy. I have to stop and stretch my hand to the wall for support. The voices go on, in a language I do not understand, yet I seem to hear the words quite clearly.

'You hit her! Laura, what were you thinking of?'

'I gave her a smack, that's all. She's got to learn to do as she's told.'

'But there are other ways . . .'

'She's your daughter too, you know! Perhaps if you stayed at home . . .'

'Stay at home? What have I got to stay at home for? A grizzling kid and a wife who's always plastered.'

'Do you blame me? Why should I sit around here, so you can go swanning off every day looking for your lady love? I was going to say

your little bit on the side, but she's much more than that, isn't she? I'm the little bit on the side, the afterthought, the note in the margin!'

'Oh, for God's sake! How many times do I have to say it? There isn't anyone else. I've had enough! I'm going, and if I don't come back you've always got the bottle for company!'

'Go then! What do I care? . . . Now see what you've done? This is all your fault! If you hadn't been a naughty girl Daddy wouldn't have gone away. If he never comes back it'll be because of you.'

I open my eyes. A young man has come out of a door a short distance ahead of me. A woman stands in the doorway, holding a snivelling child in her arms. They all stare at me. I take in a deep breath and stand up straight. Then I force myself to walk on past them. They respond to my murmured 'Good morning' with wordless nods, and I can feel their eyes following me until a bend in the road takes me out of sight.

When I get back to the hotel the man behind the reception desk hands me my key and says, 'I have a message for you. Dr Mezeli was looking for you. He is on the terrace by the pool, if you would care to join him.'

My first instinct is to make an excuse. I feel too raw and wounded to want company. But as I turn away he comes into the lobby and greets me with a smile.

'I'm so glad I've caught you. I looked for you at breakfast but you were nowhere to be found.'

'No, I . . . I went out to see the Wentworths. You know, the people who live in the house my parents owned.'

'Of course. You have your own researches to pursue.' He fixes me with that sharp, attentive gaze and I find I enjoy the feeling of having his undivided attention. 'Is everything all right?'

'Yes, of course. Well . . . why do you ask?'

'You look a little . . . strained. I hope you haven't had bad news.'

'No, no. It's just . . . well, I've had rather an odd experience.'

'Would you care to tell me about it? Let me buy you a drink. Have you had lunch?'

It occurs to me that I have not eaten all day except for a rather dry roll I bought on the way to pick up the car.

'No, not yet. Is it too late?'

'Of course not. Shall we go outside?'

He touches my elbow and a thrill of pleasure goes up my arm to the shoulder and then straight down to the pit of my stomach. He leads me out onto the terrace and calls a waiter over. They speak briefly in Turkish and then Karim says, 'Do you like fish?'

'Yes, very much.'

'And to drink?'

I ask for a beer. He orders Coca-Cola.

As we wait a small boy, four or five years old, comes running along the terrace, catches his foot in the leg of a chair and would have fallen flat on his face had not Mezeli leaned forward and caught hold of him. He sets the child upright and says, smiling, 'Careful, little one! Just take it gently. All right?'

The boy nods, round eyed, and Mezeli tousles his head and lets him go. In spite of myself I ask, 'Do you have children of your own, Karim?'

He turns to me as if the question has taken him by surprise, then the sudden smile flashes out. 'No, how would I? I am not married.'

I feel my heart bounce and come down with a thump. 'I'm surprised. I thought you would be — married, I mean.'

'Why? You aren't — at least, I assume . . .' He glances at my left hand.

'No, but — Well, I suppose I thought that out here attitudes would be . . . very traditional. You know what I mean?'

'Oh, I know what you mean,' he agrees. 'And you're right. But perhaps that is exactly why I am not married.'

When the drinks arrive he says, 'So, what was this odd experience?'

For a moment I am silenced by the contrary impulses of embarrassment and the urge to confide in someone. Then I say, 'Karim, do you believe in reincarnation?'

His eyebrows shoot up. 'Reincarnation? I'm a Muslim, not a Hindu.'

'No, sorry. I didn't mean it like that — not as part of your religion.'

'So why are we discussing theology?'

'We're not. It's just that one or two of the things that have happened to me lately . . .' I trail off and try again. 'Ever since I've been on the island I've had this weird feeling, a sort of déjà vu.'

'But of course. You have been here before.'

'But it's not just that some places look familiar. OK. You're going to think I'm bonkers but I'll try to explain. Twice, when I've been listening to one of your talks I've sort of dozed off . . .'

'I'm sorry. Am I that boring?'

'No! No, that's not what I'm trying to say. It's more like going into a sort of trance and then I find I'm making up stories, except that I'm not making it up. It's more like being told by someone else. Oh, this is hopeless! You're going to think I'm schizoid, hearing voices . . .'

He leans over and touches my hand. 'I don't think that. These stories, are they connected with what I was talking about at the time?'

'Oh yes. It's like the people you were talking about speak . . .' I stop myself but he is not shocked. He is nodding thoughtfully.

'There is a condition known as hypnogogia. It occurs when people are somewhere between sleep and waking, and makes them highly suggestible. Sometimes people have hallucinations or hear voices. It's the origin of a lot of ghost stories.' He smiles at me. 'I don't think your experiences are evidence of reincarnation. I think they just mean that you have a very vivid imagination and you aren't sleeping too well.'

I think about this for a minute. It's reassuring, but . . . 'OK. But there have been other things, nothing to do with your talks.' I tell him about the angel boy and the explosions.

He smiles. 'What sort of tree were you sitting under?'

'What? A fig tree, I think. Why?'

'That was your mistake, you see. There is an old island superstition that if you fall asleep under a fig tree you will always have bad dreams.' He stops and leans over to touch my arm with his fingertips. 'I'm sorry. I shouldn't joke. I can see it has upset you. Did you say you left the island in 1974?'

'Yes.'

'Then I think this was not a dream but a memory.'

'You mean I really was out there, while the bombs were dropping?'

'The Turkish troops landed at Five Mile Beach. It's a cove about five miles from here along the coast towards Lapta. The Greek Cypriot National Guard met them and almost drove them back. The fighting went on for several days and Turkish planes were bombing the National Guard positions. If you were in Lapta then you would have been quite close.'

I gaze at him. 'But surely I would never have forgotten an experience like that.'

'Oh, it's quite possible,' he replies. 'After all, we know that people can suppress the memory of traumatic experiences.'

My fish arrives, red snapper grilled, with chips and a side salad. I realize that I am ravenous. He watches me eat for a minute, then says, 'Will you have dinner with me tomorrow night?'

I don't hesitate. 'I'd like that very much. Thank you.'

'Excellent! I'm delighted. About eight? I'll take you to one of my favourite restaurants.'

'That would be great.'

'Good. Are you coming with us tomorrow? We are going to Gazimagusa.'

'Where?'

'You would call it Famagusta. You'll want to see it because of *Othello*.'

'*Othello?* Of course! I'd forgotten the play is supposed to take place in Cyprus.'

'I'll show you Othello's tower.'

'His tower? He didn't really exist, did he?'

His enigmatic smile returns. 'Well, that's a matter for conjecture. All that is known is that once, during the time when Venice ruled the island, there was a lieutenant-governor called Cristoforo Moro, which I suppose might be interpreted to mean he was a Moor. He mysteriously returned to Venice minus his wife. I suppose there may be some basis in that for the story of Othello, but no one knows for certain.'

'Minus his wife. Do you think he murdered her, like he does in the play?'

'Who knows? She might have died in childbirth, or of some infectious disease. Or gone off with another man, perhaps. Will you come — to Famagusta?'

'Yes, all right.'

'Good! And then we'll have dinner. Oh, by the way . . .'

'Yes?'

'Remember to wear a hat.'

'For dinner?'

'No, silly! When we go to Famagusta. I don't want you passing out from the heat.'

I laugh, pleased by his concern. 'Don't worry. I'll remember.'

In bed that evening the reference to *Othello* comes back to me; it is not Shakespeare's play but Verdi's opera that drifts into my mind. The strains of Desdemona's heartbreaking 'Willow Song' run through my head as I settle down to sleep. *Oh, salce . . . salce . . . salce . . .* This time, the dream, or whatever it is, does not take me by surprise.

CHAPTER 11

The coach journey to Famagusta is a jolly affair. All the people in the group are behaving like old friends and seem happy
to include me, and I make an effort to join in. However, the
city itself has a sobering effect on all of us, including Karim.
Usually he is brimming over with enthusiasm and information, infecting everyone with his own fascination with the
history of his island, but today he is much less forthcoming,
as if there are things about this particular place that he pre-
fers not to recall. I feel in sympathy with him. The ruined
walls of the old city, with their potent reminder of defeat and
decay, seem to be echoed in the bleak prospect to the south,
where the empty shells of luxury hotels in the no man's land
between the two halves of the island look out onto golden
beaches that were once alive with colour and movement but
now lie deserted and silent.

Back at the hotel I take a long shower, order a spritzer
from the bar and lie down for half an hour, listening to Verdi
on my headphones. When I get up to dress for dinner, I
cannot make up my mind what to wear. The clothes I might
have worn for a night out with friends in London seem too
flamboyant, exposing too much naked flesh. I do not want
to appear too formal but I have an instinct that Karim will

expect me to have made an effort. In the end I opt for a new summer dress that I bought specially for the holiday and have not yet found an occasion to wear. The fabric is patterned in shades of blue and green, which I know flatters my colouring, and the cut is good. I have lost weight recently, and my breasts were never big, but the low, scooped neckline gives a hint of cleavage, while the smooth, flowing line emphasizes my newly slim hips. Then I can't make up my mind how to do my hair. During the day I wear it wound into a thick plait; now I try putting it up, then take it down again. Finally I take my hot brush and work it into soft waves, so that it frames my face in a halo of pale gold. By the time I have finished my make-up and darkened my eyelashes with navy mascara I feel almost satisfied. But no amount of foundation or powder will obliterate the faint violet shadows under my eyes.

Karim is waiting in the hotel foyer when I come down and I see from his eyes that I have not wasted my time. I sense that he enjoys the appreciative looks from the hotel staff as we go out to the car. The car, to my surprise, is a Mercedes convertible; admittedly not new, but still not the sort of vehicle I associate with a local tour guide. We drive up into the hills above Kyrenia, to a building which looks more like an English manor house than the typical Turkish restaurant I was expecting, and where the menu owes more to provincial France than the Middle East. I had been hoping for something a little more exotic and he senses my disappointment.

'I'm sorry. Don't you like this kind of food?'

'Oh, yes. I'm sure it will be delicious,' I say hastily. 'I just thought perhaps you might introduce me to some of the real local cuisine.'

He smiles. 'Perhaps another evening, if I may. Not everyone is happy to try Turkish food, so I thought I would play safe for tonight. And the food here really is excellent.'

And so it is. We eat crayfish, followed by a deliciously tender and piquant steak *au poivre* and Karim orders a bottle of smooth, full-bodied Turkish wine that surprises me by its quality. As he fills my glass, I notice that his contains only mineral water.

'You don't drink?'

'Alcohol? No.'

'Never?'

'Never.'

'Is that a matter of taste, or of principle?'

'A matter of religion.'

'Of course.' I feel myself blush. 'I should have thought. Muslims don't drink, do they?'

'Not officially. Though I know plenty who do.'

'But not you.'

'No.'

'Are you a very devout Muslim?'

'No, I'm afraid not. I can't remember the last time I was in the mosque. But I was brought up that way. My parents are believers. What about you? Are you a devout Christian?'

I shake my head. 'Far from it, I'm afraid. The only times I go into a church are for weddings and—' For a moment, memory catches at my throat '—and funerals.'

'Well,' he says, smiling, 'we have that much in common, anyway.'

For a moment we are both silent. Then he says, 'What did you think of Famagusta?'

'It's fascinating, but it makes me shiver. So many terrible things have happened there.'

'Yes, indeed. It has seen a great deal of suffering.'

'You mentioned that siege, when the Turks took the city from the Venetians. I started reading *Bitter Lemons* on the plane out here and Durrell talks about Famagusta in the first chapter. Is it true they promised the Venetian governor safe conduct and then arrested him and tortured him to death in that horrible manner?'

Immediately I could kick myself for my lack of tact. His expression has changed and when he speaks there is a harshness in his voice that I have not heard before. 'Ah, of course! The savage and perfidious Turk! I should have known you would have read that story.'

'Isn't it true, then?'

He meets my eyes. 'Oh yes, it's true — so far as I know. It was 1571, for heaven's sake! Things like that happened in those days.'

I struggle to make amends. 'Karim, I'm not trying to criticize you, or your people. I didn't mean it that way at all.'

'No?' His eyes are smouldering and his mouth is set in a hard, combative line. 'No, you're just accepting the general British line that the Turks are backward, untrustworthy savages who still live in the Middle Ages.'

'Karim!' I am embarrassed and angry, with myself and with him. 'I never said that — or implied it!'

'Have you ever heard how the Crusaders behaved when they conquered Jerusalem?' he goes on, as if I had not spoken. 'They killed every man, woman and child in the city. They speared Muslim babies and roasted them to eat!'

'Oh God, that's sick!' I protest. 'Don't, Karim!'

He looks at me and takes a gulp of water. 'I'm sorry. I got carried away.'

There is a pause. Then I say, 'You really are passionate about all this, aren't you?'

He gives me a wry grin. 'I can't help it. I suppose I'm particularly sensitive about Famagusta because I grew up there.'

'I didn't know. Whereabouts?'

'In the old city. My father had a business there.'

'And you don't have happy memories?'

He shakes his head. 'Don't get me wrong. I had a wonderful childhood, and a wonderful family. I'm the only son, so I suppose you could say I was spoiled rotten. But at the same time, other things were happening . . .'

'Such as?'

'Oh, political things mainly.' He puts his fork down. 'Enough! Tell me about you. How's life in London? Do you enjoy it?'

'Yes, very much. After growing up in rural Hampshire it's great. At least . . .'

'At least?'

'Oh well, I suppose the excitement wears off after a bit. But I can't imagine living anywhere else.'

'Do you like being a teacher?'

'Most of the time. I read English at university and it seemed the obvious career. But I didn't grow up with a burning desire to teach. Not like you. I imagine you always knew what you wanted to do.'

'More or less, yes. Did you ever have a burning desire to do something else?'

I take a sip of wine. 'Well, yes. What I really wanted — still want — is to be a writer.'

'Fiction?

'Oh, yes.'

'Plays? Novels?'

'Novels, mainly. And short stories.'

'Have you had anything published?'

'Just a couple of things, in fairly obscure magazines. But I don't really have the time, or the energy, to write after a day in school.'

'What do you do in your leisure time?'

'Oh, the usual things. Theatres, discos, parties . . .'

'No wonder you're tired!'

'Not every night! Actually, most evenings I'm too tired to do anything except flop in a chair and watch telly, or listen to music.'

'Would you like to go dancing?'

'Tonight?'

'If you are not too tired. We have some very good discos in some of the hotels.'

I feel my pulse quicken. 'Yes, all right. I'd like that very much.'

We drive back to the coast, to a large new hotel west of Kyrenia. The disco is in the basement and as we enter the intensity of the sound hits us like a solid wall. The dance floor is already crowded with bodies gyrating under the strobing lights, the white shirts of the men glowing blue as the

UV catches them. Karim throws off his jacket and leads me into the melee. I should have guessed he would be a natural dancer. I give myself up to the pleasure of matching my movements to his, feeling the common rhythm that flows through us both. For a while I am able to ignore the growing sense of exhaustion, until I suddenly stumble and he has to catch hold of me to stop me from falling.

'What is it? Are you feeling ill?' He has to put his mouth close to my ear for me to hear him.

My head is spinning but I try to hide the fact. 'No, it's nothing. I'm just a bit tired. Can we sit down for a bit?'

'Of course. Come outside, where it's quieter.'

He leads me up into the open air and we sit on a low wall with the sea breaking in hushed waves below us. The scent of orange blossom from an orchard across the road hangs in the warm air. Karim takes my hand and feels for my pulse. I force a laugh.

'You should have been a medical doctor.'

He does not laugh. 'I'm concerned about you, Cressida. Are you sure you're not ill?'

I feel the sudden crawl of fear in my stomach. 'What makes you say that?'

'You're so pale, for one thing. And the other day by the pool, I thought you were going to faint.'

I try to shrug it off. 'It's nothing to worry about. The doctor who looked after my mother said he thought I might be a bit anaemic.'

'Then when you get back to England you should have a blood test. Will you do that?'

'Yes, all right. I'll do that. I promise.'

He lifts my chin and looks into my face and I think, *He will kiss me now*. And I feel the familiar melting sensation of physical desire. I half close my eyes, sensing his closeness, his desire, but the kiss does not come. Instead he drops his hand and sits back.

For a long moment we sit in silence. Finally he says, 'How are you getting on with your researches into the family history?'

I try to swallow my disappointment and force my mind to focus on the question. 'Oh, slowly. As a matter of fact, my mother's journal is quite a revelation. It seems that my father was never really in love with her, because he'd fallen head over heels years before for a girl he met here, in Cyprus. At least, that's what my mother thought. I don't know if she was right or not. But it would make sense of my father's letters.'

He looks puzzled. 'How do you mean?'

'Oh, I don't think I told you. In the box with my mother's journal were some letters signed by my father but written in Greek. Os Wentworth looked at the first one and said it seemed to be a love letter. I've asked him to translate them for me.'

In the faint glow of the lights from the hotel I see him frown.

'Are you sure that's wise?'

'What do you mean?'

'It's all past history. Why distress yourself?'

I turn to him. I'm not sure why, but I want him to understand. 'I need to know, Karim. It's strange, but when my mother was alive I never asked her about my father. I suppose I knew that it distressed her to talk about it. But now that she's gone I suddenly find I desperately want to know about him and I'm kicking myself for not making her tell me. A child should have the right to know about its parents, don't you think?'

'Of course.' He meets my eyes and his own are serious and gentle. 'I don't blame you for wanting to find out, but you may not like what you find.'

'I'm already realizing that,' I say.

After a moment he says, 'Didn't your father have relations? You must have grandparents on his side, or uncles, aunts, cousins, perhaps.'

For a moment I stare at a floodlit palm tree rising ghost-like against the background of the dark sea. 'Do you know, I've no idea. I certainly never met any. I suppose my mother must have cut off all communication with them, if there were any.'

'You could try to find out, I suppose. You could go online, to one of those sites that help you to trace your ancestors.'

'Yes.' I am surprised that the idea has never occurred to me. 'I suppose I could.'

Once again we are silent for a while. Then he says, 'How did your father die, Cressida?'

'I don't know that either,' I confess. 'All I remember is my mother telling me he had gone away and wouldn't be back for a long time. Then, one evening, she came into my room to say good night and said, "Daddy won't be coming back, ever." I asked her if he was dead and she said, "Yes". I suppose I was too young then to ask how — but actually I think it might have been malaria. Do people die of malaria?'

'Certainly, if it's not treated. But in England he would get treatment.'

'He wasn't in England. I'm not sure where he was, but he worked as a journalist, a sort of foreign correspondent. I'm pretty sure it was in the Far East somewhere, because he brought me back a clockwork monkey once and I think he said it came from Singapore. And I do remember him being very ill once, when he was at home, and my mother told me then it was malaria. I remember, because I thought it was such a funny name.'

'Well, if he was working in that area, perhaps Malaysia or Korea or Vietnam, he might have picked up a resistant strain of malaria and if that was left untreated it would have killed him.'

'Perhaps that was it, then.' My mind is half on something else. 'Do you know, I'd completely forgotten that monkey until just now. Isn't memory an odd thing?'

'Is it?'

'You remember what I told you about that sort of dream I had about the air attack, which you said was probably a suppressed memory?'

'Yes.'

'I had another, similar experience last time I went to Lapta. I was just wandering around the streets, and I heard a man and a woman quarrelling and a child crying. I couldn't understand what they were saying, and yet it was as if I was listening to my own parents shouting. My father was saying that he refused to stay in the house with a squalling brat, and when he'd gone my mother told me it was all my fault and if he never came back she would blame me. Do you think that could be a genuine memory too?'

He takes my hand and says softly, 'Who can say? It might just be something you overheard as a child and misunderstood.'

Suddenly I feel tears pricking my eyelids and I find myself voicing the thought that has been torturing me since that day. 'Did he leave home because of me, Karim? Was it all my fault?'

He puts his arm round me and draws me against his shoulder. 'Of course not. You mustn't think that. A man doesn't leave home because his child cries. He may get irritated and say things he doesn't mean, but he doesn't leave. There have to be other, much deeper reasons.'

I gulp and draw a deep breath. 'Yes, there must be, mustn't there? It's stupid, but I've just realized that all my life, at the back of mind, I've been blaming myself. So you see, I really need to find out the true reason. If he went because he was in love with someone else, then it's nothing to do with me, is it?'

'No, of course it isn't.' He releases me and looks into my face. 'I didn't know it was so important to you. If there's anything I can do . . .'

I am shaken by the ideas that have just crystallized in my brain, but I manage a smile. 'I don't suppose there is.'

'I'm not so sure,' he answers. 'I could ask around. Someone may remember your parents and be able to throw some light on the matter.'

'That's very good of you.' I don't believe there is any likelihood of that, but I am touched by the offer.

He gets up and draws me to my feet. 'Now, I'm going to drive you home. You've had quite enough for one evening.'

'I'm sorry to be such a wet blanket,' I say. 'Usually I can dance all night.'

'It was my fault,' he says, leading me towards the car. 'The disco was a stupid idea. I should have seen you were tired.'

We say little on the way back to my hotel but as we draw up outside he says, 'Can we have dinner again tomorrow, if I promise to take you to a Turkish restaurant?'

I feel a flush of happiness. 'That would be great. I'd love to. And thank you for a wonderful evening — and for being so patient and understanding.'

On an impulse I lean across and kiss him quickly on the cheek. For a moment he sits quite still and when he speaks the old formality is back.

'No, I should thank you. It's been a great pleasure.' He gets out and comes round to open the passenger door for me. 'Tomorrow then? About the same time?'

'I'll be ready,' I tell him. 'Good night, Karim.'

'Good night.'

I wait a moment, giving him one last chance, but he simply bends his head in a stiff little bow and waits until I turn away and go into the hotel.

CHAPTER 12

Next morning there is no sign of Karim, so I wander into town and buy a few souvenirs as presents for friends at work. As I come back into the hotel, the receptionist hands me an envelope.

'A Mr Wentworth left this for you.'

I take it out onto the terrace, order a fresh lemon juice, and open it. Inside is one of my father's letters, together with several sheets covered in small, neat writing and a note from Os Wentworth.

Dear Cressida,

This is as far as I've got at the moment, but I thought you might like to see the results. They certainly make interesting reading! I'm getting in touch with some ex-colleagues who may have been more closely involved with the matter of your father's disappearance in '74 than I was. They may be able to shed some light on the mystery. Of course, his later letters may make everything clearer. We shall have to wait and see.

With a tremor of excitement, I put the note aside and pick up the first sheet of Os's translation.

My only beloved,

At last it seems there may be a chance of getting a letter to you, to tell you that I am still alive and have never for one moment stopped loving you and missing you. Though whether I shall still be alive when this letter reaches you is rather more questionable. Iannis is holding me prisoner and I have no idea what his intentions are, but at least now I have news of you and a chance to send this letter. Evangelos will bring it to you. Of course, he has no idea who I am and I will say nothing unless it becomes unavoidable. I only realized the truth myself yesterday, when he told me Iannis was his uncle. He is confused and frightened enough, without me adding to it. Iannis has convinced him that this is his patriotic duty and he does not dare to disobey. Remembering what EOKA used to do to anyone they regarded as a traitor back in the fifties I'm not surprised! But he is a good boy and we have become friends, so I think I can trust him to deliver this when the time comes. He has supplied the paper and pen, at great risk of his uncle's anger, but so far he thinks I am writing to my wife.

Yes, I have a wife — and a little girl just four years old. Don't think me faithless. In the end I just couldn't go on alone and I thought it might help me to forget. The years have shown me what a fool I was to imagine that was possible. You know, you must *know, that I did not leave the island of my own free will. Somehow my commanding officer found out about us, and I was immediately confined to barracks and then shipped back to England almost before I knew what was happening. I wrote you letter after letter, but each one was returned unopened. Did you ever know they had been sent? I am sure that it was your father and your brother who prevented you from reading them. I still had almost a year to serve in the army so all I could do was write. As soon as I was free I came back to Cyprus and went to your house, but your mother refused to open the door to me. I was still pleading with her when Ferhan came running up and almost dragged me away to her house. She told me that your father and Iannis might return at any moment and that if they found me there they would kill me. That would not have been enough on its own to make me give up, but then she told me that you had gone away; that you were in Athens and married.*

My darling, I know the marriage cannot have been of your choice. Please believe me when I say that I hope it has been a happy one, or at least not too unhappy. I cannot bear to think of you suffering all these years through my fault.

What an extraordinary chain of events it is that has given me the chance to write this letter. I followed you to Athens, of course, but I could never find out where you were. I didn't even know your married name! Eventually my money ran out and I had to go back to England to find work but I had persuaded Ferhan to keep in touch with me and let me have any news of you that came to her. For years she wrote to me every six months or so, so that I learned of the birth of your children and that you seemed to be well and not in any kind of distress. So the years passed and I tried to forget Cyprus and all that had happened here but the island wouldn't let me go.

I've been to Ayios Epiktetos. Strangers live in your old house but by chance I met an old man who told me you had returned to the island. He said he had seen you, but he didn't know where you were living. I went to Ferhan, but she refused to give me your address. She thinks it would only cause trouble if I suddenly reappeared in your life. Perhaps she is right. Then, two days ago, Evangelos said that there was someone who wanted to meet me secretly. I thought for a wonderful, crazy minute that it might be you. To say it was a shock to find myself face to face with Iannis would be an understatement! At first I thought he was going to carry out his old threat and kill me on the spot, but it seems he has other plans for me. I don't know what is going on, but he is clearly still involved up to his neck in EOKA and I get the impression that they are planning something big. Perhaps they have some idea of holding me to ransom. If so, my chances are pretty slim as we have no money to speak of.

Of course, it is a deliberate, cruel irony that he has chosen this cave as my prison, but I am kept in the rear chamber, far from the warmth of the sun. Iannis comes occasionally but he is obviously too important now to waste his time on guard duty. That is left to an old man and a couple of almost inarticulate shepherd boys with Kalashnikovs. Evangelos comes every day with supplies. It's hard to believe that here we are, twenty years on, and

(The letter comes to an abrupt end here. I think we can assume he was interrupted. O.W.)

I put the paper down and gaze unseeingly across the pool. There is too much information here to take in. Who was this Iannis, the brother who was mentioned as wanting to kill my father? I re-read the letter, more slowly, trying to piece together a consistent narrative from the disjointed fragments. Some of it is hinted at in Mother's journal. Why had Evangelos come to the bar looking for work? Was it pure coincidence, or had he been sent by his uncle? And why had my father been kidnapped? My first impulse is to drive out to Lapta after lunch to see if Os has translated any more of the letters. Then I remind myself that I have no right to expect him to devote his life to the task.

Instead, I fetch my mother's journal, and flip the pages in search of some mention of my father's disappearance. The acronym EOKA jumps out at me.

2 July

More political upheavals! Makarios has released a letter to the press in which he more or less accuses the junta in Athens of backing EOKA B and of trying to assassinate him. He has also demanded that all the Greek officers commanding the National Guard should be recalled. Stephen reckons the Athens regime can't afford to be seen to climb down so it will be a stalemate. He doesn't think it will come to a civil war, because the forces are so unbalanced but, of course, the big danger that everyone is afraid of is that Turkey will get involved on the pretext of protecting the Turkish Cypriot minority. There are very few Turkish Cypriots around here, but there is a big TC enclave in the Kyrenia area and several others to the west, so if that happened we should be in the thick of it. I have been trying to persuade Stephen to sell up and let us get out while we still can, but he points out, quite rightly, I suppose, that no one is going to buy property out here in the present state of things and all our capital is tied up in this place. He would be quite prepared to let me go back to England with Cressida, but I can't leave him here to cope on his own. If things get really bad we'll just have to pack up and run and hope we can come back when the trouble has blown over.

7 July

I don't know what has happened to Stephen. I am writing this at midnight, after closing the bar, hoping to hear the car coming up the hill at any minute. He went off this morning, saying he had to meet someone in connection with his research. I saw him talking to Evangelos just before that and I assumed Angel was coming for his usual English lesson, but instead he went off with Stephen. I wasn't surprised when they didn't come back at lunchtime because Stephen often disappears for most of the day, but until now he has always come back to help out during the evening, when we get busy. He has never been this late before. I find myself oscillating between two horrible suspicions and I am ashamed to say I don't know which is worst. Either he has finally found the woman he has been looking for and is with her or . . . or what? Everything is unsettled here, and we know EOKA is active in the area. God forbid he has been caught in some terrorist bomb attack or something. I keep telling myself he's met an old friend and they are drinking in a bar somewhere — or maybe the car has broken down. Oh God, I wish he would come home!

8 July — 10 a.m.

Still no sign of Stephen. Angel hasn't put in an appearance either, though he usually comes about this time. Does this mean they are together somewhere? If it does, there must have been some sort of accident. I've tried telephoning the police but they say there have not been any reports of road accidents or terrorist activities. I don't know what to do next. I'm sick with worry, and Cressida keeps asking where Daddy is. She misses Angel, too. He is always so good with her and amuses her for hours.

The worst part is the awful suspicion that this may have something to do with that dreadful row we had the other day. Stephen walked out in a huff then, but he came back later that same evening. He gets these moods but normally they don't last long. I can't believe he's been brooding over it ever since and finally decided to leave. Perhaps he thinks he is teaching me a lesson, getting his own back for some of the things I said. Well, he's certainly succeeded there. I sat up waiting for him till God knows what time last night — this morning — and of course I got through a couple of bottles of the local vino, so I feel doubly awful now.

Perhaps I'm being unjust. Stephen has never been the vindictive type and I don't think he would really intend to make me suffer. But he has always been a loner and sometimes I think he just has to get away until he gets his head together. I put it down to having a lonely childhood. I know he hated boarding school and never forgave his adoptive parents for sending him there. He says he can't understand why they wanted to adopt him in the first place if they were just going to send him away. I'm sure they really only wanted to do what was best for him, according to their lights, but he can't see that. I've never met them, of course. Stephen hasn't seen them or spoken to them since he left Oxford and went into the army. I feel very sorry for them.

I'm rambling, I know, but at least writing keeps my mind off the real anxiety and helps me to put off making a decision. I don't know if I should report his absence officially to the police, or perhaps contact the British Consul. The trouble is, he's a responsible adult and he's only been missing for 24 hours, so I don't think they will do anything. After all, if he has just 'gone walkabout' to think things through and turns up again tonight or tomorrow, I'll look a real idiot. And it will be even worse if it turns out that he's tucked up in some cosy little love nest with his girlfriend.

So, all I can do is try to behave normally and wait.

15 July — 11.15 a.m.

I've just heard some extraordinary news on the radio. It seems the National Guard have attacked the Presidential Palace and killed Archbishop Makarios! Now what will happen? Civil war? Will the Turks intervene? I'm terrified. And there's still no sign of Stephen. Something terrible must have happened to him. If he was still alive and free I know he would have come home by now. He wouldn't leave me to cope alone in this situation. What should I do? One minute I think I should pack up and get on the next plane back to England, while I still have a chance. I can't risk staying here with Cressida if there's going to be a war. But how can I go away, not knowing if Stephen's dead or alive? I've spoken to the police, and the British Consul, but they're no help. I can see them thinking I'm just another sozzled ex-pat whose husband has run off with a younger woman — and who can blame him? Oh God, I wish we'd never come here!

5 p.m.
The Greeks have appointed a man named Nicos Samson as president. All afternoon the local Brits have been congregating in the bar to discuss the situation. According to some of the old hands Samson was once sentenced to death for terrorism when the island was under British rule. How can a man like that be president?

Later.
Makarios is not dead after all. He has just broadcast from Paphos and appealed to the United Nations to step in. Most people here think that that means we are definitely in for a civil war, unless the UN acts very fast. It's too late to get out now. The airport is closed. All we can do is sit tight and hope.

I close the book and try to imagine my mother's panic and despair. I am amazed yet again that I remember nothing. Could I have wiped it out so completely? Or did my mother succeed, in spite of everything, in hiding her fears from me?

In the evening, Karim picks me up and drives me to a village on the coast, where he leads me into what looks like the front room of a small private house. There are four tables and a tiny bar and a glass-fronted refrigerated cabinet full of sticky cakes. I suppose my surprise shows in my face and Karim laughs.

'I'm sorry if this isn't what you were expecting, but I promise you, Mehmet produces some of the best Turkish Cypriot food on the island.'

A dark-faced woman in a white headscarf comes out of a back room and greets Karim with evident pleasure mingled with respect. There is no menu, but Karim and the woman exchange a few words in Turkish and she disappears into the kitchen, to return with a bottle of wine and another of mineral water. These are followed by a series of tiny appetizers — little cigar-shaped rolls of filo pastry stuffed with cheese, tiny spicy meat balls, a dish of roasted aubergines and tomatoes, cucumber in a garlicky yoghurt dressing. We follow these with veal cutlets and finish with a sticky almond pastry which I recognize as baklava.

As we eat, we talk, casually, about nothing in particular. Then, over the dessert, he says, 'So, what have you been doing today?'

I have been waiting for an opportunity to bring this up. I put down my fork and take the papers out of my handbag. 'Reading this.'

He glances down at the sheets, then raises his eyes to mine with a slight frown.

'Your father's letters?'

'Well, the first one. Os hasn't got any further at the moment.'

'Are you sure you want me to read this?'

'If it wouldn't bore you too much.'

'It wouldn't bore me at all, but it is rather personal.'

'I'd like you to read it. I'd really like to be able to talk it over with someone.'

'Very well.' He lowers his eyes again and does not speak until he has read the whole letter. Then he looks up, his gaze inscrutable. 'So, how much of a shock has all this been to you?'

'Well, considerable,' I reply. 'I'd never suspected any of it until the other day.'

'So what do you want to do?'

'I'm not sure. I wish I knew who she was — the woman my father loved. He doesn't even mention her name. Do you think there is any chance of tracing her?'

'Not without a lot more information,' he says. 'And even then it would be difficult.'

'We know she lived in Ayios Epiktetos.'

'Which is now Catalkoy. But all the Greeks from there left years ago. Anyway, she had moved to Athens.'

'Yes, but she came back — and she had a mother and father, and a brother.'

'A terrorist, it seems.'

'Who kidnapped my father, apparently. Why would he do that?'

'To avenge the family honour? To have had an affair with his sister would be an insult only death could avenge.'

'But he didn't kill him. I know he survived, because he came back to England with us.'

'You're quite sure about that? You couldn't be mixing up the time?'

'No, because he used to take me to school and I didn't start school till after we came back.'

'Right. But I don't see that it gets us any farther. Why do you want to find this woman, anyway?'

I hesitate and shrug my shoulders. 'I don't know, Karim, to be perfectly honest. Curiosity? What was it about her that made her so special? My father spent the rest of his life regretting that he lost her, so it must have been a very intense affair.'

'But suppose you did find her. Suppose you gave her the letters. Don't you think it might just cause her pain? She will have made a life for herself. She has a husband, children. How are they going to react?'

'What about us — my family? My mother drank herself to death because my father could never really love her as she loved him, and I've grown up feeling that in some way it was all my fault. I want to see this other woman face to face and tell her that she ruined three people's lives.'

Karim reaches across the table and lays his hand on mine. 'I understand that. But it isn't going to be easy.'

'Perhaps the other letters will help.'

He turns his attention to the letter again. 'There's a name here — Ferhan. That's a Turkish name. Catalkoy . . . Ayios Epiktetos . . . used to be a mixed village in those days. Greek and Turkish Cypriot children would have grown up side by side, so it's quite possible that your father's mistress had Turkish friends. Ferhan might still be there, or someone may know where she is now.'

'Could we go there and ask around?'

He shakes his head. 'People are inclined to be suspicious of anyone who asks too many questions, particularly a foreigner. Leave it with me. I have friends in Catalkoy. I'll make a few discreet enquiries. If I find anything helpful I'll let you know.'

I feel warm with gratitude, and relief. This makes us more than casual acquaintances. 'That's really good of you, Karim. Thanks.'

He returns my smile. 'Listen. Tomorrow I have a day off. I'd like to show you *my* island. Can I?'

'I'd love that.'

'Good. I'll pick you up at ten. OK?'

CHAPTER 13

'Up there? What do you think I am, a mountain goat?'

'Come on! It's not so far.'

I stare up at the sheer-sided crag above us. This morning Karim collected me, not in the usual Mercedes but in a Range Rover, and we headed up into the mountains east of Kyrenia. At the top of a pass we swung off the road and onto a narrow, stony track which clings to the top of the saw-toothed ridge I had seen from the coast. For several miles we wound our way around the sides of the precipitous gorges that carve themselves into the flank of the mountain, bouncing and jolting over the potholes, with Karim chuckling at my gasps of alarm. Now we are standing in an empty, level square of dusty ground, which seems to be as far as we can go.

'But there's nothing up there,' I protest.

'Look again!' he says, laughing.

I screw up my eyes against the intense blue of the sky and slowly begin to make out shapes that are not the work of nature, but which yet seem to grow out of the honey-coloured rock as if an organic part of it. Little by little, as I concentrate, what had appeared to be a jumble of boulders, cracked and fissured by wind and weather, resolves itself into walls and towers.

'There's a castle up there?'

'Buffavento. Come on.'

He takes my hand and leads me up a steep, rocky path. By the time we reach a paved road and a solid, imposing gate tower I am already gasping for breath.

'How on earth did they ever get the supplies they needed up here to build a place like this?'

'Who knows? How did the builders of Salisbury or Lincoln Cathedral manage?'

'At least they started at ground level. Why would anyone want to build up here?'

'A watchtower to warn of invasion, originally. The Byzantine rulers built it as a defence against Arab invasion in the twelfth century. Later it became a handy place to stick your political opponents.'

We pass under the archway, following a cobbled street that climbs still higher and higher, past the ruins of buildings whose purpose I can only guess at. Eventually, we emerge onto a level platform that gives us for the first time a view to the seaward side of the mountains. I gasp. On all sides the rock drops away sheer for hundreds of feet, so that we look out over the tops of the pines that clothe the steep ravines. A raven, disturbed by our approach, rides a current of air on a level with our faces and caws a sinister warning. Far below to the north lies the sea and the clustered villages of the coastal plain and beyond, where the distance dissolves in an amethyst haze, there is a faint suggestion of snow-capped peaks.

Karim touches my arm. 'Turkey. Those are the Taurus Mountains. Now you see how close we are.'

He turns to point in the opposite direction, where the slope flattens out into a dun-coloured plain.

'That's the Mesaoria, the bread-basket of the island. It doesn't look like it now, because the harvest is over, but in spring it is covered in wheat. And there, in the far distance — can you see? — that is Lefkosa.'

'Nicosia?'

'If you insist.'

I put up my hand to my hair. On the climb the sun beat down fiercely but now, without the shelter of the mountain-side, we are catching the full force of the west wind which, even at sea level, constantly sets the waves dancing and the flags outside the hotels rippling and cracking. Up here it makes my ears sing and, looking down at the vertiginous view, I feel suddenly dizzy.

I feel Karim's arm round my waist. 'What is it? Are you feeling faint again?'

For a moment I cannot answer. Then I say, as calmly as I can, 'No, I'm all right. Just a bit giddy for a minute. I'm not very good at heights — and I think I must be out of condition. That climb . . . the heat, you know . . .'

His voice is contrite. 'I'm sorry, I should have thought. It was silly of me to bring you up here when I know you're not well.'

I pull free of his supporting arm. 'I'm all right! Honestly. I was just out of breath. Look, I'm fine now.'

He studies my face for a moment, then turns and leads me into a huge, vaulted chamber.

'Take care, there's a hole in the middle of the floor!'

I peer down into an apparently bottomless shaft. 'What is it? A well?'

'An oubliette. Somewhere to throw things you wanted to get rid of — rubbish, or an inconvenient prisoner.' He moves to an arched window in the opposite wall. 'Look, there's our car, right down there. See?'

'Oh yes! God, I knew it was a long climb, but I didn't realize we'd come that far.' I squint at the winding thread of track. 'The road seems to go on. Why is it blocked off down there?'

'It leads to a military base. We're not allowed to go any further.'

'Another one! Everywhere I go I seem to pass army camps.'

I see his face harden in a way I am beginning to recognize. 'It's necessary. Without the Turkish army we should all be pushed into the sea.'

I say sadly, 'This is such a beautiful island, yet it seems to be full of the relics of wars.'

Suddenly his face relaxes into a smile. 'Not everywhere. Come on, I'll show you somewhere that was built as a place of peace.'

'Bellapais. The Abbaye de la Paix. Built in the aftermath of the Crusades as a place of peaceful contemplation. Beautiful, isn't it?'

I gaze up at the soaring Gothic arches framed by the dark spires of three tall cypresses. 'Yes, it is. It must have been wonderful to come back here, away from the desert and the fighting. Why did the monks leave?'

We stroll along the cloister, the air heavy with the scent of thyme and the endless whirr of cicadas. Karim says, 'The monastery was closed down by the church authorities. The last few monks were found to be living a life of luxury and each in possession of several wives.'

I laugh. 'Oh dear! I wonder how they squared that with their vows.'

Karim grins in return. 'I imagine they didn't try. I'm afraid the atmosphere here didn't lend itself to austere contemplation. Too easy, too warm. Or perhaps the goddess Aphrodite resented the intrusion of our celibate, male deity and set out to subvert them.'

'Ours?' I query.

'Yahweh, God, Allah. Essentially the same. Are you thirsty? Let's go and have a drink under the Tree of Idleness.'

'Where?'

'It's the name of the bar in the square.'

We sit in the shade of the huge tree which gives the bar its name and sip lemonade, looking across to where the arches of the ruined abbey frame a distant view of the sea. I lean back in my chair and sigh.

'What a perfect name for this place! I could sit here all day. No wonder the monks forgot their vows! Peace and idleness. It makes all our working and fighting and rushing about seem pointless.'

'Be careful,' he warns, smiling. 'You're in danger of succumbing to the temptation of the lotus eaters.'

'If only! Do you realize I've only got a few days of my holiday left? I hate the thought of going back to work.'

'I thought you enjoyed your job.'

'I did — I do. Oh, I suppose everyone regrets coming to the end of a holiday. But I have to admit this place does seem to have a special magic. I can understand why my father had to come back.'

Karim gets up and takes some money from his pocket to pay for the drinks. 'Come on. I'll show you the house where Lawrence Durrell wrote *Bitter Lemons*.'

When we return to the square he says, 'Now, how about lunch?'

'Here? Under the Tree of Idleness?'

He shakes his head. 'No. I've got a better idea. Jump in. It's not far.'

We drive out of the village, past a cluster of new villas embowered in bougainvillaea and hibiscus.

'Holiday homes,' Karim says. 'The tourist trade is an important part of the local economy, in spite of efforts to cut us off from civilization.'

A little further along the steep hillside he turns the car in through some gates and pulls up outside a large, white-painted house. I follow him up the steps, assuming that this is another of his favourite restaurants. We enter a spacious, cool hallway with white walls and a floor covered in tiles of an intricate design in exquisite shades of blue. On one wall hangs a beautiful rug in similar shades, but there is no other decoration. A woman in a black dress and a white headscarf appears and greets Karim in Turkish, then bows and smiles at me before retreating.

Karim says, 'Welcome to my home.'

I gaze at him, stunned. 'This is yours?'

'My father's. But I live here. This way.'

He leads me out into a courtyard enclosed on three sides by the house and on the fourth by a wall which rises to first-floor height and is pierced by a series of archways, each one supporting a profusion of jasmine and roses and framing a view of the coast and the distant mountains of Turkey. A table is set for lunch under the shade of an acacia tree.

'Karim,' I murmur, 'this is beautiful!'

He nods. 'Yes. I am fortunate.'

'Are your parents here?' I ask.

'No, no. They live most of the time in London. My father's main business is there. They come out from time to time, for a holiday or to check on the staff in Gazimagusa.'

'What is your father's business?'

'He's a merchant. He imports and exports, mainly from the Turkish mainland.'

The woman, who seems to be a housekeeper, returns with wine and mineral water. Embarrassed, I say, 'You don't have to give me wine, you know. I'm quite happy with water.'

He shakes his head. 'There's no reason to deprive you, just because I have this odd little habit. Please, let me pour you some.'

As he fills my glass I ask, 'Have you always lived here? I thought you said you grew up in Famagusta — Gazi . . . what do you call it?'

'Gazimagusa. Yes, so I did. We only moved here after—'

'After the invasion?'

He gives a slight, ironic grimace. 'After the peace operation.'

'What made your parents move to London?'

His face darkens. 'Things were very difficult in Gazimagusa prior to the division of the country, especially where we lived. There was a lot of hostility, a lot of trouble. We — the Turkish Cypriots — were confined to the Old City. People were being massacred in the surrounding villages, and we were virtually under siege. My father already had an office in London. He managed to get us on a flight. He won't come back here to live. Too many bad memories.'

'So why this house?'

'When things settled down, after the fighting was over, there was a lot of property left vacant by the Greek Cypriots. My father had the opportunity to . . . acquire some land. To begin with it was just olive groves, some citrus orchards. Then he saw that the tourists were beginning to come back. There was a shortage of accommodation. He built villas, like those we saw on the way here. It was a shrewd move, from a financial point of view.'

I look around me. 'Your father is obviously a very successful man.'

'Fortunately for me,' Karim agrees. 'Otherwise I could never have been educated in England. The government here cannot afford to pay for students to study abroad.'

The woman reappears with a selection of *mezes*. Karim encourages me to try various dishes, but I can't help noticing that his face, as so often, is shadowed as if some unwelcome memory has been reawakened.

I say, 'You must have been too young to remember much about the fighting.'

His dark eyes flicker up to my face and then drop again. 'Oh, I remember it all right.'

I hesitate, not wanting to pry, but I have a strong desire to share whatever it is that troubles him. I say quietly, 'What happened, Karim? Tell me about it.'

For a moment he is silent, then he begins. 'Before the fighting started we lived in the outlying suburb of Karakol. When the invasion came, the Greek National Guard arrived and surrounded us. An officer told my father, "If the Turkish army comes here, they will find only the dead." That night some of our resistance fighters came to the house and told us we must leave, bringing only the barest necessities with us. My mother woke me and told me to get dressed. My sisters were crying, but my mother slapped them and told them they must be silent or we should all be killed. We crept out of the house and found the street was full of people. All our neighbours had been brought out of their houses in the same way. In that terrible silence we followed the fighters through the dark streets towards the walls of the Old City. I was very frightened, but I dared not speak or cry. When we reached the city a miracle happened. We were led into the mouth of a tunnel that had been dug under the walls. No one knew it was there, except the resistance people. When we reached the other end we were taken to one of the buildings which had been used by the old Venetians to store grain or stable horses. The city was under siege and that stable was home to us and dozens of others for three weeks. By the end there were only three days' supply of food left in the Old City. More than twelve thousand of us were crammed inside the walls. Twice a day we got a bowl of watery soup and a little rice. I was hungry and afraid all the time. The National Guard were pounding the city with their heavy weapons. They had mortars and "tank buster" rifles. We dared not go out and the noise went on day and night. My father was trying to find a ship, or someone who would take us to the British air force base. We heard that the British were evacuating people and he offered to pay whatever was required to get us out, but no one would risk trying to break through the National Guard forces. We prayed daily that the Turkish army would come to our aid, or the United Nations, but it seemed no one heard or cared about what happened to us.' He stops and shakes his head, without looking at me. 'It's not a subject for a day like this.' Then he draws a deep breath and looks up, smiling that sudden, bewitching grin. 'Eat your lunch. I thought you liked Turkish food.'

'I do.' I quickly turn my attention to my plate. 'And this is delicious.'

For the rest of the meal we talk of other things — of music and films and my life in London. When we have finished he says, 'Now, I am a great believer in the tradition of a siesta. Come with me and I'll show you where you can rest.'

He leads me into the house and to a white-walled room on the ground floor with long windows whose light curtains billow softly in the breeze from the sea. Seeing the big double bed, its sheets turned down ready, I experience a sudden lurch at the pit of my stomach. Am I about to be seduced? Normally the prospect would be delicious but today, as so often recently, I feel only a deep longing to lie down and sleep.

I need not have worried. Karim says only, 'There is a bathroom through that door. If you would like to take a shower after your sleep please feel free to do so. There is no hurry. Sleep as long as you like.'

Before I can thank him the door closes behind him. I slip off my dress and lie down, revelling in the cool air on my skin and the crisp freshness of the sheets. As I drift towards unconsciousness it occurs to me that perhaps it was a mistake to drink wine at lunch after all. On the other hand, there is something seductive about this delicious drowsiness. I picture Karim, leaning towards me, tempting me with tasty morsels of food, smiling and attentive. Then I remember his face when he spoke of his early memories and, on the edge of sleep, I twist over in bed and murmur, 'Poor boy, poor boy!'

When I wake the patch of sunlight from the window has moved across the floor to the opposite wall. There is a tap at the door. Expecting Karim, I pull the sheet across my body and call. 'Come in.'

It is the housekeeper, carrying a tray.

'Dr Mezeli asks if you would like some tea.'

I sit up. 'Oh, lovely! That's just what I need. Thank you.'

The woman puts the tray on the bedside table. 'He asks also if you would like to go swimming later. If you have not brought your costume, he says there are some belonging to his sisters but—' She pauses, looking at me with a glimmer of a smile behind her grave composure, 'I think they would be too large for you.'

I smile back. 'It's very kind of Dr Mezeli, but there's no need. I have my costume with me — just in case. Please tell him I should love to go swimming, and I'll be ready in ten minutes.'

Karim is sitting under the acacia tree reading a book when I join him, freshly showered and wearing my bikini under my dress. He rises as I approach.

'Did you sleep?'

'Yes, I did. I don't know what you put in that wine. I can't usually sleep in the middle of the day.'

He smiles in return. 'Well, I think it has done you good. You were looking tired.'

It strikes me that his story of a habitual siesta was fabricated for my benefit and also that my need of it had been anticipated.

'You're very thoughtful,' I say. 'Thank you.'

I had been slightly disappointed by the beaches close to Kyrenia but Lara Beach, along the coast to the east, to which he drives me, is much more attractive. A shallow cove encloses a crescent of sand bisected by a smooth outcrop of rock on which children clamber and young men stretch themselves to sunbathe. The water is like green crystal, fringed with the creamy effervescence of waves. We spread our towels on a patch of dry sand, strip off our outer garments and run down to the water's edge. His body is as I guessed it would be — lean, lithe and deeply tanned — and he swims with powerful strokes that soon carry him beyond the breakers. Normally I would have matched him stroke for stroke, but today I content myself with splashing around in the shallows. He comes back quite soon and we sit quietly in the edge of the waves.

'Do you regret leaving England?' I ask.

He clasps his arms round his knees. 'Sometimes. I miss the things we've talked about: the music, the theatres, even the climate when it gets too hot here!'

'But you never considered staying?'

'Oh yes. I nearly did. I was offered a fellowship.'

'Why didn't you take it?'

'Oh, various reasons. Mostly because I felt I was needed more here. I came here to take up a post with the Department of Antiquities and Museums.'

'But now you work as a tour guide.'

He shrugs. 'The department can't afford to pay me to work full-time. The tour guiding fits in very well.'

'So you wouldn't want to come back?'

'I . . .' He hesitates. 'I'm not sure. Much of the work I came here to do is in hand. There is not the same urgency. But I wanted to get away from London. Any ex-pat community can be a bit claustrophobic, you know, and as you said, living between the two cultures can be difficult at times.' He looks at me. 'Don't sit too long in the sun. You'll burn.'

I laugh, touched by his concern. 'Do stop worrying about me! Anyway, the sun will be down any minute.'

It is true. I have slept away half the afternoon and now the sun is dipping towards the headland that closes the western end of the bay. We sit on until it has disappeared in a sudden upsurge of blood-red clouds and then drive back towards Kyrenia.

We eat dinner at a restaurant called the Harbour Bar and towards midnight find ourselves sitting at another café table, sipping thick black Turkish coffee. The café is right at the end of the quay, close under the castle wall, where few tourists penetrate. A little group of local men argue animatedly inside the bar but we have the outside tables to ourselves. The wind has dropped and the waters of the harbour lie still and black, reflecting the lights along the front like a mirror. The air has the texture of warm milk.

After a silence, Karim says, 'Why aren't you married, Cressida?'

The question takes me by surprise and for a moment I don't know how to answer. Then I say, 'The usual reasons, I suppose. Too busy building a career, not wanting to be tied down . . .'

'You've never wanted marriage?'

'No. Well, not until . . . I suppose lately I have thought about it more.'

'There must have been boyfriends. Wasn't there anyone special?'

'No. Yes . . . Well, I thought he was, for a while. But it was all a mistake.'

'Tell me about him?'

'His name was — is — Paul. He's good-looking, intelligent, fun. We had some good times together. He's got a good job, too, in computers.'

'Were you together long?'

'Almost a year. I'd begun to think it was going to be permanent.'

'What went wrong?'

'It was when my mother got ill. I had to spend a lot of weekends down in Hampshire, looking after her and coping with her affairs. Paul hated that. He's a party animal. He lives for the weekends.'

'Didn't he come down to Hampshire with you?'

'To begin with he did. Then, when she had to go into hospital, he just couldn't hack it. Hospitals frightened him. After that he stayed up in town. When I came back to the flat after my mother's funeral I found a note from him. He said he needed to get away, to think things out. Actually, I found out a few days later he'd gone to Spain with a girl he met at a party while I was away.'

'He left you, while you were at your mother's funeral?' Karim's voice is heavy with incredulous disgust.

'Yep.'

He is silent for a moment. Then he says, 'The man is not only a bastard, he's a fool! Forget him.'

'I have,' I say. Then more honestly, 'I'm trying.'

'Were you . . . living together?' There is a hesitation in his voice.

'Oh yes.'

After a moment he asks, 'Was he the first?'

My first reaction is annoyance. What right has he to quiz me like this? Then something tells me that this is a time to be honest. 'The first? No.'

He goes on as if compelled to ask, against his better judgement. 'Have there been many others?'

I glance at him. Why is he asking? 'Two or three — well, three.' It was almost true, if you didn't count the boy who, out of pity, relieved me of my virginity on a sixth-form field

132

trip, or the Finn at that party whose name I was too drunk to remember.

He doesn't look at me. In the silence I study his profile, trying to work out what is behind his questions. I have never met anyone quite like him before. In the end I decide to turn the tables.

'Why aren't you married, Karim?'

He withdraws his gaze from the dark water and meets my eyes. 'Not for the reason you're thinking of.'

'Why then?'

'You have to understand,' he says slowly, 'marriage is not a simple thing in my society. You do not meet a girl at a party and live with her for a year and then decide to marry. In fact, it's not easy to meet a good Muslim girl at all.'

'So how do you find someone to marry?'

'Usually an introduction is arranged. Not an arranged marriage, you understand. Neither party is obliged to proceed further. But parents agree to introduce children who they think may be compatible.'

'So, what went wrong in your case?'

He gives a rueful, self-mocking grin. 'Every time I go home my parents have found some suitable new girl for me to meet. I'm afraid I have offended most of their friends by failing to pursue the connection. That's one reason why I don't go back to England very often. It's a curious fact that expatriates of my parents' generation are far more conventional and rigid than our people who have stayed here.'

'What about the girls themselves?' I ask. 'Were they offended?'

He laughs briefly. 'Oh no, I think most of them felt they had had a lucky escape.'

'I don't believe that for a minute,' I say and momentarily our eyes meet. I press on, 'You must have met lots of girls at uni.'

'Oh yes.' There is something almost wistful in his tone. 'No shortage of pretty girls. But none of them would have been . . . suitable.'

133

'Because they weren't Muslims? Is that so important to you?'

'It's important to my family. And I think it is important to the success of the marriage. An English girl, a non-Muslim, might find it difficult to accept our ideas, our way of life.'

'But you wouldn't expect your wife to wear a veil or . . . or live in a harem?'

He laughs. 'Good Lord, no! How many veiled women have you seen out here?' Then his face sobers. 'But just the same, there are differences of attitude, different values.'

We are both silent for a moment. Then I say, 'So there's never been anyone — for you?'

'Not really, no.'

'But you're not — you can't be . . . !' The words are out before I can stop them.

He holds my gaze. 'A virgin? No, not quite. Thanks to a kind girl in Newcastle and one or two . . . professional ladies since. But I don't like that kind of relationship. On the whole, I prefer continence.'

It is my turn to look away. Suddenly I see how vast the gulf must seem to him between my lifestyle and his own and I wish I had lied about the previous boyfriends, or could in some way erase them.

Karim gets to his feet. 'I'll walk you back to your hotel.'

We walk in silence, past the now empty tables. At the hotel entrance he takes my hand.

'Thank you for a very enjoyable day.'

'No,' I respond, 'I should thank you. It's been a lovely day, and you've been very kind and thoughtful.'

Our eyes meet again and I long to reach up and press my lips to his but find myself held back by an unfamiliar restraint. He raises my hand and kisses it lightly.

'Good night. Sleep well.'

'Good night, Karim.'

In the foyer of the hotel I turn and watch him through the glass of the doors, walking away towards his car. It comes to me that he has not asked me to go out with him again.

134

CHAPTER 14

When I come down to breakfast the following morning, I find that the tour group has already left on a day trip to Nicosia. I pass the day idling around the town, explore the castle, then lie by the pool. When I come back into the hotel I find another envelope waiting for me from Os Wentworth. Inside are translations of two more of my father's letters. I take them to my favourite spot on the terrace and discover that my hands are shaking as I unfold the first one.

My darling,

I had to break off last night because Iannis suddenly appeared. Luckily I heard him speaking to the sentry outside the cave and so was able to hide the letter before he came in. Perhaps I should not be writing at all. I don't care what he might do to me if he found out but I could not forgive myself if it caused trouble for you. God knows, you've suffered enough because of me. And yet, I cannot let this one last chance of communicating with you slip away. I do not expect anything to come of it. I know you would never betray your husband and your family. After all these years I am probably only a distant memory to you.

I am rambling, I know. The fact is, I can feel a fever coming on. For years now I have suffered from bouts of malaria that recur from time to time, particularly when I am under stress. The damp and chill in

135

this cave are not helping, either. It doesn't matter. When I have served whatever purpose Iannis has for me he will dispose of me. The malaria may save him the trouble!

What I want to do, what I must do while I have a chance, is set the record straight. Yes, I was responsible for the ambush. I had to give my superiors some concrete proof that I had really been following up a useful lead. I came across the arms cache one day when I was waiting for you. Of course I realized that you had not the faintest suspicion of its existence. How could I have possibly guessed that Demetrios was involved? He was my friend and your brother. I would never have harmed him. You must believe that!

My head is splitting. I shall have to stop. Good night, my darling girl.

The third letter was brief and Os had written at the top of his translation, 'The writing on this page is very erratic and quite difficult to follow. I think your father was in a bad way when he wrote it. I've done my best with it but there were bits I couldn't make sense of at all.'

Iannis is convinced I am still working for British Intelligence . . . (Indecipherable) Can't make him understand . . . Strong arm tactics are useless. Have to persuade him I don't know anything. Not making much sense anyway. High fever . . . delirious some of the time. Must find a chance to give these to Evangelos before it's too late. Should I tell him the truth? What could he do, poor kid? (More indecipherable scrawl, then the writing becomes steadier again) Just woken up. Head a bit clearer but think I must still be hallucinating. Thought for a minute I was back in Vietnam. Keep thinking I can hear gunfire.

(The letter breaks off here. My guess is that what your father was hearing was probably the beginning of the Turkish invasion. This is bound to be distressing for you. I'm sorry. If you want to come out to Lapta and talk it over Meg and I would be delighted to see you. Os.)

I look at the back of the letter and feel sick. Those rust-coloured blotches that I noticed before have taken on a much more sinister significance. 'Strong arm tactics.' What did that mean?

I shut my eyes tightly and try to force myself to remember those last days on the island. There are only fleeting, disjointed images. Bags, suitcases, my mother shouting at someone — and running. That recurring nightmare. Running with my mother, being dragged along by the hand, a bag banging against my legs. 'Hurry! Come on! You can run faster than that! We can't stop here!' Then something I had not recalled before. A beach, crowded with people, but not sunbathing, not swimming. 'No, you can't go and paddle! Sit here and don't move. Do you understand? Don't move from this spot. I want you to look after the cases.' Legs moving around me — men's, women's — cases being picked up and dumped down again — voices. Then someone lifting and carrying me, a man, a stranger. Not my father. In all the confusion there is no image of him. And yet I remember him in England, walking me to school along the Hampshire lanes. Surely I can't be mistaken about that.

I take a taxi to Lapta, where the imperturbable Meg insists that I stay for lunch. When I describe my memories Os says, 'That makes sense to me. When the invasion happened the navy was sent in to rescue British nationals. They couldn't use Kyrenia harbour because the EOKA guerrillas were firing into the town from the hills above and the castle itself was still in Greek hands. So people were taken off by launch and helicopter from the beaches to the east of the town. It was a pretty chaotic scene, I should imagine. That's probably what you were remembering.'

'But where was my father at that time?' I ask. 'The last thing we know, he was being held prisoner in a cave somewhere, half dead with malaria. How did he get away?'

Os shrugs gently. 'We shall probably never know. Perhaps the Turkish army rescued him when they took over. Maybe his captors just disappeared and he managed to get himself to a road or a village. He may not have left on the same ship as you and your mother. What matters, surely, is that he did get away.'

137

'I suppose so,' I agree reluctantly. 'But I would love to know the full story. It's awful to think of what he must have been through — and I never knew anything about it.'

'What still perplexes me,' Meg remarks, 'is how those letters came to be here. He meant to give them to Evangelos to pass on to this other woman — whoever she was.'

Suddenly I have a vivid mental picture of the 'angel boy' who rescued me from the bombing. 'Of course! He did give them to Evangelos! And Evangelos brought them to my mother by mistake. He must have misunderstood.'

I describe the dream/memory I experienced under the fig tree. 'I can picture him carrying me back to the house. There was another explosion and I think he must have been wounded. Blood was running down his arm and he was carrying some folded papers. Those marks are Evangelos's blood, not my father's!'

'Well, that would certainly explain how the letters got here,' Os agrees. 'You and your mother would have had to leave in a hurry so they were probably shoved into a box or a drawer and forgotten about.'

Meg says thoughtfully, 'The fighting in this area was pretty fierce — well, you obviously remember that. And yet Evangelos braved the shelling to get those letters to your mother. I suppose, if your father was delirious at the time, it's not surprising that Evangelos misunderstood who the letters were for. But he must have felt very strongly about your father to bring them, under the circumstances. Unless it was that he felt he had an obligation to you and your mother.'

'I wonder where he is now,' I say. 'I suppose it would be no use searching for him.'

'Not on this side of the dividing line,' Os says. 'If you want to pursue your enquiries you'll have to come back to the Greek half of the island for your next holiday. Only make sure that the Turkish customs and emigration don't stamp your passport when you leave. Otherwise they'll never let you into the Greek sector.'

As I collect my key from the hotel reception desk I try to suppress a hope that there might be a message from Karim. There is not, and I spend the evening trying to fight off a growing sense of depression. Alan and Mary call me over and invite me to join their table at dinner. There are four others and conversation is lively. They all seem to have bonded and are full of enthusiasm about the island and its history — and full of praise for Karim — but their bonhomie only serves to make me feel more solitary. Afterwards, we adjourn to the terrace and order more drinks. A Turkish belly dancer has been brought in to entertain us and as the evening progresses the mood becomes more and more raucous. These people can certainly put away the alcohol and I find myself wondering what Karim would make of us if he were present. I totter off to bed at midnight with my head swimming.

The next day at breakfast, Karim comes over to my table.

'I've found someone you might like to meet,' he said. 'Someone who remembers your father.'

I gasp in surprise. 'How wonderful! You are clever, Karim. An Englishman?'

'No, one of my people. He lives in my village. I remembered that he used to be in the police force so I asked him if he recalled anything about an Englishman disappearing around the time of the peace operation. He recognized your father's name at once. Do you want to meet him?'

'Of course! When?'

'I have to take the group to Lambousa this morning, but it's only a half-day tour. I'll pick you up about four o'clock this afternoon and take you to his house. Will that be OK?'

'That will be fine. Thank you, Karim.'

Rauf Demirel is a corpulent man in his late sixties, as near as I can guess. He welcomes us courteously into his small, whitewashed house and offers apple tea. After the exchange of some necessary small-talk, Karim brings up the subject of our visit.

Demirel responds at once in fluent though heavily accented English.

'Mr Stephen Allenby? I met him only briefly. But I remember his wife — your mother — very well. She came to see me a few days before the peace operation began.'

'Why did she come? Was she looking for my father?'

'She came to report that he had disappeared, yes. At that time I was in charge of the police depot in Kyrenia. It was a difficult period. I'm not sure how much you know, but the situation was . . . volatile, shall we say. If I remember correctly your mother came to the police station on the tenth or eleventh of July. She was obviously very worried. She told me your father had not been home for several days and asked for our help.' Demirel spreads his hands. 'You understand, your father was a grown man, in full possession of his senses. Normally we would not follow up such a case, except to check the hospitals and circulate his name to other police stations. If a man wishes to disappear . . .' He shrugs expressively.

'So you don't know what had happened to him.' Is that all? I try to keep the disappointment out of my voice.

'Ah, but wait!' Demirel goes on. 'That is not the end of the story. As you perhaps know, a few days later the Greek National Guard attempted a coup against President Makarios. From then on there was civil war — Greek against Greek — as the supporters of Makarios fought the National Guard. We Turks were told to keep out of it, that it was nothing to do with us. But we knew whichever side won we would be next to suffer. Kyrenia was taken over by the National Guard. My officers and I were mostly Turks. We decided to withdraw from the city, up into the hills near the pass that leads to Lefkosa. We stayed in a village called Agirdag and waited to see what would happen. Then, five days later, the Turkish army arrived. I watched the paratroopers coming down out of the sky onto the mountain slopes right in front of me!'

I try not to fidget. It is obvious that Demirel is wrapped up in his memories, but I can't see what relevance they have to my father. Karim catches my eye and makes a slight, pacifying movement of one hand.

'The fighting went on for two days and nights,' Demirel continues. 'The planes came over by day, dropping bombs and strafing the Greek positions. And the ships off the coast kept up a constant bombardment. It was high summer and very hot. Soon the hillsides were ablaze. The Greeks had prepared positions in caves, where they had stashed large quantities of arms and ammunition. We could only wait and watch. Then, on the third morning, during a lull in the bombing, a farmer arrived in the village. He was driving a tractor and pulling a trailer on which were his wife and children and everything he had been able to salvage from his home. There was also an Englishman — a very sick man.'

'My father?'

'Yes, Miss Allenby. Your father. The farmer told us how the previous night, during a lull in the fighting, he had heard a knocking at the door. When he opened it, he found your father slumped on the threshold. He was delirious and unable to stand, so obviously someone must have brought him to the farm, but whoever it was had already disappeared.'

'What did you do?'

'We did what we could, but we had no medicine and no doctor. Of course, all communications were cut. So I sent him with two of my men with instructions to try to get through to the British base at Dhekelia. I believe they had some difficulties, but they reached the base eventually. I assume your father was cared for there until he was well enough to be flown home. He reached you all right, in the end?'

I hesitate. It seems ridiculous that I cannot be sure. 'I suppose he must have done. I remember him in England, soon after that.'

'Dr Mezeli tells me he died a year or two later,' Demirel says sympathetically. 'My commiserations. Perhaps he never recovered from his ordeal?'

I struggle to remember whether he was ill during that brief interval. 'Perhaps not. But thank you. Thank you so much for helping him — and for filling in part of the mystery for me. I suppose you have no idea why he was kidnapped?'

'What makes you think he was kidnapped?'

'Some letters he wrote — letters I have only just come across. It seems he was being held in a cave somewhere, but I don't know why.'

Demirel shrugs again. 'I can only guess. The EOKA terrorists were very active at that time. What they might want with your father I do not know, but kidnapping and murder were part of their trade. If they were holding him, perhaps his captors were killed in the bombing, or went off to join in the fighting, and he was able to escape. But someone must have helped him.'

'I wish I knew who. I should like to thank them.'

Demirel raises his palms. 'There, I'm afraid, I cannot help you.'

We leave soon after that. In the car Karim says, 'Shall I drive you back to the hotel? Or would you like to come back to my place for some proper tea?'

My mood lifts immediately. 'Tea would be lovely.'

Once we are seated in the shade in the courtyard of Karim's house I say, 'Thank you so much for taking the trouble to find Mr Demirel for me. At least now I have one more piece of the jigsaw.'

'Enough pieces to make up a picture?'

'I'm not sure.' I assemble my thoughts with an effort. 'The one thing we haven't been able to discover is the one thing I should really like to know.'

'Which is?'

'Who the girl was. I wonder if she's still alive. And Evangelos. I wonder where he is now.'

Karim shakes his head. 'I'm afraid I can't help any further. If there are answers to those questions, then they are on the other side of the Green Line, in the Greek sector.'

I sigh. 'There's no more time, anyway. I have to go home the day after tomorrow.'

Karim gets up. 'Come on. I'll drive you back to the hotel.'

I decide on a last throw of the dice. 'Actually, I thought we might have dinner together. My treat, this time.'

For a moment his eyes narrow. Then he says, 'I'm afraid not. Thank you for the invitation, but I have a talk to give tonight.'

I follow him out to the car, raging inwardly but whether at him or myself I do not know. As we drive away from the house I try once more, against my better judgement.

'Well, if not tonight, how about tomorrow?'

For a moment it seems he is looking for an excuse to turn me down again. Then he says, as if the decision has cost him a struggle, 'Very well. But you will be my guest. I cannot allow a woman to pay for me.'

That night I can't sleep. I am beset by confused emotions that refuse to submit to rational examination. What did I expect from Karim? What did I want? A holiday romance? A one-night stand? Am I that desperate? I feel a hot flush of humiliation at the thought of how obvious I have been. No wonder he cooled off! He was attracted to me to begin with. I am quite sure of that. And I know exactly when it all went wrong. It was when I confessed to having had several former lovers. I feel a rush of exasperation. What did he expect? I am twenty-eight and this is the end of the twentieth century. If he is looking for a virgin bride, it is no wonder he is still single. He had better settle for one of the nice Muslim girls his parents keep finding for him. Anger comes to my rescue. Sod him! It's his loss. There is no way I am going to settle for the kind of marriage he would want. My train of thought hits the buffers with an almost physical jolt. Whoever mentioned marriage, anyway?

I turn over and make a determined effort to get to sleep. But as I drift off, a small voice somewhere murmurs, 'First your dad, then Paul. Now Karim. What's wrong with you?'

The next morning I make a last visit to Lapta, to say goodbye to the Wentworths. They are solicitous, commenting that I look tired and joking that I have been enjoying the nightlife too much and need to go home for a rest. I do not disillusion them. Os promises to pursue his enquiries about my father with other ex-pats and I give him my address in London.

As we part Meg says, 'I'm sure you'll be back one day. This island casts a spell on people, you know. And when you come back, you must promise to come and visit us again.'

I promise and say goodbye. Then I have a last wander around the village, hoping that it might awaken some further memories, but it seems that the curtain between me and the past, which briefly became transparent like the painted gauze in a pantomime, has now resumed its illusion of solidity and I cannot see beyond it.

I spend the afternoon packing and then lie down for a while before getting ready to meet Karim. The feeling of exhaustion, which this holiday was supposed to cure, has grown worse with every passing day, and is now so acute that I am almost tempted to call him and cancel the arrangement. Only the thought that I will never see him again if I do forces me out of bed and into the shower. My hand shakes as I apply my make-up and the dark rings under my eyes are stronger than ever.

I know from his expression when he picks me up that I have not succeeded in concealing how ill I feel but he makes no comment. He takes me to the tiny Turkish restaurant again and, under the influence of food and wine, I manage to put on a show of vivacity. Underneath I could weep with frustration. This is not me! What has happened to all my natural joie de vivre? No wonder he doesn't want to spend time with such a wet blanket!

All through the meal I keep hoping that he will make some reference to a possible future meeting, or at least ask for my address, but he says nothing and my pride will not let me be the first to raise the subject. In England I would have been quite brazen about it — might even have suggested that he come back to the hotel with me, if I could raise the energy — but instinct tells me that to make such a proposition to Karim would be to kill any faint hope that still exists. When the meal is over I am not sorry that, instead of suggesting that we go on somewhere for coffee, he drives me straight back to the hotel.

He stops the car a short distance from the main entrance and for a moment we sit in silence. Then he says, 'What time is your flight tomorrow?'

'Just after ten. We're being collected from the hotel at seven.'

'You'll need an early night, then.'

Silence again. I contemplate asking him in for a coffee but know that he would refuse. At length I say, 'Well, thank you again for all your help. You've been very kind.'

'Not at all.' The response sounds automatic. 'I'm sorry we couldn't fill in all the details.'

'I suppose this is goodbye, then.'

'Yes, I suppose it is.' He turns suddenly towards me and for a moment I think he is going to kiss me but he only lays a hand on my wrist.

'Cressida, promise me that you will see a doctor as soon as you get back. And don't let them fob you off with platitudes about taking it easy and having a glass of wine with your meals. Make them do all the necessary tests.'

'Tests?' I try to read his expression in the half darkness. Then, as if he has thrown me into icy water, I understand. For a moment I cannot speak. 'You think . . . ? My God, is that what you think? Is that what you're afraid of?' Fury, sheer unreasoning rage, sweeps over me 'You think I'm some sort of slut who picks men up off the street! Do you really imagine I'm such a fool? That I haven't got the sense to take precautions? And you haven't got the guts to come right out with it and tell me what you're thinking. You bastard!'

I scramble out of the car and run to the hotel entrance. Then I stop and look back. He has got out of the car and taken a few steps, as if he intended to follow me, but now he stands immobile, gazing in my direction but making no attempt to come to me. I plunge through the doors into the foyer, choking back sobs, and sink, shivering, onto the nearest chair.

Next day I go through the formalities of checking out of the hotel and checking in for my flight like an automaton. I keep telling myself that I shall be all right once I get home. It's this island! It captures your senses and your imagination and twists them. The magic of the lotus is dangerous and must be resisted.

As the plane banks over the parched landscape of the Mesaoria, I look down and my thoughts return to the girl whose memory lured my father back. Who was she? What was her story?

PART FOUR

LONDON, 1998

CHAPTER 15

'Come in, please, Miss Allenby. Take a seat.'

Dr Prentiss, the consultant, is a slender, fragile-looking woman, with blonde hair fading to ash-grey and a fine-boned, sensitive face. I glance round the room. A nurse is sitting to one side. She smiles at me but does not speak. I find her silent presence unnerving but the consultant makes no attempt to explain it. Instead she closes the buff folder on the desk in front of her and folds her hands on top of it. Her eyes seek mine.

'Miss Allenby . . .'

'Please, call me Cressida.' The response is automatic. My heart is beating so hard that it is difficult to concentrate.

'Thank you. I'm afraid the news is not good, Cressida. The tests show that you are suffering from chronic granulo-cytic leukaemia.'

'Leukaemia?' I feel an overpowering rush of relief. 'Then it's not . . . not . . . ?'

'Not what?'

'I thought . . . I thought it might be something else.'

'Such as?'

'No, it doesn't matter. Sorry! Please go on.'

Dr Prentiss leans forward.

'You do realize how serious this diagnosis is? This form of leukaemia does not progress as rapidly as more acute forms but you appear to be in what we term the accelerated stage, which means that urgent action is required.'

The words hit me as if I have crashed into a brick wall. 'Are you telling me I'm going to die?'

'No, I'm not saying that. There are treatments — of course there are. But we do have a battle on our hands and there's no point in pretending otherwise.'

'It's a kind of cancer, isn't it? Does that mean radiotherapy?'

'Not initially. We will start you straightaway with a blood transfusion and that will be followed by a course of chemotherapy, which should bring about a temporary remission, but your best hope of a cure is a bone marrow transplant. Do you have any brothers or sisters?'

'No, I'm an only child.'

'Pity. How about your parents?'

'They're both dead.'

'Cousins, aunts, uncles?'

'No, I'm afraid not. Both my parents were only children too. That is—' I stop abruptly, remembering that entry in my mother's journal. 'Well, I don't really know about my father. He was adopted, you see. I suppose he may have had brothers or sisters but I've no idea.'

'He never contacted his birth mother?'

'Not as far as I know.'

'Are his adoptive parents still living?'

'I don't know. I never met them. I think he must have quarrelled with them before I was born.'

'It might be possible to trace his birth mother. I know adopted children can do that now. I'm not sure whether that applies to the next generation. I really think it would be worth your while to try.'

'And if I can't find anyone?'

'We can put your name on the Anthony Nolan Register. That's a register that tries to find donors who match up with leukaemia sufferers. There's a chance that we might come up with a match for you.'

'How much of a chance?'

'A fairly slim one, if I'm honest.'

'And if that fails?'

'Then we must rely on the chemotherapy. If we can revert the condition to the chronic stage it would give us more time to find a suitable donor.'

The doctor pauses and I sit staring at the buff folder. Suddenly I am desperately thirsty. Ever since I got back from Cyprus I have been trying to convince myself that my weakness is due to some simple deficiency and my GP has encouraged me in that thought. 'Best to get the tests done, just to be sure, but I'm sure it'll turn out to be something quite minor.' Now, from the mouth of this gentle-looking woman, has come a sentence of death.

Dr Prentiss says gently, 'You're not married, are you?'

'No.'

'Boyfriend? Partner?'

'Not at the moment.'

'That's a pity. You will need all the support you can get over the next few months. And you have no children?'

'No.'

'Well, perhaps this is irrelevant, in the circumstances, but I have to warn you that the chemotherapy will almost certainly render you infertile — for a time, at least. Under certain circumstances it is possible to harvest eggs and freeze them but that is a long process and I'm afraid in your case we don't have the time. It's possible that you will never be able to have children.'

I look back at her mutely. I want to say, 'That isn't going to bother me if I'm dead, is it?', but I don't.

From that moment I have the sensation that my voice and actions have been taken over by some alien robot. This other self answers questions and listens as the doctor outlines a course of treatment. When I am handed into the charge of the nurse it smiles in a reflex response to her professional cheeriness. Meanwhile, the real I, naked and exposed as a snail dragged out of its shell, huddles howling somewhere within the robot's unfeeling form.

'Do you live alone?' the nurse asks.

'Yes.'

'Is there someone who would come and stay with you — a relative or a friend, perhaps?'

'No, not that I can think of.'

'You really shouldn't be on your own, you know.'

'No. I'll — I'll think of someone.'

Back at my flat, I drop into a chair and sit for a long time staring at the wall. The nurse's words come back to me. *'You shouldn't be on your own . . .' 'No, I shouldn't!'* I almost shout the words aloud. *'There should be somebody. Why am I all alone?'* Karim's face floats in my imagination. I hear his voice, sometimes amused and ironic, on other occasions passionately enthusiastic. *Damn him!* At least this sickness isn't what he thought it was.

I try to think of other contacts. I could pick up the telephone and call Paul. But Paul has Julie now. Paul left me for Julie because I put caring for my dying mother before having fun with him. So why now would he want to leave Julie to care for me while I am dying? Guilty conscience? Pity? God, no! I would rather suffer alone to the end than call Paul.

I think of friends from work. I always thought of myself as the gregarious type. A month ago, if I had been asked if I had many friends, I would have replied with an unhesitating yes. Now I'm not so sure. The connection feels fragile, superficial. I was away from school on compassionate leave for a week after my mother died and when I came back there were only a few days of term left. They pretended to understand when I pulled out of the holiday to Corfu, and I did find someone else to take my place, but it must have seemed like a slap in the face that I preferred my own company to being with them. I couldn't explain, even to myself, why I needed to be alone. They are a nice crowd but I can't imagine any of them wanting to cope with what is happening to me. There is bubbly Lisa, always good for a laugh, and clever, determined Sue with one eye on the next step up the promotion ladder. But Lisa was reduced to helpless tears by the death of her cat and Sue has never been one to suffer the infirmities of others with patience. There is Angie, of course. She is always sympathetic to anyone in trouble. I try to imagine myself telling them my news. How would they react? They would be supportive, of course. Lisa would hug me and cry; Sue would get on the net and come up with a list of organizations that might provide help or advice. Angie would fuss over me, buy me flowers, offer to do my shopping. But how long would it be before I became a nuisance to them? I picture myself growing increasingly dependent, increasingly demanding, and the idea revolts me. I am used to thinking of myself as a strong, attractive personality — and soon I shall be weak and ugly. I make up my mind to conceal my illness from them to the last possible moment.

I find I am gazing at the window. The late afternoon sun slanting through the glass shows up smears and dusty patches and the bunch of flowers which I picked up on impulse in the supermarket yesterday looks tawdry and garish against the murk. There is a pile of papers on the table — mock exam scripts that need to be marked before the start of the new term. I haven't even looked at them and there are only a few days of the holiday left.

I get up and go over to the table, pull out a chair and take the first paper from the pile. For a few minutes I force my eyes to follow the words on the page but I cannot make them mean anything. The sun through the dirty windowpane annoys me. I leave the papers and go into the kitchen. The cupboard under the sink is a jumble of washing powder and cleaning products and I drag them out, swearing, until I find the spray for cleaning the glass. I take it to the window, climb onto a chair and begin to polish. The physical effort makes me feel sick. The bottle of spray slips from my fingers and when I make an automatic grab for it my arm catches the vase of flowers and sends it crashing to the floor. I stand on the chair, staring down at the spreading puddle. Somebody, somewhere is producing a high-pitched, animal whine. It takes several seconds to realize that it is my own voice. It dawns on me that I will not be going back to school next term. I throw myself off the chair, seize the pile of papers and rip the top sheet into pieces, throwing the torn remnants into the water. Then I am suddenly aware of what I am doing and collapse on the floor and give way for the first time to sobs that shake my body and flay my throat until it is raw.

When I eventually calm down, I boot up my laptop and type a letter to the head master, explaining the situation and enclosing the medical certificate from the hospital. I ask him to keep the information confidential.

When I am admitted to St Thomas's Hospital two days later, I am given a blood transfusion, which makes me feel better than I have done for some time. Then comes the first shock. The registrar comes to my bedside.

'Cressida, you are going to need repeated intravenous injections of the chemotherapy drug. You don't want to go through the painful business of having a canula inserted every time, so I suggest we put in a Hickman line. That's a tube inserted into a vein in your chest, so that the drug can be administered directly into it.'

'You mean I'll have a permanent tube sticking out of my chest?'

'For a while. It can be removed when the course of treatment is finished.'

The idea of this disfiguring invasion of my body makes me feel sick. My only comfort is the thought that at least there is no one else who need be revolted by the sight.

When I get back to the flat after three weeks of intensive treatment, the light on the answering machine is blinking non-stop.

'Cressida, it's Sue. The head says you're off sick and not expected back for some time. What's wrong? Do get in touch!'

'Cress? Lisa here. Why don't you answer the phone? Call me

as soon as you get this.' 'Cressida? It's Tom Westwood here. I don't know if you remember, we met at Jane's party a couple of months ago. I know you've been away but I guess you must be home by now. Could we have a drink, or dinner, perhaps?' 'Cressy, it's Angie. We're all really worried about you. Please get in touch.'

I hit the delete button and go through to my bedroom. I feel sick and more exhausted than I ever imagined possible. Later, after a rest, I record a new message for the machine.

'Hello. It's Cressida here. I'm afraid I'm not available at the moment. I'm going to be out of town for a week or two so I won't be picking up messages. Leave your name and number and I'll call when I get back.'

There is a letter from the head telling me not to worry about anything at school. They have got a supply teacher in who is 'very well qualified and obviously very keen' so I need have no anxiety about my classes. So much for any idea I may have had about being irreplaceable! Actually, it occurs to me that I have hardly given a thought to the matter since my diagnosis.

My life contracts to a basic routine: the fortnightly visit to the hospital, the plunge into nausea and exhaustion, then the slow, painful recovery to something approaching normality before the next injection. In between I try to read or listen to music but I can't concentrate. My mind, like a hamster on a wheel, revolves round and round the one question. Why me? I tell myself rationally that there is no reason. These things happen to people. I have no belief in God or fate or any other external influence with the power to decide the course of human lives. The staff at the hospital are relentlessly upbeat but they make no secret of the fact that, even if the chemo succeeds in reverting my condition to chronic rather than acute, statistically there is a one in three chance of the acute phase recurring. I am not afraid of what might happen in the afterlife. There is no such thing. Soon I shall be extinguished, like a torch whose battery has run out, and that will be that. What troubles me most is the thought that

I shall leave nothing behind except a memory in the minds of a few friends, which will soon fade. I have created nothing. What is the point of my existence?

This attitude alternates with days when life seems infinitely precious and every extra day is a bonus to be cherished, but I do not have the strength to take full advantage of these highs.

Then one day, coming back to the flat from the hospital, I find a letter on the mat bearing a Turkish Cypriot stamp.

My dear Cressida,

I hope you will forgive me for writing to you. You did not leave me your address so I presume you were not expecting to keep in contact but I think I have some news that you would wish to receive. I asked the Wentworths and when I told them the reason they agreed that I ought to write to you.

I have found Ferhan, the Turkish girl who is referred to in your father's letters and who was obviously a close friend of the woman he fell in love with, whoever she was. Of course, she is middle-aged now and married. She and her husband keep a shop in the village of Karaman, not far from Kyrenia. I have not spoken to her, because I thought you would prefer to do this yourself. She would probably be more willing to talk to you than to someone like myself with no direct connection to the case.

Can you find the time to make another visit to Northern Cyprus? A few days should be sufficient. I know it's a long journey for such a short time but I'm sure you would find it worthwhile.

If you can't get away, or don't think it is worth the effort, I could, of course, talk to Ferhan myself and see what I can find out and then pass it on to you, but I doubt very much whether that would prove to be a satisfactory solution. I do hope you will come. Quite apart from anything else, I should be very happy to see you again.

Yours,
Karim

My hands are shaking so much that it is hard to keep the words on the page in focus. He wants to see me again! He has

155

gone to the trouble of searching out Ferhan in order to have an excuse to write to me. What other explanation could there be? '*You did not leave me your address* . . .' Did he expect me to offer it and was his failure to ask simply an extreme example of his courtesy? Was what I interpreted as coldness simply self-restraint? '*I do hope you will come* . . .' Of course I will go! I will see him again. The chance of meeting Ferhan will be a bonus but we shall both know it is only a pretext.

I force myself to stop and think. Of course I cannot go. I do not have the strength for the journey. It is true that, towards the end of each fortnight, when the effects of the chemotherapy begin to wear off, I have a few days when I feel a little stronger — but they do not last long enough to cover even a brief visit. Besides, do I really want Karim to see me like this? My hair is coming out in handfuls and the bones in my face stand out like a skeleton's. What good could come of it for either of us? There is no question of a long-term relationship and I have no desire for a brief affair. I remember the Hickman tube dangling from my chest and shudder.

I cannot decide how to reply to Karim's letter. Should I tell him the truth? At least that would put him right about the cause. But suppose he really does care, enough to jump on the next plane? I can't cope with that. I could write and say that I cannot get the time off for another visit to Cyprus and ask him to speak to Ferhan for me, but of course he will know that there is the summer holiday coming up soon. He will conclude that I don't want to see him again and I am just making excuses. But I owe him greater honesty than that. As each day passes I put off the task of writing.

A letter has come from the hospital giving me an appointment with the consultant. I enter the room with a sense of numb foreboding, to be greeted with an encouraging smile.

'Sit down, my dear. How are you feeling?'

'I — I'm not sure. Some days I feel better, some days worse.'

'Well, I'm happy to be able to tell you that your latest tests look promising. It seems that you may be in remission, or at the very least that the disease has reverted to the chronic stage.'

My breath catches in my throat. 'So what happens now?'

'We'll give you a rest from the drugs for a few weeks and see how you get on.'

'So it could all start up again?'

'Yes. I'm afraid that this is likely to be only a temporary respite.'

'How long?'

'There's no way of knowing. It could be weeks, it could last up to a year. Your best chance is still a bone marrow transplant. Have you had any success in tracing a relative?'

'No. No, I'm afraid not.'

'What about your father's birth mother? Have you been able to trace her?'

'No, I haven't.'

I shift uncomfortably under the doctor's gaze. The fact is that I have made no attempt in that direction. The whole enterprise seemed so complicated and so unlikely to succeed that I never mustered the energy to try.

'That's a pity. Well, we must just keep hoping that something will come up on the Anthony Nolan register. Meanwhile, you must rest and gather your strength. And remember, you are still at great risk of infection. You must be very, very careful.'

'Can I get rid of this thing?' I ask, indicating my chest.

The doctor smiles. 'Yes, of course. I'll get one of the nurses to remove it.'

When I get back to the flat the first thing I see is Karim's letter lying on my desk. The sight sends a sudden sharp, physical thrill go through my body. I will go to Cyprus after all! I know it's mad, that I am taking a risk that is unjustifiable by all normal standards, but it doesn't matter. The remission may only last a few weeks. This longing has been gnawing away at me ever since the letter arrived. While I have the chance to satisfy it, I will grab it. After all, I am not infectious. There is no risk to anyone else. Of course, no travel insurance will cover me, but I have money. The sale of my mother's house has left me with a useful nest egg and I am still getting sick pay. I can pay my own expenses. I will see Karim again — and he will see me . . .

I sit at my dressing table. I am thinner than ever. The mirror shows me hollow cheeks and skin of a lifeless pallor. But make-up will help and at last I am as slim as a catwalk model. I never thought I would achieve size zero! I might invest in a new dress, something expensive and fashionable. After all, I might as well spend what I have. There is no point in saving. I comb what is left of my hair. The scalp shows pink. The hospital has given me a wig, which looks almost like my own hair, but I hate wearing it because it makes my head uncomfortably hot. Imagine that in Cyprus in mid-summer! I could wear a hat, of course. Karim was always on at me to wear a hat. But even indoors, or at night?

I drop the comb and turn away from the mirror. What am I thinking of? Even if I could disguise the way I look, what right have I to deceive him like that? He needs to see that the relationship has no future. I make my decision. I shall go to Cyprus. I shall see Karim once more but we will meet honestly, without any attempt at concealment. And it will be for the last time.

CHAPTER 16

The journey takes my last reserves of stamina. The flight, with its long, pointless wait on Turkish soil before taking off again for Cyprus, seems interminable, and when we land I almost faint in the stifling heat of the arrivals hall while queuing for immigration checks. I have not told my consultant, or anyone at the hospital, what I am doing, knowing that they would forbid it because of the risk of infection. It's my life — I'll take my chances. When I finally get through customs I see Karim waiting for me and my heart begins to pound. He comes towards me, his face, usually so guarded in its expression, alight with pleasure. Then I see it change as he gets close enough to see me properly.

'Cressida! What is it? You're ill! You shouldn't have come.'

It is too much. The heat and the light and the noise overwhelm me and my legs give way. I feel myself caught in his arms and held tightly against him. For a moment I close my eyes. This is where I want to be, where I have wanted to be since we first met. His arms are strong and he smells of aftershave and sweat and that indefinable personal scent, which every individual has and which I would have recognized among a thousand others.

I manage to mumble, half coherently, 'You're right, I shouldn't. But I couldn't not.'

He holds me away and looks into my face. 'What is it? No, don't try to answer now. This isn't the place to talk. Can you walk? My car is quite close. I could get a wheelchair . . .'

'No! I can manage. Just hold on to me. I'll be OK.'

I let myself be half carried out into the pitiless sunshine and helped into the passenger seat of the Mercedes.

'Just relax. We can talk later. All that matters for now is to get you somewhere you can rest.' He speaks calmly but I can hear the underlying anxiety in his voice.

I close my eyes and feel the sweat beginning to evaporate in the cool rush of the air conditioning. Karim drives without speaking and I drift into a half-doze in which I am dimly aware of the change in the engine note and the varying pull of g-forces as the car leaves the flat plain of the Mesaoria and begins the tortuous climb into the Kyrenia Mountains. The sun was low when I landed and when I open my eyes it is dark. As we crest the pass I see the lights of the town far below. At the bottom of the hill Karim turns, not towards Kyrenia as I expect, but in the direction of Bellapais.

'Where are we going?'

He glances sideways. 'I thought you had gone to sleep.'

'No. Just dozing.'

'All the decent hotels are fully booked. I thought you could stay with me. I hope that's all right?'

I think of the house on the hill with its cool white rooms and its courtyard brilliant with bougainvillaea and oleanders. 'That would be perfect.'

When we arrive, the housekeeper in her dark dress and white headscarf comes forward to greet us. If she is surprised by my appearance she gives no sign of it. Karim gives instructions in Turkish and, as if in a dream, I find myself effortlessly transferred to the bedroom where I rested on my first visit. Karim has disappeared and the woman, with unobtrusive efficiency, helps me to undress and settles me between clean, white sheets. I sleep almost at once.

I wake to sunlight and the scent of thyme from the hillsides beyond the house drifting in through the open window. I lie still, waiting for the nausea, which is always worst first thing in the morning, to abate. I think back to my meeting with Karim the previous evening. We said so little. He caught me in his arms, but that was because otherwise I should have fallen. I remember how his face changed at the sight of me. Is he regretting the impulse that made him write to me? He disappeared as soon as we reached the house and left me to the housekeeper's care. Perhaps he was repelled by my appearance. Probably he is more than ever convinced that I am suffering from AIDS and wants to keep as far away from me as possible. At least I can clear up that misunderstanding, for all the good that will do.

There is a tap on the door and the housekeeper comes in with breakfast on a tray. I drag myself out of bed and take a shower, then carry the tray out onto the little balcony outside the window. As I set it down I see that there is a note propped against the coffee-pot.

Dear Cressida,

I have to work this morning. I am booked to take a party of tourists to Salamis. I'm very sorry about this. I tried very hard to find someone to take my place, without success. Please don't be angry with me for not being around to entertain you. I would have told you last night, but I thought it better to let you go straight to bed. I do hope you are feeling better this morning. Probably it will be a good thing for you to have a quiet day. Please use the house as if it were your own and ask Kezia for anything you need. There are books in my study if you need something to read. I shall be back about the middle of the afternoon and then we can talk. Look after yourself till then.

Karim

I fold the paper and pour myself a cup of coffee. I cannot decide whether I am disappointed or relieved. All through the flight I buoyed myself up with the thought that I would soon see Karim again. Now, faced with the reality, I realize that somewhere along the line I convinced myself, on the flimsiest evidence, that Karim was in love with me. I remind myself of the resolution I made before leaving England. If I was mistaken about his feelings, so much the better. I can finish the relationship without hurting him. Soon there must be a conversation that will resolve matters one way or the other and part of me is anxious for the moment to arrive. On the other hand, the prospect of a morning spent relaxing in the beautiful garden without the pressure to explain or the emotional turmoil that must follow is seductive.

I take my time over breakfast. Then I dress and make up with great care. He has seen me at my worst. I might as well make the best of myself now.

Karim returns, as promised, in the early afternoon. I am dozing in a long chair under the shade of an orange tree in the garden with a book in my lap and wake to see him coming down the steps from the terrace. The sight of his lean figure with its dancer's movement sends a stab of pleasure and desire through me. He squats beside me and takes my hand.

'You look better today. Did you sleep?'

'Like a log. And I do feel better. Yesterday I was very tired.'

'That was obvious. I feel bad about asking you to come. If I'd realized . . .'

'No, I wanted to come. I need to . . . to make some kind of conclusion. What the Americans call "closure", I suppose.'

Instead of drawing up a chair, he sits down on the grass close to me.

'Cressida, tell me. What is wrong with you?'

I tell him, simply, without attempting to minimize the seriousness of the condition, and see his face tighten and grow pale beneath the tan.

'It's not all bad news,' I add. 'I'm in remission, thanks to the drugs. It could last quite a long time — up to a year the doctor said.'

'A year? That's good. But there must be something more permanent. There must be a cure . . .'

'A bone marrow transplant from a compatible donor. But as you know I haven't got any close relatives and the chance of a match from anyone else is very small.'

He kneels up and takes both my hands. 'What can I say? Sorry is such a futile word! If only I'd known before . . .'

'Did you think it was . . . something else? Something worse?'

'Worse? What do you mean?'

'Did you think it was AIDS?'

'No! The thought never entered my head, I swear! Is that what you meant, on that last evening?'

I study his face. There is no hint of reserve now, only open distress and — yes, love. 'Then why? Why were you so . . . aloof?'

He lets go of my hands and turns away. 'I thought it would be better if we didn't see each other again. Better for both of us.'

'But why?'

He makes a gesture with his shoulders and arms that encompasses not only the two of us but the island and its people. 'We come from such different worlds. I couldn't imagine you giving up your life in London to settle out here and I couldn't see any future for myself in England. Besides, I knew my parents would never accept you as a daughter-in-law. I told you, they are very traditional. If we . . . if we wanted to make a life together I could only see that one or the other, or both, of us would have to make great sacrifices. I didn't think it would work — but . . .'

'But?'

'Once you had gone I began to realize what I had lost, what I had thrown away. And now . . .'

'Now it's too late. I suppose it was always too late. Probably it's better this way.'

He shakes his head. 'I won't believe that.'

'You must,' I say. 'You were right all along, Karim. There is no future for us.'

He puts his arms round me and kisses me very gently on the lips. My body responds tumultuously but the very strength of my desire exhausts me. How bitterly ironic it is that now that what I longed for is within reach I am unable to grasp it.

He strokes my face. 'Never mind the future. We must squeeze every last drop of happiness out of the present. At least now we understand each other.'

I nod and swallow. 'Yes, at least we have that.' It is tempting to lie in his arms and forget my good resolutions. I draw a long breath and extricate myself from his embrace. 'Have you spoken to Ferhan?'

'Yes. She is ready to talk to you tomorrow, if you feel up to it.'

'Good.'

He takes my hand again. 'Are you sure this isn't going to be too much for you?'

'No, it's OK. After all, it's what I came for.'

'Is it?'

I look into his face. 'No, not really. That was just the excuse.' There is a moment's silence and he touches my cheek with the tips of his fingers. I turn away. 'I'm sorry. I'm just not up to — anything physical.'

He sits back. 'Of course. I understand. Don't worry about it.'

The village of Karaman is perched halfway up the steep slope of the mountains above Kyrenia, its houses clinging to the hillside in a series of terraces. Karim stops the car outside a small shop that appears to double as a bar, though the tables outside are empty at this time in the morning. He helps me out and leads me into a dim interior that smells of spices and grain and leather. After the sunlight outside it is a moment before I am able to make out the features of the woman who comes forward to greet us. As my vision clears I see a slender, erect figure with a strongly boned, dark face, a complexion lined and weathered by the sun and dark hair touched with

164

grey at the temples. Karim speaks a few words in Turkish and then turns to me.

'This is Ferhan Osman. Ferhan, this is Cressida Allenby.'

The woman extends her hand and I shake it.

'Dr Mezeli tells me you are looking for information about your father.' The voice is unexpectedly deep, the English only slightly accented. 'I don't know how much I can tell you. I have often wondered what happened to him myself. But you look tired! Come through to the back room and sit down. Will you have something to drink? Coffee? Or apple tea, perhaps?'

I ask for coffee and sink into the chair Ferhan draws out for me. I feel her looking at me, but her dark eyes under the heavy lids give nothing away.

'So! You are Stephen's girl.'

'You knew my father?'

'Not well. Ariadne was my friend and she spoke of him often.'

'Ariadne! That was her name? The girl my father fell in love with?'

'You didn't know?'

'No. I didn't know she existed until I came across some letters my father wrote to her and he never mentioned her name. What was she like?'

'Oh, it wasn't hard to see why he fell for her. She was beautiful — very beautiful — and clever. She had — how would you say it? — great spirit. I used to worry for her, even before she met your father. She was too independent, too much of a rebel. But then, she was very young. Not yet eighteen.'

'So young! I'd imagined her as much older. I think my father really loved her, but somehow it all went wrong. What happened?'

The other woman shrugs. 'How could it have been different? The situation was very bad here, between the Greeks and the British. Many people were getting shot. Your father was confined to the camp. Then, suddenly, he was gone, without a word.'

'I know he didn't mean to abandon her. He says so in his letters.'

'She never got any letters. She never heard from him again.'

I look away. In spite of Ferhan's courtesy I can sense an underlying hostility. 'But he came back to look for her.'

'A year later, after her father had sent her away to Athens.'

'Her father sent her away?'

'To marry a man twice her age. An old friend of the family.'

'How terrible! Why?'

'He found out about her affair with your father. Ariadne was lucky. It was not unusual for the bodies of girls who behaved as she had to be washed up on the beach — and for much less reason.'

I stare at the inscrutable face. 'That's awful!'

'That's how it was, in those days. What she had done was a disgrace to the family.'

I reach into my bag and take out Os's translations of my father's letters. 'My father says here that you took him back to your house, because Ariadne's father would have shot him if he had seen him. I suppose that's why.'

'He was desperate to find her but I could not help him. I did not know her address or even in what part of Athens she was living. I told your father to go home and forget her. There was nothing he could do that would not bring greater grief than she had suffered already. He accepted that but he begged me to write to him if I had any news.'

'And you did. He mentions it here.'

'Yes, it went against my conscience but he was very persuasive. I still heard about Ariadne from her mother, as long as the family remained in the village, and I used to pass on what I learned to your father.'

'I don't remember him getting letters from Cyprus.'

'He gave me an address to write to — a Post Office box number. I think he travelled a good deal.'

'Yes, he did. And I suppose after he married my mother and settled down he didn't want your letters turning up at home. But that was years later. Were you still writing then?'

'From time to time, when I had news. Then, one day, almost eighteen years after she left, Ariadne walked through that door. She told me that her husband, who was in poor health, had retired and sold his business in Athens and she had persuaded him to bring her and their children back to live in Cyprus. By that time, her father was dead and her mother had gone to live with a brother who kept a hotel in the Troodos Mountains. Iannis, her brother, had gone off somewhere with the EOKA people, so no one was left in the village who knew about the affair.'

'Did you write to my father and tell him she was here?'

'No, I did not! I could see that it would only cause trouble.'

'Then that wasn't the reason he brought my mother and me to live here.' I am thinking aloud. 'Or could he have learned that Ariadne was back?'

'Not from me. But he found out somehow. He came to see me again and begged me to give him her address. I refused, of course, but he wouldn't take no for an answer. He kept searching, asking anyone who might have known her where she was. He did not find her because they had settled in the Troodos, where no one knew her. Then the Turkish army arrived and everything was confusion. When the fighting was over I heard he had taken you and your mother back to England.'

'And what happened to Ariadne?'

Ferhan shrugs again. 'I told you, she and her husband had settled in the south. Once the island was divided there was no way to contact them.'

'So you don't know where she is now?'

'How should I?'

I fold the papers covered in Os's immaculate handwriting and put them back into my bag. I feel tired and depressed. It seems that I have struck another dead end in my search. Karim gives me a sympathetic look and turns to Ferhan.

'Cressida is not very well. I think I should take her home now. But thank you for your help.'

I add my thanks but I sense as we shake hands again that there is still something unspoken, a secret yet to be revealed.

When we get back to his house, Karim insists that I must rest, but later on I persuade him to drive me to Lapta.

'I promised the Wentworths that I would call and see them if I ever came back and I feel I ought to keep my promise. They were very kind to me.'

As soon as Meg Wentworth opens the door I see the shock on her face that I have come to dread. But both she and Os are far too well bred to comment and when I explain the situation they are sympathetic but controlled, which I find much easier to cope with than overt displays of emotion. I explain why I have returned to Cyprus and give them the gist of my conversation with Ferhan.

'So you are not really much wiser,' Os comments.

'Well, at least I have a name for her now,' I reply. 'Ariadne. Wasn't she the one who was sacrificed to the minotaur?'

'No, no.' Os chuckles briefly. 'You're on the right track but it was Theseus who was supposed to be eaten by the minotaur. Ariadne was the king's daughter. She fell in love with Theseus and saved him. The minotaur lived in the middle of a labyrinth, so that even after he had killed the beast Theseus might have perished because he couldn't find his way out. Ariadne gave him a ball of thread to unwind as he went along, so he was able to retrace his steps.' He pauses and sighed. 'I'm afraid he treated her badly though. She ran away with him when he set off back to Athens but he abandoned her on a remote island on the way home.'

I wince inwardly. 'That sounds too much like history repeating itself.'

'Oh good Lord!' Os looks abashed. 'My dear, how very tactless of me! I didn't mean to imply a parallel between Theseus's behaviour and your father's.'

'Anyway,' Meg fills the momentary silence, 'you still don't have an address for her?'

'No, I don't. But perhaps it's just as well. I don't know what I'd do if I had.'

'But don't you want to meet her? Aren't you curious?'

'I did at one time. I wanted to confront her and tell her what she'd done to my family. But now I'm not so sure. I'm beginning to see that she had a pretty bad time herself.'

'Anyway,' Karim says, 'even if you had an address you couldn't get there. Not if she's still living in the south.'

'Only by flying back to Ankara and then taking a plane to Athens and flying back from there to the other side of the border,' Os agrees.

The idea appals me. 'I couldn't possible manage that.'

'It's ridiculous!' Karim exclaims. 'I could drive you there myself in an hour or two. I know the Troodos well. We used to go there for holidays when I was a child. Banned from half of my own island!'

'I sympathize,' Os says. 'The whole situation is ridiculous.'

For a while Karim and the Wentworths discuss the political situation but I drift into the half-waking state that is becoming more and more familiar. I can imagine how that young girl must have felt as she faced the coming confrontation with her family.

169

CHAPTER 17

'What would you like to do today?' Karim asks at breakfast the next morning.

I think for a minute. I slept better than I have done for weeks and woke feeling a little stronger.

'I don't know. Yes, I do. I'd like to go to some of your favourite places again. I want to sit under the Tree of Idleness and wander round the abbey — but I can't manage Buffavento this time.'

'Very well,' he says. 'I'll take you to another place I love — somewhere we didn't find time for on your last visit.'

An hour later he helps me down a short, steep track to a tiny church hidden in a fold of the mountainside. Built of a reddish brick that echoes the colours of the soil around it, its arched cloister and central dome seem to have grown organically out of the earth.

'This may seem a strange place for a Muslim to treasure,' Karim says, 'but as an archaeologist I have to revere the artistry that went into decorating this church — even though the pictures go against everything I have been taught by my faith.'

He pushes open the heavy door and leads me inside. For a while I can make out nothing but the outlines of pillars and the vault of the dome but, as my eyes become accustomed to the dimness, I begin to see that the ceiling and walls are frescoed with pictures of saints and angels, while from the dome itself the face of Christ gazes down upon us. Closer examination shows that many of the frescoes are damaged, the faces pock-marked by what look like bullet holes.

'What happened? Was there a battle?'

'I'm ashamed to say,' Karim replies, 'that immediately after the peace operation some fanatics came in here and tried to deface the images. You know that for us it is blasphemy to portray the face of God, or of men, who are made in his image. But now the authorities have come to their senses and realized that we have been entrusted with the guardianship of a great artistic heritage. Its preservation has been a large part of my work here and this glorious place is now protected.'

I look at him. 'Karim, you love everything about Cyprus, don't you? I understand why you would never want to leave.'

He reaches out and draws me to him. 'I would go if I could take you with me.'

When we return to the house the housekeeper hands Karim a note. He glances at it and exclaims, 'A-ha! I thought so!'

'What did you think?'

'I had a feeling yesterday that Ferhan was holding something back. This is a message from her. She wants to see you again, today if possible. Do you want to go?'

'Yes, if there is something else she wants to say. I suppose it would be silly not to.'

Ferhan greets us with the same reserve but I sense a softening in her manner. When we are seated at the wooden table in the back room with tiny cups of bitter coffee, she says, 'You are ill, I think.'

'Yes,' I reply tersely. I want to tell her to mind her own business.

Ferhan seems to understand. 'I will not ask questions, but my conscience has troubled me since you left yesterday. You asked me if I knew where Ariadne is and I said no. It is true that I do not know for certain where she is now. But I did have an address.' She gets up and takes a dog-eared envelope from a shelf. 'One day, about two years after the fighting was over, this letter arrived from her. It had been smuggled across the Green Line. She told me that her husband had died and she had moved in with her mother and uncle in the hotel. She asked me if I had seen Stephen. She had met someone from her old village who had been evacuated to the south and this person had told her that Stephen had been on the island, looking for her. She told me she had never forgotten him and had always wondered why he had never tried to get in touch with her.'

'What did you tell her?'

'I didn't know what to do. I had no means of getting a letter back to her. But I lay awake for many nights after that, wondering what would be the right thing. In the end I wrote to your father and gave him her address. But I never had a reply.'

'What year would that have been?' I am struggling to piece together a sequence of events.

Ferhan frowns. 'The fighting was in 1974, so that must have been '76.'

It begins to make sense. 'I thought so. My father had left home by then. He went back to being a foreign correspondent. He died somewhere in the Far East that year. He probably never read your letter.'

Ferhan lays her strong, brown hand over my wrist. 'I am so sorry. What a tragedy, for you and your mother.'

'It's a tragic story all round, isn't it?' I say. 'So neither of them ever knew that the other had gone on remembering and loving all those years.'

Ferhan nods gravely. 'Yes, I am afraid that is so.'

I say nothing, overpowered by a deep sadness. Eventually I make an effort and look at the other woman. 'Do you still have her address? Perhaps I should write to her.'

'I have not heard from her for more than twenty years. She may not live at this address any longer. But you can try.' She hands me the yellowing envelope. 'This gives the address of her uncle's hotel. You can write there. If she has left, someone may know where she has gone. I am sure she would like to hear from you.'

When we return to the house I go to lie down and fall into a deep sleep. When I wake it is evening. I find Karim in the courtyard, standing by one of the archways that form the fourth side of the square. He beckons me to join him.

'Look. The sunset is particularly fine tonight.'

I stand beside him and look westward along the coast to where the distant violet mountains stand in silhouette against a sky of crimson fading through indigo to the palest duck-egg blue and streaked with amber and gold.

'It's magnificent,' I say. 'We don't get skies like that in London. Or, if we do, you can't see them for the tall buildings.'

He puts his arms round me from behind and I lean back against him.

'Then don't go back to London.'

'What?'

'Stay here, in Cyprus, with me.'

For a moment I keep very still. Then I pull away from his embrace and turn to face him. 'Karim, you know that's not possible. I have to go back.' I am looking for an excuse. 'I have to go back to the hospital, for a check-up.'

He steps back, his face once more the polite, formal mask I know so well. 'Of course. That was selfish of me. Of course you have to go back.'

I reach out and touch his sleeve. 'Don't look like that, please! Don't you know how much I want to stay?' My resolution wavers. 'Perhaps I could. After all, what's the point . . .'

'No!' He takes me by the shoulders. 'No, my darling! It's too much of a risk. It was stupid of me even to suggest staying. While there is the slightest chance of a cure you must take it. Listen, sit down. There is something important I want to say to you.'

He leads me to a chair and kneels in front of me, taking my hands in his. 'I told you I realized when you left that

173

being with you was more important than my family or my job. So, I took steps. I started looking for another job. And I found one. I've been offered a fellowship at an American university — Illinois, to be exact. Cressida, my darling, marry me! Marry me and come to America with me.'

I stare down into his face, stripped now of its mask to reveal tenderness and urgent desire, the image blurred by the hot tears rising in my own eyes.

'Karim, don't. Oh, how I wish I could! There's nothing in the world I want more than to say yes. But it wouldn't be fair. I can't let you marry a dying woman.'

'You mustn't say that! You don't have to die. And there are doctors in America. Good ones. They may have some treatment you don't know of . . .'

'There is only one treatment that could cure me. A bone marrow transplant from a compatible donor. And the chances of finding one are so remote that it's hardly worth thinking about.'

'What about me? Let them test me.'

'No, it isn't even worth trying. Your genes must be so different from mine.'

He rises and turns away. 'There has to be some way! I can't let you give up.'

'There is one slight chance. There's a register of volunteer donors. If they happen to come up with a match for me . . .'

He swings back. 'Then there is hope! You told me the remission could last a year. Before then, who knows what might happen? You must hold on to that.' He catches my hands again. 'Cressida, promise me you won't give up.'

I force a smile. 'I promise. It's only a small chance but I promise you I'll try to hold on as long as I possibly can.'

The sunset has faded and it is almost dark. In the fields below the house, the frogs have started their nightly chorus. The housekeeper materializes among the shadows that now fill the courtyard and murmurs something in Turkish to Karim.

'Dinner is ready,' he says, offering me his hand. 'Come along. You must try to eat. We can talk more about this tomorrow.'

Perhaps because of the rest, or perhaps just because I am with Karim, I feel better than I have done for weeks and over dinner I am almost my old self. He has ordered wine for me but I stop him from opening it.

'I'm not supposed to drink — at least not more than one unit of alcohol a day — and red wine tastes horrible for some reason. I'll be quite happy with water.'

Instead he plies me with mouthfuls of delicious food and tells me stories about some of the tourists he has to escort that make me laugh. Nevertheless, by the time we are sitting over coffee in the cool, jasmine-scented evening air, my eyelids are beginning to droop again. He takes my hands and pulls me to my feet.

'Come along. It's time you were in bed.'

I get up and, suddenly dizzy, sway against him. Immediately I am swept up into his arms and carried towards the house.

I protest, half laughing. 'Karim! Don't be silly. Put me down. You'll injure yourself.'

'Nonsense,' he responds, his lips close to my ear. 'You weigh no more than a bird.'

'Yeah! A scruffy old London pigeon,' I say.

He carries me to my bedroom and lays me gently on the bed, then stands for a moment looking down at me in silence.

'Can I stay with you?'

How I long to say yes! I stretch out my hand to him. 'Oh, darling! It would be wonderful. But I can't. I just can't!'

He sits beside me. 'I know. I don't mean to make love to you. Let me just stay with you and hold you. Please!'

'It wouldn't be fair. It's asking too much of you.'

'No. I promise you, that's all I want. Let me stay.'

'If that's really enough for you . . . Yes, stay. Please.'

He undresses me with a gentle deftness that surprises me. I shudder at the thought of how pathetically thin I must look to him but he makes no comment. He covers me with a sheet and stands up. The room is lit only by moonlight through the long window, where the curtain billows softly in the night wind. I watch as he pulls off his shirt and steps out of his trousers, his body lithe and muscular and shadowed with dark hair. Then he slides into bed beside me and takes me in his arms. The night is warm but I still welcome the heat of his body, its vital solidity against my own. It seems a bulwark against the encroaching tide of mortality I feel in my own flesh. I nestle my cheek against the satiny smoothness of his shoulder and feel his hand gently caressing my head. Suddenly, physical desire wells up within me, like a spring in parched earth. I move against him and he murmurs, 'Be still, my love. Sleep now.'

I lift my head and look at the dark outline of his face. 'Make love to me, Karim.'

He turns his head to me. 'No, not tonight. You're not strong enough. It wouldn't be right.'

'Please,' I beg. 'I want you so much. And it might be our last chance . . .' Then I regret the phrase and amend it. 'Our last chance for some time.'

He rolls onto his side. 'Cressida, are you sure about this?'

'I've never been more sure of anything.'

'I don't have a condom.'

'It doesn't matter. There's no risk.'

'I don't know . . .'

I stop his words by pulling his head down and kissing him on the lips. He folds me in his arms and the kiss deepens and prolongs itself as if each of us is exploring the very depths of the other's being. His hand caresses my back and moves downwards to my buttocks. Then he turns me gently onto my back and begins to kiss my breasts. His hand strokes my inner thigh and then moves delicately between my legs. The touch sends liquid fire through my nerves but I recognize at the same time that I can only sustain this intensity of feeling for a brief moment. I pull him into me and sob aloud as my body convulses with pleasure. He comes with a groan that seems wrenched from the depths of his body and for a moment collapses across me. Then he lifts himself on his elbows.

I whisper, 'Thank you.'

He lowers his head and nuzzles his face against mine. 'Oh, my sweet! Don't thank me. You have no idea how long I've wanted to do that.'

He turns on his back and draws me against his shoulder again. I lie still, feeling at peace with my own body in a way I have not experienced for many months.

I say, 'I thought this was never going to happen. I had really begun to believe that you weren't attracted to me.'

'How could you think that? I wanted you from the first moment I saw you.'

'Did you? You were always so formal. I suppose I'm not used to that. All the men I've ever known just wanted to jump into bed at the first opportunity.'

'But for me it was too important. I couldn't bear the idea that for you it might be just another holiday romance.'

'I thought you disapproved of me — thought I was a loose woman.'

'No, not that. But I couldn't share you with another man.'

I rub my face against his neck. 'You won't have to. I promise.'

He kisses my forehead. 'That's all I need to know. Good night, my love. Sleep now.'

And very soon I sleep.

When I wake I am alone and the sunlight is falling across the floor beside the bed. For a while I lie contentedly, remembering the feeling of his arms around me. Then, as I wake fully, the implications of what I have done strike me with painful force. What has happened to my good resolutions? I promised myself that the purpose of meeting Karim again was to set him free. I intended to make it clear to him that there could be no future for us and I held to that until last night. Now I have undone it all. I have committed myself and allowed him to make a similar commitment and I know very well that for him that is no light matter. I think of the future and imagine him tending me as I sink into ever greater helplessness and become more and more demanding. He would never give up, I know that. He would leave his job and his beloved island and in the end he would be left with nothing. I understand, with a chill at the centre of my being, that I can never allow that to happen.

The housekeeper comes in with my breakfast tray and a note from Karim.

My darling,
Forgive me! I had forgotten until I woke up this morning that I have to work today. It's the tour to Lambousa and I can't let people down. I do hope you will understand. I shall be back this afternoon. Have a quiet morning and then we will do something together later.
I love you!
Karim

I dress and then make a telephone call to the airline. By the time Karim comes home my bag is packed and my story prepared.

'Karim, I'm sorry. Try not to be angry with me. I'm flying home this evening.'

'This evening! But I thought you had another two days!'

'I know, but I've changed my flight. I have to be at the airport by eight o'clock.'

'But why? Why? Is it because of last night?'

I intended to tell him that last night had been a mistake and that I am leaving so that it can never happen again but looking at his face I find the cruel truth impossible to utter. Instead, I choose the obvious lie.

'I've been feeling bad all day. I have to take my temperature every day and this morning it was over thirty-eight degrees. I need to be near the hospital in case I have to have emergency treatment.'

'It's my fault!' he cries. 'I should never have let it happen. It's been too much for you.'

'Perhaps that's it,' I agree. But I can't sustain my resolve. 'But I'm so glad it did.'

'No, it was wrong. I can't forgive myself.'

I put my arms round him. 'Karim, darling! It isn't your fault. Probably the whole journey and everything has been a bit too much for me. I just need to get home. You mustn't blame yourself.'

He does not try to persuade me to stay but I know my sudden change of heart has wounded him beyond words. He drives me to the airport and in the departure hall he takes me in his arms. 'I'll phone every day.'

I step back and look into his face. 'No, Karim. Don't do that. I think . . .' Finally I find the courage to utter the words I have been rehearsing all day. 'I think it would be best if we said goodbye here. Let's leave it at that, shall we?'

'Goodbye?' He looks puzzled. 'But we are saying goodbye. What do you mean?'

'I mean for good, Karim. There's no point in you pinning your hopes on something that isn't going to happen. No point in you giving up a job you love and leaving your home just to be with me, if I'm not going to be around.'

'Don't say that!' he cries. 'How can you ask that? I won't let you give up this easily. There is still a chance and we have to grab it.'

'Not *we*, Karim. There is no *we*. There might have been and it would have been wonderful but I can't bear the thought of you putting your life on hold on the tiny chance that I might get better. I can't carry that burden, Karim.' I have to fight back tears to continue. 'Please don't ask me to. It's hard enough to struggle on from day to day, without dragging your hopes and fears with me. Please, Karim! Let's say goodbye now.'

The tannoy announces the last call for my flight. He stands for a moment looking at me in silence and the distress on his face stabs me with an almost physical pain. Then he turns away abruptly and begins to walk towards the exit. I almost call after him but I fight down the impulse and walk towards the barrier that leads to the flight gates. I have almost reached it when I hear hasty steps behind me and feel myself grasped in his arms. He presses his face against my own with a fierce intensity.

'Goodbye, my darling, my dearest love. But don't think this is the end. I shan't impose my worries on you, but whatever happens I shall be waiting — waiting for you to contact me. Be merciful, my darling! Don't let me wait in vain.'

CHAPTER 18

I re-enter my flat in a fog of exhaustion. I spent most of the flight home pretending to sleep, so no one would notice that I was crying. The journey and the emotional turmoil of the last few days have drained me completely and now I am incapable of feeling anything.

Amongst the junk mail and the bills on the doormat is a folded slip of paper.

Cressida,
We're all desperate to know what's happened to you! Please get in touch!
  Sue, Angie and Lisa

I dump it in the bin, along with most of the mail, and fall into bed.

When I wake it is evening and it occurs to me that I have not eaten since yesterday. The contents of my suitcase are strewn across the floor, and the laundry basket is overflowing with unwashed underwear. The kitchen presents an equally unattractive prospect. There are dirty mugs in the sink and the remainder of a loaf of bread is growing mould on the counter-top. A search in the fridge reveals nothing except some sour milk and tuna paté that is well beyond its sell-by date. I consider dialling out for a pizza or a curry, but the thought of anything highly seasoned revolts me. I find a last tin of tomato soup and I am just trying to raise the energy to open it when the doorbell rings. I freeze, afraid that any movement might reveal my presence, and wait for the caller to go away. The bell rings again and then the letterbox rattles and Sue's voice calls, 'Cressida! We know you're in there. Your neighbour said he saw you come in this morning. Please let us in. We're not going away until we know you're all right.'

There is a pause and then the letterbox rattles again. This time it is Angie. 'Cressy, please! We're all really, really worried about you. Please talk to us!'

I put down the tin and open the door. The exclamations of 'There you are!' 'See? I said she was home . . .' die on their lips and then Lisa says in a strangled voice, 'Oh my God!'

There is a moment of terrible silence and then Angie reaches out and puts her arms round me. 'Oh, you poor thing! Whatever's happened to you?'

While I struggle to find my voice, Sue says, 'I knew something was wrong!', and marches past us into the flat.

There seems to be no point in holding out any longer and I let them lead me into the sitting room and settle me in a chair. I had not realized what a relief it would be to come clean about my illness. But I do not mention Karim or my visit to Cyprus.

'But why leave without saying a word to anyone?' Lisa protests. 'We're your friends. We want to help.'

'I know,' I say. 'I know. I'm sorry.' The effort of explaining is too much.

Within minutes I am being spoon-fed soup by Angie, Sue has set off for the supermarket and Lisa is in the kitchen dealing with the washing up. By the time my three friends leave, the flat has been cleaned, the cupboards stocked and my dirty laundry washed and tumble dried. What is more, they have drawn up a rota so that one of them will visit every evening to make sure that I am not left to 'mope on my own'. I hear the front door close behind them with relief. I know I should be grateful but their energy and easy capability only serve to remind me of my own weakness. Not long ago I was as efficient as any of them and it hurts my pride for them to see me in this state.

The next morning I sit down at my desk and boot up my laptop but then sit staring at it until the screensaver clicks into blackness. I finally have an address for the woman whose mysterious existence has obsessed me for so long but now I no longer know what I want to say to her. I reach into a drawer and take out the brittle sheets of paper on which my father wrote his impassioned declarations. I run the tips of my fingers over the unintelligible characters and wish that I could read them. I know Os's translation by heart but it is not the same as being able to read the words for myself. If I write to Ariadne I will have to send her the letters. They are all I have left of my father, except for those faded photographs I found hidden in my mother's bureau. Do I have to give them up? Unable to reach a decision, I put the papers back in the drawer and switch off the computer.

Karim's first letter arrives a few days after my return from Cyprus.

My darling Cressida,
I know I promised not to burden you with my anxieties but I find I cannot keep that promise. I must know how you are. As things are I have no peace from the questions that plague me night and day.
You know that our one night together meant more to me than anything else that has ever happened to me. I have never been in love before and you are more important to me than any person or place. Let me come to London. I can give up my job here at a day's notice. What do I care what other people think? I have considered simply getting on a plane without waiting for your permission but I know I must respect your wishes. I don't want to add to your burdens and if you feel you must be alone at this time, so be it. But please, my darling, write to me and let me know how you are. I shall be watching for every post.
With all my love,
Karim

183

I sit for a long time staring at the letter. The temptation to pick up the phone and call him is hard to resist. In a matter of hours I could be in his arms. But then what? What can I offer him but long, dreary days of waiting? I have made my decision and in this one thing I will not allow my weakness to overcome my will. It will be kinder to Karim in the long run not to reply.

I am in the shower one morning when it strikes me that my period is late. In recent months they have been very heavy — a symptom, I have been told, of the leukaemia. Now, I am four or five days overdue. But that is probably a lingering effect of the chemotherapy. I was told that my periods would probably stop altogether if I continued on it for long.

For weeks my friends keep faithfully to their schedule. My every physical need is catered for and they chatter to me brightly about school politics and the latest gossip until I long to yell at them to shut up. They try to persuade me to go out with them — for a drink or a meal, or to the cinema — but I always find an excuse not to go. I have this intense feeling that my life is in a phase of transition and that I need to be quiet and alone until the process works itself out. I realize that my response to their kindness is ungracious but the guilt only serves to feed my growing resentment. They are trying to run my life and I refuse to permit that.

Eventually my lack of response has its effect. Sue is the first to telephone and apologize for not calling in that evening. She has a huge pile of marking to do. Can I manage without her? Some days later Lisa calls. Her parents are in town for the weekend and have booked tickets for a show. As September draws to a close the excuses become more frequent and I allow myself the bitter self-justification that I always knew it would be like this.

Matters come to a head one evening about six weeks after my return from Cyprus. None of my friends have been to see me for five days and then Sue and Angie arrive together. In their absence I have taken a perverse delight in allowing the flat to descend into chaos and I sit hunched in my easy chair while they fuss around, uttering exclamations which are, to begin with, good humoured and teasing but rapidly become more and more exasperated. 'Cressida, don't you ever wash up?' 'Oh, Cress, really! When did you last change the sheets?' 'You haven't been eating this jam, have you? It's got whiskers on it.'

Eventually Sue comes into the living room and stands over me.

'Cressida, you've got to pull yourself together. You're perfectly capable of cooking yourself a proper meal and washing it up. And look at you! You've been wearing that tracksuit for a week and when did you last have a shower? OK, I know you're ill and we're all sorry for you but what's the point of sitting here wallowing in self-pity? You've been given some extra time. You ought to make the best of it.'

It's the final straw. I uncoil myself from the chair like a spring released and get to my feet.

'What do you know about it? The way I choose to live is my business — and the way I choose to die, if it comes to that. Nobody asked you to come poking your nose in!'

For a long moment Sue stands silent. Then she turns away and picks up the carrier bag she has brought with her. Lisa has come to the door, hearing the altercation. Sue walks past her.

'Come on, Lisa. We're wasting our time here. Like Cressida says, if she wants to pass the rest of her time living in a dung heap that's up to her.'

As the front door slams behind them, the phone begins to ring. I stand gazing at it like a rabbit menaced by a snake until the answering machine cuts in. Karim's voice comes over the line, jagged with emotion.

'Cressida, please pick up the phone! You don't answer my letters. You don't respond to my phone calls. I don't know if you're dead or alive! I can't bear it, Cressida. For the love of Allah, if you are there, answer me!'

I stand paralyzed until the line goes dead. Then I make my way slowly into my bedroom and throw myself onto the bed. Tears come slowly, painfully at first, then faster until I am sobbing without control. I cry myself into exhaustion and fall asleep.

When I wake my throat is parched and my limbs are stiff from lying in the same position but my mind is clear. I see myself with sharp objectivity, as my friends must see me — self-absorbed, bitter and ungrateful. I get up and shower and wash my hair and get dressed properly for the first time in days. Lisa restocked the fridge before she left and I force myself to eat a proper breakfast. Then I go to the telephone and thumb through Yellow Pages until I find a nearby florist's number. I order three individual bouquets to be delivered to my friends at the school, each bearing a card with the single word 'Sorry'. Then I go to my desk and open the drawer where I keep Karim's letters. I struggle for some time with various forms of words until I finally have a version that comes close to saying what I want to express.

Dear Karim,

I have finally realized how badly I have been behaving towards you and I want to apologize. Please believe me when I say that I really only wanted to do what is best for both of us. If circumstances had been different I think we could have had a wonderful relationship but as things stand at the moment that is just not possible. It is my fault that you have been hurt so badly. I should never have come back to Cyprus, or at the very least I should never have persuaded you to make love to me. It is a memory I shall always treasure — nothing can take away from that — but all the same it was wrong, because it gave you the impression that something permanent was happening between us. You must understand that I cannot commit myself to anything. I may only have a short time to live and I do not want you to give up everything you love about your job and your beautiful island just for the trauma of watching me fade away.

Please, Karim, try to forget you ever met me. It will be better for both of us in the long run. But so that you will not have to pass months wondering what has happened to me I will write another letter and give it to a friend to post when . . . (I pause for a long time here before I can bring myself to write the next words) when it is all over. That way at least you will know the final outcome.

I shall always love you but, unless some kind of miracle happens, we can never be together. One day you will find someone else, probably someone much more worthy of you than I am, and have a wonderful life.

Take care, my darling.

Cressida

As I put Karim's letter back in the drawer I see the yellowing bundle of my father's letters. I take them out and smooth their creases with my hand. In the drawer with them is the letter Ferhan gave me with Ariadne's address. I understand for the first time that the letters are not mine. They were addressed to that frightened eighteen-year-old girl whom Ferhan conjured up for me. Admittedly, that girl had grown into a mature woman by the time the letters were written but that must have been the image in my father's mind as he wrote. It was a last, desperate attempt to explain that he had not abandoned her of his own free will, written at a time when he was in fear for his own life. I picture him, sick and shivering in that dark cave where he was imprisoned, frantically scribbling those words of apology and undying devotion. It was not his fault that he had fallen in love so completely that no other woman could ever fill the gap left in his life by the loss of Ariadne. And she must have loved him with the same abandon. Is it not my duty, as his daughter, to set the record straight? At last I come to a resolution. I will send the letters to Ariadne, with a note explaining how they had come into my possession. It will be a final tribute to my father's memory — an act of forgiveness and reconciliation. I pick up my pen and begin to write.

Over the next weeks I exist in a kind of limbo. As September turns to October there is an autumnal gentleness to the sunshine that I find soothing. I make myself go out for a walk every morning and each day I am able to walk a little farther. At times I almost begin to believe in the possibility of a cure but then a sudden fit of dizziness or bout of nausea reminds me that the disease could take me in its grip again at any moment. I read voraciously, but only the kind of light popular novels that I would once have considered beneath my notice. Then, one day, booting up my laptop to deal with some routine bills, I come across the brief historical vignettes which I typed out with the sense of transcribing words that were not my own. It occurs to me that it might be possible to work them up into a series of short stories. Once I start, the idea takes a hold of me and the work gives a focus to my otherwise idle days.

I am sitting curled up in my easy chair, half watching some inane television quiz show, when the doorbell rings. I swear under my breath. Sue and Angie and Lisa have forgiven me for my outburst but they have taken the hint and made their visits less frequent and I am not expecting anyone to call this evening. Muttering bad-temperedly to myself, I get up and stomp to the front door.

The man who stands outside is a complete stranger. He is a little above middle height, solidly built, thickening slightly round the waist. I guess he is somewhere in his mid-forties. He has a mane of hair that must once have been silver-blond but has faded to the colour of straw and the softening of the flesh along the jaw line cannot obscure the perfect regularity of his features. I stare at him. A stranger — yet there is some- thing about him that I feel I ought to recognize. His good looks and smart suit make me painfully aware that I am wear- ing ancient, sagging jogging bottoms and a stained sweat- shirt and that I have no make-up on and my hair, which has started to grow back, is once again badly in need of washing.

I see the shocked expression that I have come to expect and say abruptly, 'Yes?', then regret my lack of courtesy. I push a strand of hair back behind my ear and add, 'Sorry. I wasn't expecting visitors.'

He is visibly disconcerted. 'Of course. I'm sorry. I should have telephoned. It was thoughtless of me.' His English is perfectly correct but there is a faint hint of a foreign accent.

I moisten dry lips with a tongue that feels like a piece of old carpet. 'Did you want something?'

He hesitates and clears his throat. 'You are Cressida — Cressida Allenby?'

'Yes.'

'You don't remember me, do you?'

'I'm sorry.' In my head I am going through a card index of old acquaintances — ex-colleagues, old friends from university, casual pick-ups at parties . . .

He goes on, 'Of course, why should you? You were only a small child.'

I feel the solid floor lurch under my feet. 'It's you! You're Evangelos — the angel boy!'

He laughs suddenly and the intervening years evaporate. 'Yes, that is what your mother used to call me.'

I have to reach for the edge of the door for support. He comes into the hallway. 'You're not well. Can I get you something — a glass of water, perhaps? Would you like to sit down?'

His concern recalls me to my duties as a hostess. 'I'm sorry. Please come in. I'm so glad to see you. Would you like a drink?'

But I sway as I move towards the sitting-room door and he catches my arm and supports me into the room. When I am seated he murmurs, 'Stay still. I will find some water.'

A moment later he is back with a glass. I sip gratefully and get myself under control.

'I'm sorry about the state of the place. I'm — I've been ill.'

He looks down at me, his brow wrinkled with concern. 'I hope it's not serious.'

'No, no. Just a nasty bout of flu, that's all.' It is the lie I usually tell to shopkeepers or other strangers. 'Look, please sit down. Or wait — just a minute. I think there's a bottle of white wine in the fridge. The glasses are in the cupboard above. Would you mind?'

'Of course.'

While he is out of the room, I try to order my thoughts. His sudden reappearance has shaken me. It is as if my own recollections of that long-past time have conjured him out of thin air.

He returns with the wine and pours out two glasses. He sits down opposite me and raises his glass. 'Here's to a speedy recovery!'

I take a tiny sip and find my voice. 'I don't understand. How did you track me down?'

He leans forward, nursing his glass between his hands. 'You don't know? Surely you must have guessed that I am not just the boy who helped out in the bar at Lapithos.'

'What do you mean?'

'I found you because you wrote to my mother.'

'Your mother?' My brain struggles to process the information. 'You are Ariadne's son?'

'Yes. But not just hers. You still don't know?'

'Know what?'

'The letters you sent her were written by my father — *our* father.'

Suddenly that phrase in my father's letter comes back to me. *'Of course he has no idea who I am.'* 'Our father? You mean, Ariadne had a child with my father?'

'Yes. I am Stephen Allenby's son. My stepfather gave me his name, so I am called Evangelos Charalambous — but that is who I am.'

'That makes you . . . my half-brother!'

'Exactly. I am so happy to meet you at last. Though of course we did meet, more than twenty years ago.'

'Did you know — then?'

'No, I had no idea. It was only when . . . only several years later that my mother told me the truth. It was kind of you to send the letters. She asked me to come and tell you how grateful she is for all the trouble you took to find her.'

'You came all the way from Cyprus?'

He laughs. 'No, no. I live here, in London. I own a restaurant in the Fulham Road.'

'Oh, I see.'

For a moment neither of us speaks. Then he says, 'You didn't know that my mother was pregnant when our father disappeared?'

'No, I had no idea.'

'You spoke to Ferhan. Didn't she tell you?'

'No. She must have known, I suppose, but she never mentioned it. But I think she felt quite protective of Ariadne. I'm sure she blamed Dad for abandoning her. Is that why she was sent to Athens and married off to a man she had never met?'

'No doubt.'

I feel myself flush. 'I'm sorry. That was tactless of me. Of course, you must have grown up thinking of that man as your father. Was . . . was it a happy marriage?'

'Tolerable, I think. My stepfather was a good man.'

'Stephen . . . our father . . . didn't leave of his own free will. You know that now. I'm so glad your mother got the letters. I wanted her to know that he never forgot her.'

He looks at me in silence for a moment. Then he says, 'You wrote that your own mother died recently. I'm sorry. I liked her very much.'

I say, 'What I don't understand is, how did you come to work for my parents all those years ago? Was it pure coincidence?'

Evangelos shakes his head. 'Oh no, far from it. But it's a long story. Perhaps you don't feel up to it tonight.'

'No, please! I want to hear. It's all been such a puzzle and I'd like to know the full story before . . . before you go.'

'You know a little of what was going on, politically, at the time your mother and father brought you to Cyprus?'

'Yes, I've heard about that.'

'My mother had two brothers . . .'

'Iannis and Demetrios. I know. They are mentioned in the letters.'

'Ah yes, of course. So you know that my Uncle Iannis was involved with EOKA B, the terrorist organization.'

'Yes.'

'He was a fanatic, Uncle Iannis. He gave his whole life to the struggle for *enosis*. When my stepfather brought us back to live in Cyprus, I was seventeen. Iannis talked to me about the cause. He persuaded me that I should do my patriotic duty by joining EOKA. I was impressionable and he seemed a very glamorous and exciting figure. The outlaw! The freedom fighter! I joined and swore an oath that neither torture nor the threat of death would force me to disclose what I knew. At the time, I thought I was doing something fine and noble. I discovered very soon that it was neither of those things.'

He takes a sip of his wine. His expression has darkened and he seems for a moment to have forgotten my presence.

'Go on.'

'When our father returned to the island and began asking questions, Iannis was convinced that he had come to spy for the British army. He told me to go to the bar when he was away and offer to help. I was to try to find out everything I could about him — where he was going, what he was doing . . .'

'Did Iannis know who you were?'

'Of course. That was the real reason behind it. He needed me to act as a decoy.'

'What do you mean?'

'He intended all along to kidnap your father — partly to find out what information he had been passing back to the authorities but partly, largely I think, as revenge for what had happened with my mother.'

'So, how did he do it?'

'Iannis told me that he needed to talk to your father but he couldn't be seen going to the bar himself. I was to tell him that someone wanted to meet him, secretly, and then take him to an old church up in the hills.'

'Not the church of St Antiphonitis?'

'Yes! How did you guess?'

'It's just a coincidence. I was there not long ago. Go on.'

192

'Of course, Stephen thought that his messages had got through to my mother and that she wanted to meet him. He came with me and Iannis was waiting for him, with two other men. They held him at gunpoint, tied him up and drove him to a cave up in the mountains.' Evangelos gazes into his wine glass. 'He looked at me, just once, and I knew I had betrayed him. I have never forgotten that look.'

'You weren't to blame. Your uncle deceived you, as well as him. And you did try to look after him, didn't you? He wrote about that in his letters.'

'I did what I could. I would have let him go, if I could, but there were always a couple of Iannis's men on guard.'

'But you did get him paper and a pen.'

'Yes, that was one thing I could do for him. Then, when the invasion started, Iannis and his men rushed off to fight and I was able to get him out of the cave. He was very ill by that time. I got him on to a donkey, somehow, and took him to a farm. There was total chaos by then — heavy fighting along the beaches and on the road between Kyrenia and Nicosia and Turkish planes coming over all the time, bombing and strafing. It was particularly heavy all round Lapithos and anyway I didn't think Stephen would make it that far. It was hard enough keeping him on the donkey even for a short journey. The farm was owned by Turks and I could see that the Turkish forces were going to win, so I reckoned he'd be safe there.'

'So it was you who left him there.'

'I felt bad about just leaving him,' Evangelos says. 'But I was afraid that, under the circumstances, the owners might decide to make me a prisoner of war.'

'Just a minute,' I interrupt. 'I remember you rescuing me when the bombs were falling. Was that before or after you left my father at the farm?'

'After. Your father had made me promise to deliver his letters.'

'But they were for your mother, not mine!'

'I know that now. But when he first asked me for paper he said they were for his wife. Then he got delirious with the fever. I suppose he intended eventually to tell me the full story but once he got ill he really didn't know what he was saying. I had no reason to think that the letters were for anyone but your mother. It was night time when I left him. As soon as it got light the next day I set off for Lapithos. That's when I found you under the fig tree. Your mother was desperately trying to pack and half out of her mind with worry about your father. You must have wandered off. I took you home and gave her the letters but the Turkish army was advancing and I didn't dare stay. I could see myself being shot, either as a spy by the Turks or as a deserter by my own side.' He pauses and looks at me. 'It was a great relief to know you got back to England safely.'

We are silent for a moment. Then I say, 'It must have been a shock for your mother, hearing from my father . . . our father . . . again after all those years. A voice from the grave!'

Evangelos makes no reply but after a moment he says, 'It doesn't upset you, that he had a love affair with someone else, before you were born?'

'It did, very much, to begin with. Now — now I just feel terribly sorry for everyone. I hope those letters have given your mother some comfort. And I'm so glad to have met you again before—'

I stop myself but after a pause he says, 'This illness — it's not just flu, is it?'

I shake my head. 'No. I've got leukaemia.'

'Oh no! I'm so sorry! But that's treatable, isn't it? Have you seen a specialist?'

'Yes, I've been having chemotherapy and it seems to have helped. But it's only a temporary remission.' I look at him. Here, out of the blue, is the blood relative I thought I would never find. Dare I ask for his help? I empty my wine glass. 'What I need is a bone marrow transplant from a donor whose genetic make-up is close enough to mine . . .'

'Like a brother, or a half-brother,' he says at once. 'They can test for that, can't they? When can you arrange for me to be tested?'

'Very soon, I should imagine. But, Angel, are you sure you want to do this? It means an operation — not the nicest sort of process . . .'

He interrupts by taking both my hands in his. 'Cressida! You're my little sister. Of course I want to help, if I can. Ask your doctor to arrange the tests — please.'

'All right. I have to go for a check-up the day after tomorrow, as it happens. I'll ask about it then. How shall I contact you?'

'Here.' He takes a business card from his pocket and writes quickly on the back of it. 'That's the restaurant — and I've written my personal number and my mobile on the back. Ring me as soon as you hear anything.' He gets up. 'I'm going to leave you now. I think you've had quite enough for one evening. I can see you're very tired.'

'I wish I could entertain you properly. It's awful, meeting you again and not being able to invite you to a meal or something. There's so much I want to ask you.'

He presses my hand. 'We'll find the time. God willing, the genes will match up and soon you'll be well again. Then we'll have a big celebration at the restaurant. Do you like Greek food?'

'Yes. Yes, I do.'

'Then that's something to look forward to. I'll call in again, soon — but this time I'll telephone first.' He hesitates, then bends and kisses me lightly on the cheek. 'Don't bother coming to the door. I can let myself out.'

When he has gone I turn the card over and look at the name of the restaurant. It is called The Tree of Idleness.

CHAPTER 19

At the outpatients clinic I tell them about Evangelos and ask them to arrange a test, so I am not surprised when I receive a call from the hospital giving me an urgent appointment with the consultant. I walk into the room buoyed up by a tremulous optimism, but that is immediately dispelled by the expression on Dr Prentiss's face. I sit down opposite her and she folds her hands and leans forward.

'So. How are you feeling?'

'Not too bad, actually. I went through a very low patch but I seem to have come out the other side.'

'That's good.'

'You did get the message — that I've discovered I have a half-brother? Do you think there's any chance that he might be suitable?'

'It's possible. But there is something else we have to discuss first. Did you know that you are pregnant?'

'Pregnant!' I stare at her. 'I can't be.'

'I'm afraid there's no doubt about it. It shows up clearly in your recent test.'

'But you told me the chemotherapy would make me sterile.'

'I said it might. And you told me that you were not in a relationship at present.'

'I wasn't. I'm not . . .' I stumble into silence. I don't want her to think that the pregnancy is the result of some casual encounter. 'I thought it had finished but it started up again.'

There is a pause. Then the doctor says in a gentler tone, 'I'm sorry if this is a shock to you. But now you have to make a decision. If your potential donor turns out to be a good enough match, there is no question of going ahead with the transplant while you are pregnant. You are going to have to decide if you want this baby.'

I press my hand to my forehead, as if the physical pressure could still my churning thoughts. 'I don't know. How can I make a decision like that on the spur of the moment?'

'I didn't mean that. Of course you must have time to think. But we can't afford to leave it too long. Do you know when the child was conceived?'

'Yes, exactly. It would be almost six weeks ago.'

'Then we have a little time — say another five weeks. That is, if you decide to go for an abortion.'

I force myself to breathe deeply. After the initial shock my brain is starting to work again. 'Is there any chance that it could have been . . . harmed by the treatment I've had?'

'I'm afraid there is that possibility. Did the conception take place before or after we stopped the chemotherapy?'

'Afterwards. About a week after.'

'Well, that's something in our favour. If you had still been having the treatment the chances of foetal deformity would have been very high. Even now I can't guarantee that there won't be a problem. There is also the possibility of a miscarriage.'

'Can we find out? If the baby's OK, I mean?'

'We can do a scan and later, after sixteen weeks, an amniocentesis. But even then we can't be sure of picking everything up. But that is not the only, or indeed the primary, consideration.'

'What do you mean?'

'I would be failing in my responsibility if I did not warn you that if you go ahead with the pregnancy you could be putting your own life at risk. If the leukaemia returns to the acute phase we should not be able to treat you with the same drugs without endangering the child. Have you considered that?'

I hear myself say, 'I suppose I shall just have to hope that the remission lasts long enough for the baby to be born.'

'And if you succeed in carrying the child to term and successfully delivering it, at the expense of your own life, what happens to the baby?'

This is more than I can deal with at this moment. 'The father might . . . he might want . . . I don't know. I suppose there are always people wanting to adopt, aren't there?'

'Well, if that is your decision, after you have had time to consider all the factors, I shall respect it, of course. We can start you on a course of alpha-interferon, which should slow the progress of the disease and will not harm the foetus, and I'll refer you to a colleague of mine in the gynaecology department. We'll monitor your progress and hope for the best.' She smiles, and the professional mask is replaced by a warm humanity. 'Whatever decision you come to, you can rely on my support.'

When I get home I take the letter with Karim's number on it from the drawer of the desk and stand for a long time by the telephone. Karim has a right to know, hasn't he? I stretch out my hand to the receiver. One phone call and he will be on the next plane. Then the decision will not be up to me alone. The prospect of passing some of the burden of responsibility to him is tempting. But even as the thought comes to me I know what his reaction will be. He will want me to get rid of the child. He will say that my health is the most important consideration — that he cannot allow me to do something that might mean he will lose me forever. But if I decide to go ahead with the pregnancy in spite of everything he will insist on marriage and at least then, if anything happens to me, the child will have a father. But suppose the tests show that there is some terrible deformity? Suppose I were to miscarry? And I still have no prospect of a permanent cure — less now, if anything. It would be too cruel for Karim to lose his child and his wife within months of each other. Eventually I decide to wait, at least until I have the result of the scan.

The scan shows nothing abnormal and as I enter the flat the phone is ringing. It is Evangelos.

'Have you arranged for the tests?'

'Yes — but there is something I need to talk to you about.'

'Fine. I want you to meet some people — my family, my wife. Will you come to the restaurant?'

I almost refuse. Going out means such an effort and I am in no state of mind to be sociable but I need to talk to him.

'Yes, thank you. I should like that.'

'Tomorrow evening, about seven?'

'Yes, that would be fine.'

I dress with care. I have been eating better lately and with the application of some make-up I look a little less 'like death warmed up', as my mother would have put it. I call a taxi and find that the prospect of the evening ahead is not as daunting as I expected.

The restaurant is sophisticated, with modern, uncluttered decor and subtle lighting. It is obviously successful, since most of the tables are occupied although it is still early.

Evangelos is waiting for me at the door. 'Cressida! You look beautiful! Come upstairs. We will eat *en famille*, not in the restaurant.'

He leads me to the back of the restaurant and up a narrow flight of stairs and through a door into a hallway, where a huge vase of fresh flowers stands below a large, framed photograph of Kyrenia harbour. Then he stops and turns to look at me.

'Cressida, I haven't been entirely truthful. I said I wanted you to meet someone, and it's true that I want you to meet my wife and kids, but before that there is someone else you should meet. Please, this way.'

He opens a door and ushers me into a comfortably furnished sitting room. A small, plump woman whose dark hair is streaked with grey rises from a sofa as we enter. Evangelos takes me by the arm and leads me over to her.

'Cressida, this is my mother, Ariadne.'

The solid earth seems to disintegrate beneath my feet. This little old lady is the seductress who stole my father's heart? This is the enchantress who spun a thread that kept him captive all his life? This is Circe? This is Calypso?

'Cressida, my dear! I am glad to meet you at last.'

I stammer like a schoolgirl. 'Ariadne — Mrs Charalambous — I'm sorry . . . I had no idea. I thought you were in Cyprus.'

'So I was, until a few days ago. Then, when Angel telephoned, we knew we had to come. Please, sit down.' She indicates a place on the sofa beside her. 'It is tragic that we have had to wait until you are so ill. Thank God we have found you before it is too late! How are you feeling?'

'I'm . . . a little better at the moment, thank you.'

There is a knock and a waiter comes in with a tray bearing glasses and a bottle of champagne in an ice bucket. Evangelos says, 'Forget sickness for a moment. We must celebrate finding each other again.'

Ariadne says, 'I was so touched that you sent me those letters. I think many women would have burned them.'

'Oh no,' I reply. 'They were my only souvenirs of my father. I never really knew him, you see.'

'Did you miss him very much, while you were growing up?'

'I suppose I did but children accept things, don't they? It was really only after my mother died that I realized what a . . . well, what a hole there was in my life. It wasn't that my father was dead, but that I knew so little about him. My mother wouldn't talk about him, you see, and she must have destroyed everything that reminded her of him, except a few photos I found at the bottom of a drawer.'

'And were you angry, when you found out that he had had a love affair?'

'Yes, I was initially. It broke my mother's heart, you see. Not that he'd had another love, but that he'd never got over

200

it. But then I began to realize that you must have suffered too. Ferhan told me how your father sent you to Athens, to marry a man you hardly knew. It must have been awful for you.'

Ariadne lays her hand on my arm. 'Being separated from your father was awful, but I was lucky in many ways. My husband was a good man. I never loved him but he was always kind to me and he never threw my sin back in my face.'

'You think of it as a sin?'

'In the eyes of many people it was a sin. But to me? No. I could no more have stopped myself from loving your father than I could have forbidden the waves to break on the shore.'

'Was he very good-looking?'

'Good-looking? Oh yes, he was beautiful. Tall and fair as a young god. But it was not just his looks that I fell in love with.'

'What was it then?'

'It was his smile, and the way his eyes crinkled up at the corners when he laughed — and his kindness.'

'Was he kind? He wasn't very kind to my mother.'

'You are still angry with him, then?'

'No, not any more. I think he did his best but he just couldn't forget. Why didn't he marry you?'

'He would have done, if it had been possible. My family would never have permitted it. He asked me many times. What happened was not his fault.'

We are talking as if we have known each other for a long time. I look into her dark eyes and see in them the pride and tenderness that must have enthralled my father.

'I don't think it was anybody's fault,' I say.

Somewhere out of my line of sight a door opens and Evangelos says softly, 'Cressida, look behind you.'

I turn and see that a second man has entered the room. He is tall and lean and silver-haired and his face is as lined and tanned as the leather of a well-worn brogue, but the blue eyes are as vivid as a boy's. He stands still and looks at me across the width of the room.

'Cressida?' His voice cracks slightly. 'Don't you know me?'

I get to my feet. Everything seems to be happening in slow motion, as if in a dream.

'Dad? But you can't be! You died. Mum told me you were dead.'

He comes towards me, both hands held out. 'My darling little girl! If only I'd known sooner. I can't bear it that you're so ill!'

I shrink back from his touch. 'I don't understand. What are you doing here? Where have you been?'

He drops his hands. 'Yes, you're right. I owe you an explanation. Sit down, please. Let's talk this through.'

I sink back onto the couch and realize that Ariadne has moved in order to make room for Stephen beside me.

He says, 'Years ago, soon after we got back from Cyprus, when you were only a small child, I realized that your mother and I had come to a point where it was impossible to go on living together. I had already given up my teaching job and was making a living as a journalist. It gave me a reason to be away and I thought perhaps if we gave each other some space things might come right. But each time I came home it was worse. In the end I only came back in order to see you. Do you remember that at all?'

'You brought me a clockwork monkey. I remember that.'

He smiles briefly. 'Oh, that monkey! I'm glad you remember that.'

'But then you went for good.'

'Yes. You've spoken to Ferhan. You know that she used to write to me? One day I got a letter telling me that Ariadne's husband had died and giving me her address.'

'She told me she had written, but she said you never replied.'

'No, that was remiss of me. But all I could think of was that Ariadne was now free and I could go to her. At last I could explain why I had left her without a word and tell her how I felt.' He turns and stretches a hand to the small woman

202

who was sitting on his other side. 'And she, God bless her, forgave me and took me in.'

Ariadne says softly, 'There was nothing to forgive.'

'And you have been living together ever since?'

'Yes, ever since.'

'Then, those letters . . . I need never have sent them.' The confusion of thoughts and emotions threaten to overwhelm me.

'I'm so glad you did! Without that I should never have known where to find you.'

'But why did you let me think you were dead, all these years?'

'That was your mother's wish, not mine. When I wrote and told her that I wanted her to divorce me she said that she would on one condition — that I must give up all right to see you and let her tell you that I was dead. She said it would be better for you to think that than to know that I had left you both to live with another woman. I don't know if she was right. Perhaps I should have fought her on that point. But she convinced me that it was best for you. Believe me, it was one of the hardest things I have ever had to do.'

'It was a choice between us, Mother and me, and her.' The words are choking me. I glance towards Ariadne. 'You could have chosen us.'

'Yes, I could. But your mother and I couldn't live together peaceably. Would it have been good for you to grow up in the middle of our rows? And I had a debt to Ariadne, too, and to Evangelos. Don't forget I had another child to think of.'

'Why did you marry my mother if you didn't love her?' Finally I arrive at the crucial question.

'But I did! At least, I thought I did. Or perhaps it was that I needed an anchor, something, someone to hold on to.'

'Because you couldn't find Ariadne? But that must have been years later.'

'Oh yes, many years. But I had never settled, never put down any roots. When I left the army all I could think about was finding Ariadne and when I finally had to accept that I had lost her for good, I had to find some way of occupying my life. That was when I decided to become a journalist. Things went quite well for a while. I worked as a stringer for several papers, mainly in the Far East, and later as a foreign correspondent for the *Guardian*. But it's a lonely life. I had no home to go back to and I spent far too much time in bars and hotels. Most journalists drink. I came to rely more and more on alcohol to get me through the lonely evenings. Eventually it began to affect my work. I missed deadlines and finally got the sack. At that point I came back to England, pretty well down and out. Luckily for me, a friend put me in touch with a rehab clinic and I managed to get myself dried out. But I still didn't have a job, so I decided to go back to university, do a PGCE and go into teaching — which was the career I had originally planned. My first post was in that comprehensive school where I met your mother. She was much younger than I was, of course, but we had one thing in common. We were both trying to recover from a failed love affair.'

This is news to me and I feel a physical jolt of surprise. But before I can speak my father goes on, 'I'm sorry if that comes as a shock to you, but I wasn't your mother's first lover any more than she was mine. She had just been let down rather badly and needed someone to lean on. We found mutual comfort in each other. She was bright, intelligent and fun and a brilliant teacher — and I badly needed someone to help me through a disastrous first year. I realized very quickly that I just wasn't cut out for the job. If it hadn't been for your mother I think I would have resigned at the end of my first term. Then the day came when she told me she was pregnant.' He releases Ariadne's hand and turns to take mine instead. 'I want you to believe that that was one of the happiest days of my life. I had never had a real family. The idea that I could have a wife and child of my own was wonderful to me. I knew I wasn't in love with your mother as I had been with Ariadne but I thought that I could never feel that way again about anyone. We seemed to have a reasonable basis for making a life together and when you were born I really thought everything was going to be all right.'

'You drove my mother to drink!'

'Did I? I really don't think so. You were too young to know anything about it, but she was already drinking before we went to Cyprus. Perhaps I was partly to blame for that, but not in the way you think.'

'So what went wrong?'

'I suppose it began as post-natal depression. The tragic thing was that, although having you was one of the best things that had ever happened to me, motherhood never really worked for her. To begin with she was over-anxious, over-protective. Then, as time went on, she got very bored and frustrated staying at home with no one but a baby for company. I suggested that she went back to work but that was wrong, too. She worried about leaving you with a child-minder. She didn't sleep. She'd lost all the sparkle and enthusiasm that made her such a good teacher.' He pauses briefly, then continues, 'One day I met someone who gave me a chance to go back to Cyprus — and a chance to work as a journalist again. I couldn't resist it, and I thought a new life would be good for all of us.'

'Did my mother know you'd been there before?'

'She knew I served there in the army. Nothing else.

'You didn't go there in order to look for Ariadne?'

'No! Why would I? As far as I knew then she was still living in Athens. It wasn't until a week or two after we'd moved in that I decided to go up to Ayios Epiktetos, the village where Ariadne used to live, to see if it was still as I remembered it. I didn't think anyone would recognize me, after all those years, but I hadn't been there long before an old guy came shuffling up to me and said, "You're Lieutenant Allenby, aren't you? The one who used to visit the old school master." He told me that Ariadne's father was dead and her mother had gone away and then he said, "She was here, though, the other day. The daughter who went to live in Athens."'

He turns again to Ariadne and they smile at each other with great tenderness.

Stephen goes on, 'I knew then that I had to see her, but the old chap had no idea where she was staying. He only knew that it wasn't in the village. I went and found Ferhan but she refused point blank to tell me where Ariadne was. I begged and pleaded but it was no good. All I could do was comb each village in turn, asking for her and hoping to spot an old acquaintance. It was the proverbial needle in a haystack but it became a kind of obsession. It wasn't even that I had any idea of leaving your mother and you at that point. I just wanted to explain — and make sure she was all right. At least, that's what I told myself.'

'Did you know my mother was drinking, then?'

'Yes. I soon realized that bottles were disappearing from the stock and not being accounted for. I tried to persuade her to stop. We had terrible rows about it.' He makes a small, hopeless gesture. 'That was the beginning of the end. I know I was to blame. I should have stayed with her, kept an eye on her. But whenever I did, we only fought.' He looks at me and I see tears in his eyes. 'I'm sorry, my darling. I let you both down — just as I let Ariadne down all those years ago.'

'Dearest,' Ariadne puts in gently, 'you didn't let me down. You had no choice in what happened. Neither did I. It was fate. But fate was kind to us in the end.'

I look at their faces, both suffused with love, and feel a lump in my throat. 'So you've been together all these years.'

My father nods. 'Yes. We have had more than twenty years of happiness. Was it very selfish of me? I had already made the decision that I couldn't live with your mother any more. It's true I gave up the chance of seeing you, but that was because I was genuinely persuaded that it would be better for you. Can you forgive me?'

I gaze at him. I don't know what I feel. 'I don't know. I don't think it's a question of forgiveness. We all try to do what seems best, don't we? But in the end it's like Ariadne says. It's fate. But I'm glad — I'm so glad I've found you again.'

And suddenly we are both in tears. He puts his arm round my shoulders and kisses me on both cheeks. 'Oh, my little girl! Thank you. Thank you!'

A champagne cork pops and Evangelos says, 'I think it's time we all had a drink.'

When the glasses have been filled and passed round, Stephen raises his. 'To those unseen powers — call it fate or the gods or what you will — that have seen fit to bring us together again. And to you, my darling wife, and to you, my two children. Bless you!'

I sip the wine. It tastes better than any I have drunk since my illness. Stephen turns to me. 'I've talked so long about my own life and I haven't asked you anything about yours. I can see you're not married but is there someone — someone you care for?'

For a moment I am uncertain whether to confide in him or not. Finally I say, 'Yes, there is. But I'm afraid you may not approve of him. I met him last Easter, when I went to Kyrenia. His name is Karim. He's an archaeologist . . . a Turkish Cypriot. I'm afraid after everything that's happened you will think of him as "the enemy". But I know he truly loves Cyprus and is as distressed as you must be by the political situation.'

Ariadne moves to sit on my other side and takes my hand. 'My dear, I'm the last person in the world to blame anyone for falling in love with someone who seems to be on the wrong side. We love where we must, not where it's easy or suitable.'

'The old Greeks knew that,' Stephen says wryly. 'That's why they gave Eros that bow and arrows.' He stands up and empties the last of the champagne into my glass. 'Angel, I think we need another bottle.'

'I have one here ready,' Evangelos replies. 'And then I think we should eat. My chef will be tearing his hair out if we don't go to the table soon.'

In the dining room I am introduced at last to Evangelos's wife, Ismene, whose dark beauty seems the perfect complement to his fairness, and their two sons. The meal is a delicious fusion of traditional Greek and classic modern cuisine and I surprise myself by eating most of what I am offered, though I refuse Angel's attempts to refill my glass. Over the meal I tell them how I pieced together my father's story and they beg me to describe the villages and landmarks that must once have been a familiar part of their lives and which are now inaccessible to them. We compare notes, briefly, about teaching and I ask, 'Are you still writing for the papers?'

Stephen shakes his head. 'When Ariadne's uncle died he left her the hotel. So for the last ten years running it has kept both of us fully occupied. I certainly never wanted to go back to being a foreign correspondent.'

By the time we return to the sitting room for coffee, I am almost at the end of my strength. Ismene excuses herself, saying she has to put the boys to bed, and Evangelos goes down to check that all is well in the restaurant. Stephen leads me to the sofa and takes my hands in his.

'Now, my dear, we must talk about the subject we have all been avoiding all evening. Your health. I know you have arranged for Evangelos to be tested as a potential donor. I want you to arrange for me to be tested too.'

'You?' In the welter of new discoveries and emotions, it has never crossed my mind. 'Oh no! No, I couldn't ask you to do that.'

'Cressida, I owe you that much at the very least.'

I force myself to meet his eyes. 'There's one more thing I haven't told you. I'm pregnant.'

I feel Ariadne's arm around my shoulders. 'Oh, my dear child!'

'Is it Karim's?' Stephen asks.

'Yes, but he doesn't know — yet. I haven't told him. You see, if I decide to have the baby there can't be any question of a transplant until after it's born and if — if the leukaemia gets worse they won't be able to treat it with the drugs I had before. I don't think it would be fair to ask him to make that kind of choice.'

'So what will you do? Are you going to have the child?'

'Yes.' I find that somehow I have taken the decision without being aware of it. 'Yes, it wouldn't be right to take away his life, or her life, just to save my own.'

Stephen grips my hands tighter. 'My brave girl!'

'And the child is all right? It hasn't been harmed by the drugs?' Ariadne asks.

'I've had a scan and as far as they can see everything's all right. Later I can have an amniocentesis. That should confirm it, or otherwise.'

'What does your doctor say?'

'The hospital has been wonderful. My consultant has referred me to a gynaecologist who has an excellent reputation. If the baby's OK it's just a question of whether I can go the full nine months without the leukaemia becoming acute again.'

'And after that, you would still need the transplant?'

'Yes, if . . .' I was going to say 'if I survive that long' but the words stick in my throat. 'If I'm going to have any chance of getting better.'

'Then my offer still stands.'

'But it means a general anaesthetic. At your age . . .'

'At my age what more is there for me to do, other than to pass on life to the next generation? I brought you into the world and then abandoned you — no matter from whatever motives. Now it is time for me to make reparation for that, and how could I do it better? Besides, I am as strong as a horse. There is no reason why a general anaesthetic should be any more of a risk for me than for Angel.'

I turn to Ariadne. 'Please, I don't think he should do this. You can stop him.'

But Ariadne shakes her head. 'We have talked it over. It is what he wishes and I respect his feelings. Besides, it may be that the tests will prove that he is not compatible. Perhaps Angel will be the one. We must accept what the fates decide.'

By the time I get home I am shaking with fatigue but my mind is clearer than it has been for weeks. I know what I have to do. I go to the telephone and dial Karim's number.

CHAPTER 20

LONDON, JUNE 1999

The restaurant looks beautiful! Evangelos and Ismene have done a wonderful job with the flowers and the decorations. That's one of the good things about a midsummer wedding. There are so many flowers to choose from. But everything is wonderful about this wedding. For such a long time we all thought it might never happen at all. Of course, I should have preferred it to be held in my own hotel in Cyprus but that was always out of the question.

Look at them — the happy couple! It's a fallacy to believe that all brides are happy on their wedding day. I know that only too well. But Cressida looks radiant. What a change a few months can bring about! And Karim? He looks like a man who has suddenly been released from a dark prison into the sunlight. These last months have been harder for him than for any of us, I believe. He wanted to get married straightaway, of course, but Cressida was adamant. I can understand why. Until they were both safe, she would not allow him to commit himself. Not many women in her position would have had the strength of purpose to stick to that. I admire her for it.

It's so good to see so many of their friends here, and all mixing together as if there had never been any suggestion of a difficulty. Of course, some of them have no idea what a remarkable feat this is. Those three young women, for example, Cressida's friends from the school. I've seen them dancing, first with a Greek, then with a Turk, as if it was the most natural thing in the world — which is as it should be. What would my father have thought of such girls? So independent, living alone, going from one boyfriend to another. I have to admit I find it hard to approve, myself. But they have been such loyal friends to Cressida, given her so much support, that it would be wrong to criticize.

I must go and talk to the Wentworths in a minute. It was kind of them to make the journey specially for the wedding but I know Cressida very much wanted them to be here. I shall have a long chat with them about the old days when I get a chance and ask them to describe all the places I used to know so well as a girl. How good it would be to go back to Ayios Epiktetos, or whatever outlandish Turkish name they have given it now. But perhaps it is better that I can't. It has so many memories. I should like to stand in the church of St Antiphonitis again. It would be good to go back to the place where Stephen first kissed me, but it would break my heart to see those wonderful frescoes all defaced. Karim says it is protected now but how could they let such a thing happen? And our cave in the hills? No, I don't want to go there. Those memories are too mixed.

Karim's parents seem to be enjoying themselves. We were afraid, to begin with, that they would refuse to attend. They are not at all what I expected before we were introduced. She is beautiful and sophisticated; he very urbane, very much a man of the world. He actually asked me to dance a few minutes ago! Of course, I said that in my circumstances it would not be suitable, so we sat and chatted instead. I asked him if he and his wife had been very disappointed when Karim told them he wanted to marry an English girl. He shrugged and smiled.

'Of course, we always hoped he would fall in love with a nice Muslim girl, hopefully a girl from Cyprus. But the years went by and we began to see that there were fewer and fewer suitable candidates, and he seemed not to care for any of them. We began to be afraid that he would never marry — that perhaps there was, you know, something wrong somewhere. When he brought Cressida to meet us we could see that at last he was in love. And she is everything we could wish for in a daughter, except for the question of religion — beautiful, intelligent, warm-hearted. And courageous. No question about that. She will make him a good wife. And then, of course, there is the child . . .'

Ah yes! The child. Look at him, fast asleep on Dr Prentiss's lap. So fair, like a little angel. He reminds me of Evangelos as a baby. And the doctor is so proud of him! You would think it was her own child. But she has good reason. The care she gave Cressida all through that terribly anxious pregnancy was beyond the call of duty. I shall never forget those months, watching, waiting, praying. I couldn't stay in England all the time. There were things that needed attention back in Cyprus. But Stephen stayed. He refused to leave Cressida even for a few days. That was the one good thing about that period, watching them together, getting to know each other, seeing the love and trust between them grow. He was so proud when that magazine — what is it called? *Mslexia* — accepted her short stories. That gave her the courage to start working on a novel. 'A hostage to fortune,' she said.

Several times we thought she might lose the baby, or that we might lose both of them. Then there was the trauma of the Caesarean and after that the transplant. Poor Cressida, confined to that sterile room, only able to see her baby through the glass, not able to hold him or feed him. And poor Karim. You could see that he felt so helpless, watching her, longing to be able to touch her and comfort her. My heart bled for both of them, even though I had my own grief to deal with. But the child brought us all so much joy. To see him whole and perfect was like a miracle. How appropriate that he should be born at Easter time.

Tomorrow they will be off, all three of them, to Kyrenia for their honeymoon. What a scandal it would have been when I was their age for a honeymoon couple to arrive with a three-month-old baby! Even now it will raise some eyebrows out there, though no one seems to find it at all unusual in this country. I wish I could go with them — but no, of course it would be most inappropriate, even if it were possible. I shall go back to my own side of the island. There are matters of business that need attention there. One day, perhaps, I shall be able to visit my old home again, if I live long enough. And when Cressida and Karim are settled in America they have made me promise to visit them. Something else to look forward to.

Look at Cressida! Who would believe that that pale ghost of a few months ago could turn into such a beautiful creature? Her hair is like spun gold, there is colour in her cheeks and when she smiles . . . when she smiles my breath catches in my chest because she is so much like her father. If only Stephen could be here to see this. But I must not mourn, not today. At least he had the joy of seeing the child and I feel his spirit is rejoicing with us today. When I sat with him in the hospital, while that terrible infection that no antibiotics could touch burned his life away, he told me that he had no regrets and that I must have none either.

'We were given back the lives that we thought we had lost forever,' he said, 'and we had twenty years of a happiness we had never dreamed possible. But it was at a price — a price that was paid by other people. Now it is time to make good my debt. Cressida is flesh of my flesh, blood of my blood. I gave her life once and now I have been blessed to be able to do it again, for her and her child. I am glad that we have had these few months together and I am proud that I have a daughter with such grace and courage. Whatever happened, I could not have expected to live more than a few years longer.

Now I am content to think that out of my old bones has sprung a new life — two new lives.'

I shall take his ashes to Cyprus and plant flowers on his grave — scarlet anemones, like those they say grow every year from the blood of Adonis, the young god who was sacrificed and rose again in the spring.

EPILOGUE

THE GODDESS SPEAKS

I am She, the Great Mother, Mistress of all Living Things. I am Artemis, the armed virgin; I am Aphrodite, the bringer of desire; I am Persephone, Queen of the Underworld.

Mine is the energy of Youth, the allure of Womanhood, the wisdom of Old Age. In spring I start into life the seed hidden in the ground or in the womb; in summer I bring forth increase from the fecund earth; I preside also over the decay of autumn. I am the creator of life and the bringer of death; and through me alone comes resurrection. The moon waxes and wanes at my behest, the tides rise and fall with the rhythm of my breathing, the sun grows stronger or weakens as I rise from the Underworld or decline towards it.

These women are my daughters. Let them bear witness to my power.

THE END

AUTHOR'S NOTE

In the years between the end of this story and the present day much has changed in N. Cyprus. With the influx of tourists there has been a great deal of development, not all of it sympathetic. Readers hoping to follow Cressida's footsteps may be disappointed to find how much commercialization has altered the landscape.

ALSO BY HILARY GREEN

STANDALONE NOVELS
OPERATION KINGFISHER
TWICE ROYAL LADY
APHRODITE'S ISLAND

Thank you for reading this book.

If you enjoyed it please leave feedback on Amazon or Goodreads, and if there is anything we missed or you have a question about, then please get in touch. We appreciate you choosing our book.

Founded in 2014 in Shoreditch, London, we at Joffe Books pride ourselves on our history of innovative publishing. We were thrilled to be shortlisted for Independent Publisher of the Year at the British Book Awards.

www.joffebooks.com

We're very grateful to eagle-eyed readers who take the time to contact us. Please send any errors you find to corrections@joffebooks.com. We'll get them fixed ASAP.